# Beauty Stone

## Demet Dayanch

Editors: Tara Ingman, Stefanie Kirlew
Book Design: Minel Civan


PRINT ISBN: 978-0-9957723-0-4

*For Doga*
*A dear friend and the inspiration behind the title:*
*Beauty Stone*

"Love does not fail for you when you are rejected, betrayed or apparently not loved. Love fails for you when you reject, betray or do not love. Realise that each one wants to love and to be loved by the other in love. Therefore love."

Adi Da Samraj

# One

*Autumn 2007*

In English, it's called a beauty spot; he named it a beauty stone, but to her it was her mark and one he lovingly touched.

Gently gliding his fingers along the contours of her slender frame, he watched in awe, the fair, delicate hairs rise to his command.

She had no control over this reflex, in just the same way as she had no control over her heart that recoiled with every second that bulged with the torment of his love; a love that cut so deep, wounds gaping with the wide stare of fearful eyes appeared all over her body. It wasn't a new phenomenon for her to feel watched. In fact, her afflicted mind welcomed their stares, as they didn't make her feel so alone.

With no idea about what was in store, he lay on top of her and passionately kissed her lips. His seductive eyes searched for hers, and she closed them, in case, just in case, he saw the truth.

But in the bedroom, he always won, and she bitterly parted her thin legs, giving permission for his warm hand to brush across her mound, sending waves of violent pleasure crashing into her heart.

Flooded by desire, she kissed him back and ravenously consumed the destructive passion that dripped from his mouth, into hers. Each drop was like a key bearer that released the silent pleas that had lain waiting in the dark corners of her throat; pleas that created an internal beast that both cherished and detested the intensity of his desire. One that she reluctantly shared with many others.

Her psychic gift meant that although she never saw their faces, she felt their clandestine spirits linger in his thoughts, which from time to time, she caught like unexpected disease. Thus, she knew that his love would never be enough, and she could never be his.

Tears streamed down her face as he entered her and slowly began to make love, whispering, 'I love you, I love you,' into her ear. Words she'd never heard before; words that came too late, evaporating in the vacuum of his hot breath that filled the room, crowding her, until she couldn't breathe.

Five lost breaths later, a loud orgasmic roar poured from his lungs, and she gasped sucking in his toxic life force - desperate to live, desperate to die, desperate that every time he hurt her, he freed her that little bit more.

Unaware of her tentative state of mind, he stroked the side of her face, rolled off her and instantly fell asleep.

She diligently watched his chest rise and fall with the same adornment a mother has for her newborn and felt her heart grow darker.

Holding her hand over her chest as if she might be able to prevent the darkness from seeping out, she sat up in the bed and reached between her legs. The wetness of their lovemaking streamed over her hand, and her mind drowned with the images of all the other women who'd felt his love between their fingers.

These last visions made the next action easy, and she reached for the hunting rifle that she'd cunningly placed under the bed, and aimed it at his head. He looked so peaceful, so innocent, so goddamn gorgeous, that her heart raced to have him forever – and she shot him.

Blood, bits of skull and brain splattered onto her face. She shot him again and again. Her arm held out firmly with the aim of an assassin, she stared at him, emotionless, and thought how easy it was to end it all and how it relieved none of her pain; the only emotion she'd experienced for a long time.

She closed her eyes hoping to feel something else and listened to the shrill ring of the blasts dissipate with the same tempo of his pulse and slowly give way to a penetratingly sharp silence. She felt something now, she felt him slipping away, and her ears rang with the sound of freedom. It was still too far away. She was still a mere observer. She was still a bird in the cage imagining what it would be like to fly.

Time dissolved and a light filled the room, drawing her past the crib and towards the window.

Gliding towards it, her warm toes brushed across the cold marble floor, and the angels of death lifted her over the edge. She didn't feel herself hit the ground. Her delusional mind had already transformed her pain into bliss, obliterating the final seconds of her death.

In the next undefined moment, she felt herself rise higher and higher above the trees waving her goodbye and into the clouds whose arms opened to welcome her to the other side. Moving through their embrace, she slipped through the silky darkness of the unknown.

# 

Never wanting to wake, she did. Violently jolted by the sound of screams, an earth-shattering cry of death filled the room with the breath of terror, and she ran to the window to look outside.

There, five floors below, she saw a crowd of people circling a twisted body that had congealed blood around the head, and the face of what looked like a young girl. The girl's hair, matted in the mess of blood had webbed itself to the ground and looked familiar to her. Even from that height and through the globules of blood, it looked a little like hers.

Worry trickled like tears inside of her, and she jerked back from the window and grabbed her camera from the bedside table. Her heart beating with the anticipation of what she might find, she hurriedly zoomed in on the scene below and scanned the girl's body. Terror leapt into her throat when she saw the beauty spot standing proudly on the girl's right inner thigh. Dropping her camera, she looked down and saw that her own beauty spot was fading.

She ran to the bathroom sink to splash her face with water. Glancing in the mirror, she found nothing looking back. Without any warning her knees buckled, and she fell to the floor. Her instinct drove her back to the window. An almost impossible feat, since all strength had seeped from her body in betrayal like glue, slowing her down and making every second seem infinite.

Struggling to crawl through the echo of her breath that resonated like a death march throughout the room, she wondered what the hell was going on… surely, she must be dreaming?

Finally reaching her destination, she clutched the ledge and peered out of the window. Her eyes zoomed in on the scene below, and slowly she made the connection.

Looking down at her beauty spot, she saw it completely disappear at the same time as the cover was put over the girl on the ground below.

#

He felt a slight breeze against his foot, carried by the spirit of the girl he'd reluctantly loved. Having been stirred to waking by her transitioning spirit, he lay in their bed and felt an unusual peace. Not even the sounds of the sirens roaring in the distance could disturb his state of equanimity.

As the vehicles got nearer and the sirens louder, the dissonance polluted his calm condition, and he tried to peel himself away from the bed. Although his hands were free, his head felt heavy as if some force was pressing it onto the pillow, and he wondered how he had a hangover after only a few glasses of wine.

Lifting his arm, he placed it onto his throbbing brow and felt drops of moisture fall into his palm. 'Sweating in October?' he thought, cursing at the misfortune of having a fever on a day when he had to impress his clients. Despairingly, he wiped his face with his hand; as he drew the wetness down across his cheek and lips, he was welcomed with the taste of blood.

Struck with a sudden fear, he garnered the strength to move and lift the earthly weight holding him down. Once upright, he saw the outline of his body marked by the blood surrounding him and was surprised that he felt no pain despite his loss of blood.

What he did feel was panic - and lots of it. Instinctively placing his hands over his head, he desperately followed the contours of his face, like a blind man trying to identify a person, and to his horror, found a hole.

He rushed to the bathroom where he looked in the mirror and saw only a faint blur of his reflection. Before it faded, he just managed to make out the shape of his eye hanging down his cheek, and an empty space like a bloody ditch where his nose had once been.

He trembled, backing away in the same place his lover had been moments before. Retracing her faded footsteps, he crumpled to the ground.

He'd never believed in an afterlife, in retribution, nor redemption. Death was the end, and once he saw it, he accepted his defeat.

#

She was in a place of darkness, an empty space filled with voices circling her like wolves she couldn't escape from. Torturous screams ripped through the air slicing her reality, and she had no idea where she was or how she'd gotten there.

Her twenty-one years flashed before her. When the film was over, she found herself back in her living room, in 'their' living room. Everything looked the same, except for the fact that it was filled with strangers: women, lots of them, at least forty, moving furniture, making tea, and gossiping in a way that people often did when they hadn't seen each other for a while.

She stood aghast, watching this flurry of activity as rows of chairs appeared from nowhere, facing a table with one leather, executive business chair, placed behind it. She wondered who would sit in that chair, secretly hoping that it had been placed for her. Deciding to take the chance, she moved towards it and was nearly stomped to the ground by an old lady who rudely pushed past her.

"So, you finally got 'ere then...about bloody time too."

Though quite frail in appearance, the old lady's strength sent her flying back, and she fell into the arms of a little girl.

"Hello Lucinda," said the little girl, her words slipping delicately from her fragile lips, "thank you for bringing me here."

"Err hello..." replied Lucinda, apprehensively. The little girl giggled and ran off to chase a ball that appeared only from her desire to have it.

Lucinda? So that was her name... how could she forget? Her flat had not faded from her memory, and yet her name sounded as if it belonged to somebody else. It felt bizarre to exist, and yet have no real sense of her identity.

With nothing to ground her, Lucinda's anxiety rose with the noise level in the room, swirling its notes around her head until she felt dizzy with despair.

A serious looking girl of about twelve-years-old, suddenly appeared and held up a file. A hush grew upon the women as they hurriedly took their seats.

"Welcome again everybody," said the girl.

"Again?" questioned Lucinda.

"Don't look so shocked. You, my dear, have been here before," replied the girl sternly.

Lucinda opened her mouth to object but the girl's icy stare froze the words in her throat, and she let her mouth close. The girl reminded her of The Chair at a committee meeting, and so Lucinda decided to name her, The Chair. This amused her as the girl sat down in the leather chair that she'd hoped was for herself.

Whilst following the circle of the room with her arm, The Chair remarked, "I see Martha is not amongst us anymore. Her last session freed her to be born again."

"Lucky caww," squawked the same old lady who'd earlier pushed past Lucinda and now stood a few feet away, bitterness oozing from her like a poisoned, shrunken oak.

Lucinda perused the old lady's face, looking for the secrets of life that old age might bring. Instead of a revelation, she became lost in the maze of her many wrinkles that marked the numerous paths of destruction she'd walked upon.

"I've been waiting for blooming years to go back," the old lady continued whilst pushing another woman off the seat she was sitting in, sitting down in it herself.

"Ha! Well you should have thought about that before. You had many chances, and you blew each one," was the angry reply from the little girl who'd first greeted Lucinda.

"Ah shut it! You stupid little...."

"Enough!" demanded The Chair, "we have a number of stories and trials to go through this time round. Our agendum is tight."

"Erm excuse me," said Lucinda, trying to sound brave despite feeling fearful, "I'm not quite sure what I'm doing here." She paused hoping that somebody would interrupt her and say, 'Yes, quite right dear, you can go straight on through.' The room remained silent, and her voice shaking a little, she continued, "I think there's been a mistake. Am I dreaming?"

Lucinda's question echoed in the room as a backdrop to the roar of cackles, laughter and tears that burst forth from the crowd and plunged each woman into a maddened frenzy of exaggerated responses that epitomised their deepest traits and psychoses. The young girl giggled as if she were being tickled by an octopus; the old lady, whom Lucinda internally named, 'Old Caww,' repetitively screamed, "Whores! Cheats! Scumbags!" as if plagued by Tourette's. A very sophisticated looking woman twisted her head, laughing maliciously; another woman started to pull out her hair; whilst yet another attempted to strangle herself with her own hands.

"STOP!" screamed The Chair.

Very quickly the women returned to their previous state as if nothing had happened, and The Chair continued, "I think we need to offer Lucinda a little guidance." Looking her deeply in the eyes, she smiled and said, "This place you're in now is your creation and all the people here are present to assist your growth. Though that may not be their intention, because you drew them here today, through their stories you shall be revealed. It is time to take away the mask and really see yourself."

She took a sip of water from the glass on her desk and swallowed. The sound of her gulp resonated throughout the room, and she placed the glass down and casually opened the file she was holding, leaving a shocked Lucinda to absorb what she'd just heard. Her heart was racing, and mind struggling to keep up with the tempo. One thing she was sure of by now was that she wasn't dreaming, and even though it made no sense, she had no choice but to accept that she was there in a place that was somehow of her making.

The Chair closed her file and slammed it down onto the table, interrupting Lucinda's internal turmoil. Smiling generously, she addressed the room at large, "Today we shall hear from Magnolia. A name so pretty for a woman so cunning... hmm, don't you think?" The women nodded their heads in agreement, and the room filled with an eager anticipation of what was to follow.

All eyes fixed on The Chair as she moved away from her desk and towards a girl that Lucinda could only see the back of. The girl's long black hair struck her as a little familiar. At the same time, it brought up a nasty feeling from within. That must be Magnolia, the girl who will tell her story, she thought to herself. There was something about that name that made her feel uneasy, and she questioned where she'd heard it before, wondering if it had been her least favourite flower.

Addressing Magnolia, The Chair said, "My sweet devilish flower, pray do tell of your evilness? Don't be shy and tell it all as it is, or was should I say." By emphasising the past tense, The Chair forced Magnolia to accept her fate in death, and she turned red with anger. The Chair satisfied with this genuine reaction continued, "Remember, forgiveness comes from understanding and from feeling. Have you learnt my dear, how to feel beyond your own narcissistic image? Or does your ego still suffocate your heart?"

Smiling to herself, she casually walked back towards her desk and sat down, nestling the side of her small head into the folds of the leather chair. Once comfortable, she proceeded to speak, "Now, Magnolia, we are ready to hear your story." Before Magnolia had a chance to say anything, The Chair turned towards Lucinda and condescendingly requested, "Lucinda, please be seated. You look like a peeled cucumber standing there."

Lucinda scanned the room. After finding the nearest seat, she cautiously sat down a few rows behind Magnolia. There was something dark about her, something both unnerving and exciting. Even though she could only see the back of her head and shoulders, she felt Magnolia had the power of a Greek Goddess with many secrets buried within the sexy stature of her body;

secrets that she felt were about to reveal themselves like demons in disguise.

Magnolia enjoyed being the centre of attention and confidently stood up, her tumbling dark hair falling to below her waist and resting on her voluptuous bottom. Slowly and meticulously she pulled out a folded bundle of papers from her pocket and began to read.

# Two

"Had I been an Aquarian, none of this would have happened. I might have thought about it, procrastinated, fantasised even, but like a true daydreaming Aquarian that would've been enough. I, though, am a Capricorn. My ascendant sign is Taurus, and all my other inner planets are in the sign of Sagittarius - the majority of which are cramped into the seventh house. This, I have been told, means I have a dependency on others to understand myself through reflection...ironic for an independent Sagittarian, would you not agree?"

The Chair rolled her eyes and said, "This is not a conversation. You tell your story, and the powers that be will guide you, if you allow, to the end. Now, carry on and don't be so insolent."

"Very well, I will," Magnolia paused and smiled bitchily before adding, "continue with my monologue."

Lucinda was quite afraid of The Chair, and Magnolia's bravery impressed her, but she was also quite eager to understand what was going on, and thus equally grateful to hear that there would be no more interruptions.

"Erm, where was I?" said Magnolia before pausing for a second to look over her papers and re-trace her steps, "yes, that's right. So early on in my life I concluded that I was of the bad type, since the people I attracted into my life were the tortured, violent souls of many pasts."

Resting her hand on top of the chair, she paused to find some strength before saying his name, "Joseph was one of these characters."

Lucinda stiffened and thought, Joseph? Sounds vaguely familiar. Magnolia cracked her neck and Lucinda, now even more interested than before, turned her attention back to her. Magnolia continued. "I was his silent partner whilst he viscerally expressed all my anger and frustration, my inner violence and torment. Of course, he was a boy so it was more acceptable, and he didn't write like me; he didn't know how to. Literally, as my pain spilled onto the page, his blood spilled from his veins. After a violent fight, his throbbing bruise was my thumping heart, and my words splattered across the sheet of paper, chaotically strewn, were the sprays of unuttered words from his soul. So, you see, we were the perfect match for each other, as far as reflection goes.

"I met Joseph on the first day of secondary school. He'd looked up and winked at me, while the other kids had laid their heads down low, trying desperately to dissociate themselves. It was then that I knew that he was different...that he was just like me: a troublemaker, a rebel, a fighter, a spirited person. Depending on the way you looked at it, that could either be perceived as a good or a bad thing. I was a rule breaker and that was not considered to be a good thing in school. But rules were bullshit, I believed. Like most things, they were only there to control, and control was something I fought vehemently against.

"My family didn't really care about my welfare, and pretty much ignored me, so nobody had broken me in. Secondary school was a new stable, and I was ready to gallop bareback. Initially, I'd been willing to do it alone, but then my Stallion appeared, in the form of Joseph.

"In the morning of the first hour, of that first day of school, all the first years had been instructed to file into the assembly hall. Obediently, like a herd of sheep we did and were guided by the year head to sit in rows on the floor.

"I crouched down to take my seat, but when I placed my hands onto the floor, I felt grime; it was filthy. I was sure that the teachers would be sitting in chairs, and so sought to look for another alternative. Sure enough, I found it. There, positioned directly parallel to me, was an empty chair just waiting to be filled. Without a moment's hesitation, I got up from the dirty floor and sat in it.

"Just as I had expected, within two minutes I was asked to move. The battle had begun, and I found myself in an arena - a matador facing the bull. My growing smile was the red robe, enticing them to my centre, and I gleamed. I knew secondary school would be fun. After beating them down in junior school, this was a whole new challenge.

"I smugly watched the teachers boil with anger, feeling quite justified with my actions; I didn't see why I should sit on dirt whilst they sat on clean chairs. Though I normally preferred sitting on the floor, it was the principle, and principles were a Sagittarius trait that I carried a lot of.

"Oh, how I relished watching the teachers fume at the audacity of my refusal to obey their orders. Like a mischievous bee, my battle with authority was a buzz that kept me humming all day.

"After presenting my argument, the teachers gathered around me in a disorganised group and began their spiel. They said nothing new or of any interest, which disappointed me somewhat, as I had hoped that the intelligence level of the teachers might increase with the year I was in. But secondary school teachers were no smarter than in junior school. They were the same kind of people, with the same kind of methodical, robotic responses.

"Standing defiantly against them, I showed them that I was not afraid. This somehow had a humiliating effect, with shame clearly visible in their weak eyes.

"So, it was during this event on the first day where I made my enemies. The look of insolence splashed across my face like a reckless painting, I turned away from those in authority and found my only true friend.

"Joseph caught my eye as I searched for camaraderie from my fellow pupils. He was the only one whose glare met mine, and we became locked psychically. Having met again, we acknowledged one another, and in that one moment a thousand years passed us by, and we sealed our fate for yet another lifetime.

"That was the first day of school, and I didn't see Joseph again until after Christmas because of him being sent away for a violent outburst in the school grounds, which I was not witness to. Unfortunately, at the time, I'd been sitting in the Head Master's office waiting for the first of many bollockings that I was due to receive that year.

"Joseph returned in the second term. Physically he'd changed but then so had all the children. During the two-week break, their facial features had gotten more disparate and their childlike forms fuller. I wasn't quite sure if this was due to all the excess Christmas food, or

15

just the development of puberty that had suddenly hit us all.

"The New Year had aged me as well. Having celebrated my birthday with Jesus, I was now twelve and beginning to grow breasts. I hated them. Each day I stood at the mirror disgusted with the process of adulthood spreading upon me like leprosy, and smothering me in the layers of deceit that all adults seemed to suffocate in. To save myself from this fate, I started beating my breasts to keep them down and myself afloat.

"Unlike my own, Joseph's change excited me. His soft, light brown hair which had previously splayed like a fan over the front of one eye, had been cut to a grade one, leaving the nape of his neck exposed and mourning the delicate wisps. Thankfully, it took me all of two minutes to get used to it.

"Although I'd liked his hair before, this new sharp look accentuated his fiercely handsome features, making him even more desirable. His perfect Roman nose, full meaty lips and high to heaven cheekbones had transformed him into a man. Having grown taller, his puppy fat had turned to muscle, and he had an edge about him that oozed experience of a deadly nature. I didn't know where he'd been, but sensed a trail of destruction in the history of the shadow that followed him. He was like a soldier returning from the war zone: physically in one piece but encapsulated by a world filled with experiences that can only be shared with another who has survived the same war. Having come out the other end wiser, his veteran, clear blue eyes had a faraway look to them. On the surface they were as infinite and mesmerising as the calm of the sea. But when I searched more deeply into the depth of his oceanic eyes, I saw the darkness that lurked at the bottom. And once, I swear, I saw a shark swim through his bright, blue eyes.

16

"All morning I looked at him, waiting for God to present me with an opportunity to bring him into my realm and speak to me. Joseph was already an expert assassin and before taking me with his words, claimed me with his powerful touch. That first touch marked me in a way a tattoo does, and from that day on Joseph was always going to be present. The only way to get rid of him would be to scar myself.

"Already, at the age of twelve, I knew Joseph was never going to be someone who stayed in my past. He would be around forever. His presence was so overwhelming that I had no idea how I'd even managed to breathe on this earth before he came into my world."

Magnolia turned towards the crowd and pleadingly said, "And so you see how strong our bond was."

With the exception of Lucinda, all the other women had - in their most recent incarnations - been participants in this before, and as a result were experienced in all forms of deception and manipulation. To Magnolia's dismay, they showed no reaction. She thought she must be losing her touch but didn't flounder on this point too much and continued to justify her hopelessness in her bond to Joseph.

"So, you see, Joseph was a pro. He teased me. Initially, with that wink on the first day of school, he wet my appetite for the blood of his heart, and then he took mine when he possessed me with his touch, and I had no choice but to give up my skin and crawl into his.

"It happened on the first Monday of the second term, towards the end of lunchtime when I was looking forward to my favourite lesson, English, with my favourite teacher, Mr. Lawrence. It had been raining all day, and consequently all the children had been caged in by the weather and held prisoners inside the constraints of the school building. The pressure in the heavy clouds in the sky built up within us, and we caused havoc in the classroom.

"After an hour of raised voices, tears, laughter and general mischievousness, the bell rang to signify the end of lunch.

"At the time, I was sitting on the desk waiting for the class to begin, swinging my legs rhythmically to Michael Jackson's, 'Thriller'; the chorus of which had been playing on loop in my head all day. I tried to look nonchalant as I kept my eyes on the door, eagerly waiting for Joseph to enter.

"Although it was only his first day back, he'd not been present during the lunch break having already managed to secure a detention for his 'bad behaviour' during Math. Luckily, I didn't have to wait too long. No sooner had I willed him, he appeared at the door and approached me with a conviction, held in a silent promise left over from a previous life, to take me back.

"From the moment he entered the room, his eyes never left mine, and once by my side, laid his soft, warm hand on me, and I melted under his touch. He sat down on the table opposite and caught one of my swinging legs - stopping it in its tracks - and held it firmly. I'd been captured by my keeper. Slowly and gently he stroked my shin, and the light hairs on my leg stood on end. He looked at me, smiled and said, 'I like the way that makes me feel,' then threw my leg down and flicked my ear with his fingers before walking away with the coolness of a cowboy.

"I watched him, hypnotised by the rhythm of his gait as he sat down at the back of the class with an intense look in his eyes that taunted me to swim to where he motioned for me to join him. My seat was at the front, the teachers having already established that within two weeks of my entering the school. I joined him anyway.

"At that point, we fused like Siamese twins, and I thought that nothing could sever our tie.

"We were sat so close together that I could feel the vibrations of his body surge like an ocean over my skin with the force of a tsunami that I wanted to be enslaved to. With all my might, I prayed that the teachers wouldn't ask me to move. I wasn't the only rebel in my class and hoped that somebody else would out-stake me that day, and the teachers might not notice that I was in the back with Joseph.

"First years were generally a little more cautious. We on the other hand were not in the slightest bit affected by authority. Doomed from the start, our whole class was one of rejects bunched together like left-over vegetables in a casserole.

"Our class, 1C, consisted of: The Fastest Runner (that was me); The Cripple, Todd who had one foot which slurred behind the other, dragging on the floor like a child's comfort blanket; The Retard, Penny, who suffered immensely for her sub-normality; The Most Intelligent Kid, Frankie, who was the epitome of a geek, wearing thick glasses and carrying the waft of his mother's milk on his untouched lips; The Psychotic, my beloved Joseph; The Regressive, Sonia, who played with dolls, wore flowery dresses, sucked her thumb, had no friends, and cried a lot; The Most Developed, Paula, who had the biggest tits and intentionally wore a shirt too small so that she was busting out; The Most Underdeveloped, Warren, who was actually quite uninteresting and typically childish; and The Prettiest, Sophina, who was never expected to be ugly with a name chosen for her like that. I felt certain that from the moment that she'd been born, she'd been told how utterly adorable she was, and often wondered if this positive affirmation worked in her favour to make her more beautiful. She was like a Barbie doll: blonde, blue eyes, rose lips, long lashes, and hair that flowed and followed her in awe of her beauty.

"There were some eyesores in our class too, but the ugliest of them all I think was Peter. He was so ugly it hurt to look at him. His nose was big and squashed to the right side as if he had a pane of glass constantly pressed against it. The opposite eyebrow was wonky, and had a lift at the end resembling a smirk; a wicked tilt at its own ugliness, perhaps? His top lip was non-existent, and he had the goofiest teeth I'd ever seen. They stuck out, crossed over one and other, and always had bits of food stuck in them. When I could bear to look at him, and I didn't do it often because he just made me feel guilty for not being that ugly, I would look into his eyes. They were so damn sad and dull; probably the result of looking at his own reflection over the years. Poor Peter knew he was repulsive and carried the expression of a wounded animal in need of sympathy.

"So, our class was disruptive and labelled the naughtiest in our year. Older kids talked about us and often popped their heads into our classroom just to see if we were as bad as rumour had it. Thus, we were becoming a legend and I liked this, since I had a large part to play in the drama.

"That Monday afternoon I got lucky. Mr. Lawrence was sick and we had a sub take our class. As soon as the announcement was made, Joseph looked at me and smiled in such a cocksure way that I wondered if he'd somehow orchestrated these events.

"Even though I was by his side now, he didn't look at me again throughout the lesson. Instead, he gently placed his hot hand on my leg, and I spent the entire hour enthralled by Tsunami Joseph, swept away by his force.

"After that day, and much to the horror of the teachers, we were inseparable. For the teachers of our class no day was a good day, but worst of all was Friday. Especially for those teachers who still thought that they could make a difference and affect the course of humanity. Very often, these teachers were fresh out of school themselves or in a mid-life crisis, desperate to cling onto their youth by trying to be our friend. They chewed gum, wore the latest jeans, sat back in their chairs and referred to us as their equals, by saying things like: 'Hey guys we can work together and make this fun.'

"I called these types, 'Mr. Understanding.' They would smirk with you, slag off other teachers, adolescently rolling their eyes, as they pretended to be opposed by the very authority they represented. On some days when The Mr. Understanding teacher-types were worn down, it was clear that they felt lonely. I could see it all around them as they desperately sought approval from the kids, who looked at them as if they were impostors. Often, such a look by a child who sensed this sly craving embarrassed the teacher by showing them how transparent they were, and the teacher would see that the very children they sought to befriend had no respect for them either. The children's intuitiveness and intelligence made these teachers feel foolish and like a beaten puppy, they would whimper away, mortally wounded by the children's rejection of them. Children can be so cruel! Don't you think Lilly?" probed Magnolia.

Lilly, the little girl who'd earlier greeted Lucinda, looked up with wide, scared eyes that made Magnolia smile. It always pleased her to create discomfort in another to make her feel better about herself. She didn't get to relish in this feeling for too long as The Chair grew impatient and said, "One more attempt to draw any person into your filth and you will not be permitted to carry on. You will miss your chance to leave!"

Lucinda perked up. Leave? There was a chance to leave! She'd been swept away with the drama of Magnolia's story and had even found herself enjoying it, but to hear that there was a way out of this mad place re-engaged her attention. Before she could dwell on this, she heard Magnolia sarcastically ask The Chair, "May I?" as she held up the papers that she was reading from.

The Chair smiled and said, "Why, of course my dear, your story is quite fascinating. Please do go on."

Magnolia cleared her throat and straightened out her blouse as if the creases were the guilty party and not she. With a slightly humbler tone, she continued to speak.

"All schools, even in the winter were filled with the smell of sweaty children, often infused with the touch of a fresh outdoor breeze. Our school was no different. It was a paedophiles' paradise, as the aroma of pre-pubescent sex filled every corner of the corridors. I knew this is exactly what motivated some teachers to come to work each day; silently, secretly, and maybe even latently desiring this forbidden fruit of youthfulness, so full of innocence and ripe with anarchy that it was just about to burst. Some teachers were aching to be the prick to do this.

"Bianca the Wanka was such a teacher. He stank of leather - and not the good kind, but the second-hand musty kind. His leather jacket was as stiff and impenetrable as his heart. A dark character with a short, misshapen beard, quite insignificant - a little like himself.

Although only in his forties, he walked with a stoop, as if he almost resented standing up at all. The weight of the world pressed heavily onto his shoulders, fitting into the grooves of his flesh. His eyes were constantly squinting, and his brow was permanently stressed. I often thought it would be possible to hold a pencil in the constant crease ingrained within his brow. In short, everything about him screamed, 'Fuck off!'

"Initially, I couldn't understand why he was there. My first thought was that he didn't like kids, but I soon came to realise that it was his need for them that was the draw. He wanted to consume them. In the same way a fat person on a diet might want to eat a chocolate cake, the very existence of children made him suffer. His inability to resist working in their company, to be around them, and feed off their energy, created a fire in him. This second-rate rage followed him wherever he went, as he stomped around the corridors, nostrils flared like a wild bison, constrained in a feeble man's body.

"Luckily, I had very little to do with Mr. Bianca, although he would take every opportunity he could to reprimand me: running in the hallway, wearing inappropriate jewellery or laughing aloud for no apparent reason. There was this one time when he attempted to humiliate me by asking me in front of the whole class if I had a mental disorder. I told him to 'go fuck himself,' adding that he probably wouldn't be able to as his dick was too small. Of course, I got the expected reaction from the kids, and the necessary punishment from the year head.

"At that time, I'd wished that it had been the Eighties when corporal punishment was still acceptable in state schools. Instead, I was put on report, given detentions, or suspended. I didn't care. I even liked being punished, but not nearly as much as I enjoyed antagonising Mr. Bianca.

"He hated the fact that I got to choose the morning hymns. Fiercely opposing it, he claimed that I was being given special treatment. In a way I was, but he had less authority than the educational psychologist, who'd

23

awarded me that task to give me something to be proud of. I wasn't supposed to understand the inherent relative meaning behind it, but of course I did and used it to my best advantage, choosing upbeat hymns I knew Mr. Bianca would hate. Then, during the assembly, I would take it a step further by swinging my hips and swaying my hands in a gospel fashion that really pissed him off. Whilst I sang down the light, I would feel his glare penetrating me from the other side of the assembly hall, and I loved it. I was getting to him, and I was winning."

Magnolia looked up from her papers and paused before biting her lip to contain her smile which was in stark contrast to the sincerity of what she was about to convey. "Please understand," she said, "it's not that I wasn't compassionate. It's precisely because I was that I took delight in putting a mirror up to his face, so that each time he took a shit, he could see it. He took a particular interest in Joseph; this was also why I hated him. Soon, it became clear that Joseph, too, had a bone to pick. Although at the time I had no idea how big that bone was.

"On what started out as a regular day, Joseph told me that he'd hatched a plan to get Mr. Bianca back. We were sitting in a small park near the school, and I listened intently to him. Whatever he wanted, I would do. He said that we would do 'it,' although he wouldn't tell me what 'it' was, until Friday afternoon. It would be the last Friday of the second term, and the two-week school holiday would be enough time to let the dust settle. In retrospect, I fear that 'ashes' instead of 'dust' would have been a more accurate word to use.

"It was the end of March. The year was nineteen ninety-two: The Chinese Year of the Monkey. Maybe, that's why we felt so mischievous. The last Friday at the end of the month was payday for many a man, and we too wanted compensation. Mr. Bianca had to pay, and we became the victim, perpetrator, judge, and jury." Magnolia turned to the crowded room and addressed them all by stating, "The verdict you will see, and my plea of course, was not guilty."

Her need to reiterate her defence of course made her guilty as hell, and the whole room felt it while shuddering in anticipation of what the sin might be. Magnolia ignored the tension from the people around her and carried on with her story.

"We waited for two hours after school ended and spent this time hanging around an empty lot, eating sweets and flicking through a magazine that Joseph had stolen. We were killing time, and that concept alone set the tone for what was about to follow.

"When Joseph decided to get going, he motioned for me to follow him. By now he'd briefed me, and though I knew the plan, I never really believed that we would pull it off. That we'd actually do, or would even get away with it. But Joseph had thought this through and what was a game to me was serious business to him.

"I watched from behind the hedge as he walked up to Mr. Bianca's house and rang the doorbell. I don't know whether it was because I was looking at him from a distance, but he suddenly looked small to me, standing there scuffing his feet nervously against the ground with his hands hung in his pockets.

"After a few seconds the door opened and Mr. Bianca held Joseph by the shoulders and ushered him into his home, jerking his head from side to side like a chicken scanning the area. The door closed, and I began the count. Exactly seven minutes Joseph had said. Seven was his lucky number.

"As planned, I made my way round to the back of the house and climbed over the fence. Excitement filled me.

A river of mischievousness was flowing, and one by one my morals were being drowned.

"I ducked below the window sill and could hear their voices inside. It had only been four minutes. I had to crouch for three more. Desperate to find a distraction, I set my eyes on an army of ants working together to carry a crumb. As they neared what I presumed was their destination, like a God I changed the course of their direction by transporting them with a piece of paper to the other side of where I sat. They seemed momentarily confused but within seconds were back on track. Their internal compasses had set them straight, and within a minute they were back to their original position. I felt victorious for them.

"My elation was quashed as a sudden cloud of dust shot up, burying them in dirt. They were crushed by an almighty foot. It belonged to Joseph, whose appearance brought me out of the ant drama and into my own. He pulled my ponytail, and I looked up at him. Now it was his turn to jerk his head from side to side like a chicken scanning the area, and I scurried into the pen.

"Once inside, Joseph ordered me to hide behind the kitchen door. I did. And then I heard his voice, 'Jay,' he called. It was Bianca The Wanka.

"I giggled and mimicked aloud, 'Jay... how fucking gay is that?' Joseph shot me a glare, and I knew to keep my mouth shut. Taking a fighter stance, he picked up a bat and let it hang like a giant stick insect in his hand. This mutation looked so natural that any abnormality was camouflaged, and as Mr. Bianca entered the room, he didn't even notice.

"Then it was too late. WHACK! Straight into the balls. 'How do you like that you fucking perv!' shouted Joseph, loving it. Mr. Bianca cried out and fell to the ground, rolling around in agony. Joseph held the bat high over his head and swung it down - SMACK! Right across Mr. Bianca's head. Blood squirted everywhere.

"Joseph leaned over his body. Spit was furiously running down his chin, as he savoured in saying, 'Been a while hasn't it?' His eyes were alive with revenge, and he stepped back and screamed, 'What's the matter am I getting too old for you now?' At the time, it didn't register what he was getting too old for. Plus, I was in shock. This was way out of my depth, but I knew with Joseph, no waters were too deep.

"Mr. Bianca murmured inaudibly as thick blood trickled down his face. I stood watching the red trail mark its journey from the side of his scalp to his jaw line, where it separated into drops, each one clinging like a rock climber, desperate not to fall off the edge. It sounds crazy I know, but I almost heard their cries just before they splattered onto the floor. It was a massacre crusade, as more drops plunged from the same place, creating a pool, which grew with a ferocious velocity I enjoyed watching.

"Having drifted off, I snapped back to hear Joseph's voice say, 'Come on don't just stand there, help me!' He was already dragging Mr. Bianca's body into the next room. Before I had time to think, he paused to smile and throw me some tape.

#

"It had just started to get dark outside, and the once tidy living room, now resembled the aftermath of a pyjama party from any one of the American sitcoms that I'd recently become addicted to. After raiding the paedophile's sweetshop, we were sitting on the sofa and stuffing our faces, our deadly eyes transfixed on the children's channel whilst the sweets lay in our bellies,

27

releasing their colourful chemicals of hyperactivity into our blood streams.

"Then Mr. Bianca started to come round. Joseph looked at me and winked, and I knew that he wanted to have some more fun. Rising like a sea monster from the ocean, he dropped the TV remote control from his lap and kicked Mr. Bianca hard in the shins. Mr. Bianca winced with pain, his scream trapped inside his taped mouth.

"He looked ridiculous! Having raided his 'special trunk' we'd dressed him in his favourite pink, flowery dress. Of course, he wasn't used to wearing it himself. Although I didn't know at the time, he'd had it especially made for children, and Joseph had resorted to cutting the sides of it to squeeze him in. The hem of the dress barely covered his arse, so his saggy, hairy balls stuck out like curled hedgehogs. To top off his look, and with the same excitement a child might have about putting the fairy on the Christmas tree, Joseph placed some Mickey Mouse ear warmers on Mr. Bianca's head. We'd transformed him from a miserable schoolteacher into a cartoon character, and what we'd created was as real as the Tom and Jerry Cartoon on the TV that we were watching.

"The cartoon came alive in the living room where Mickey Mouse was a special feature in the show and Tom and Jerry were, for a change, working together like the ants outside.

"Tom straddled Mickey and motioned for Jerry to pass him the broom. Taking it from Jerry's hands, he raised it over his head and repeatedly pummeled Mickey in the face before attempting to thrust it up his backside. Mickey turned white, and his ears drooped. As he twisted from side to side in a desperate but futile attempt to free himself, his arm pressed the TV remote, and the screen flicked to another channel showing a nature documentary.

"Now the teenage chimps in their ape language shouted, 'Smash his head in,' as they jumped up and down, shrieking with delight. The sheer excitement of exalted youth peered through the TV at Tom and Jerry, egging them on. The chimps thumped their chests and then turned on each other.

"Tom and Jerry turned to the TV and smiled. Mickey rolled around the floor in agony again, and his arm pressed the TV remote, flicking the channel to Newsround; news for kids. It showed the destruction and the aftermath of the latest war. The dust in the air, a symbol of lingering souls still searching for their lives - not ready to go. In the midst of it all, Mickey in his pink flowery dress and ear warmers, reaching out to the survivors who walked by.

"Leaving him in the desert to die, Tom and Jerry exited the room; while Joseph purred with the satisfaction of a cat, I was as quiet as a mouse.

"Thundercats, another favourite cartoon of ours started, and the silence was broken. We grabbed some more crisps from the cupboard in the kitchen and came back into the room. Joseph turned up the volume of the TV to drown out the muffled, tortured cries of Mr. Bianca and discounted what he'd done. And I, his silent partner, neglected the victim with my eyes open wide.

"Despite my endeavors' to ignore Mr. Bianca's pain, my head was drawn in his direction, as if some magnetic force was pushing me to face him. Reluctantly, I saw him peer to the window where freedom awaited him through a pane of glass. Out of nowhere the tune of a children's song popped into my head, playing over and over again. Without any effort, I spontaneously changed the words to fit the current setting and internally sung the tune:

29

How much is that doggy in the window, the one with the broom up his arse? How much is that is that doggy in the window, how long will his nightmare last...?

"The song got louder and faster in my head as Mr. Bianca's big, hollow eyes became swallowed up by terror, shock resonating in every one of his cells. He was petrified, unable to fight, resigned to his fate (much like poor Peter with his ugliness). I felt it must be the not knowing. The complete and utter terror of having no control or even idea of what could possibly come next that must evoke the ultimate fear.

"Mr. Bianca seemed so desperate before, but now he just looked as if he wanted to die. I wondered if any of his young comrades felt this way, having no idea of what the rules were or how to play the game of life lived under threat from an abuser.

"One of the inconveniences of being young is lack of experience, and the inability to decipher what the consequences of an action might be. Most adults know a rollercoaster ride that is making them sick will eventually end. A small child in fear may believe it could go on forever; it becomes their reality. This is where I hoped we'd taken Bianca The Wanka.

"The song faded from my mind; the pulse of the rhythm weakened with the same tempo as the victim before me. And as the rollercoaster took its last turn, I could see him reach for the door and knock to be let in by death. The door responded and opened to a hazy, bright light that filled the room.

"Finally, the victim's whimpering sound turned to silence and stained the carpet.

"Joseph wasn't even aware at first, while I sat wondering about what would happen next. It surprised me to feel no remorse, or even responsibility for his death. Instead the void was filled with a calmness that spread through me. The silence which trailed death stung my ears, until I heard God, and was drawn into my heart.

"My conscience rose another level, and I panicked. Shaking Joseph I asked him how the hell we were going to get away with this? Naturally, Joseph sustained the same cool composure as before and told me that the police would be so outraged by the pervert, they would be prejudiced against him. He would already be tainted in their eyes. They would assume justice had been served; a sick death for a sick man.

"'Besides,' he said reassuringly, 'they would never suspect children could commit such atrocities - surely they were the victims.' He smiled and gave me the same wink that had intoxicated me the second we'd met in the school assembly hall. Of course, he had my faith again. But I couldn't help wondering if anybody had seen us go in.

"'Relax, we have to believe that we had nothing to do with this,' he said already believing it himself. 'Nobody saw us – they definitely didn't see you and this sick prick's been a mate of my dads for years. I've got a reason to be here. Dropping something off? We'll get away with this.'

"I worried about fingerprints. Joseph laughed and said, 'Trust me, ours aren't the only children's prints in the house.' When I still looked scared he stroked the side of my face and said, 'I've got it under control; we're going to torch the place.'

"He got up and prodded Mr. Bianca with his foot. 'Yep, he's a goner,' he said and bent down and pulled off two red ribbons from the Mickey Mouse ear warmers. He threw one to me and said, 'Souvenir,' then smiled and walked out of the room.

"Within a few minutes he was back, carrying a canister in one hand, and the red ribbon tied around his wrist on the other.

"Gradually, the belief that we wouldn't get caught began to ferment within, and I apprehensively waited for more orders whilst Joseph fiddled with the video tapes. Finally satisfied with his choice, he pressed play, turned up the volume, and I began to douse the house with petrol to the sounds of a child 'Sucking a lollicock' and 'Begging to be filled with the magic.' At least it was Friday I thought, and I could ride my bike tomorrow.

"Back at school, Joseph wasn't there anymore. Bianca the Wanka was substituted with Hunt the Cunt. The year head walked in to remind the class not to run in the corridors. When he left we all rolled our eyes, and I smiled at the boy at the front of the class, whose cheeky face reminded me of Joseph's.

"Years seemed to melt by, as I was absorbed in the reminiscence of lost innocence, until the school bell rang and somebody shouted, 'Miss, can we go?' Looking up from my desk, I felt as though I was peering through a lens. Facing my class, they seemed so distant and out of reach. The power to release them was in one gesture, but I paused to capture this frame where the silence was timeless. Then I nodded, and the spell was broken.

"The young scrambled out of the room, barely giving me a second glance, and my stomach tightened. With each step their voices faded, only their smell lingered, and I was left empty and alone; Joseph never gave himself to me.

"My life became one long jail term as I remained a prisoner of his love. My unquenched, forbidden desire was so strong, I couldn't escape this karmic destiny. Two parts of the same sum, I stood excited and petrified for the day when I was no longer held captive and finally released to complete my sent..."

"You never got to finish it then," interrupted The Chair, who was clearly unimpressed, "and you took another way out. Tell me, how long have you been here now?"

Excited at the prospect of being released, Magnolia quickly answered, "I've attended one of these sittings and …"

She was cut off again, this time by the Old Caww. "One sitting! One lousy sitting that lasted only five hours in earthly time, and she gets to tawk. I been to a hundred of these bloody tiresome things and still, still I'm here listening to your shitty, boring, dead-end, sob stories when..."

To the surprise of many of the women an unexpected interruption came from a pertinent looking woman. "Enough you old bitch, why do you think that they are making you wait?"

The Chair smiled wryly, and in a pleased tone said, "It seems Mrs. Bruce that you, my dear, shall soon take the stand. Well done, you have found your anger. Are you ready to face it though? We shall see."

Magnolia impatiently shuffled her papers; she didn't want the attention off her. She thought this might be her chance to break free, but being unable to find the right moment, just blurted, "Can I go back now and start again? I've told my story, and I believe that I have learnt, and I do fe..."

The Chair cut her off with firm words. "Firstly, this is not your only story and secondly you feel nothing Magnolia. You are still absorbed in your drama. I feel your pleasure in the violent act. I smell and taste your desire for destruction. You still have much to learn." She paused and looked around, "all of you do."

The silent fear that descended upon the room pleased her somewhat, and she got up from her chair and walked towards the first row of women. "Here in this Divine Courtroom you'll learn lessons you failed to learn in life;

lessons you were given ample opportunities to learn, I might add. You'll learn from each other and you'll learn from me, through The Seven Universal Laws by which everything in the Universe is governed." It was clear from the puzzled look on the women's faces that she needed to elaborate.

"You see, my dears, The Universe already exists in perfect harmony. These Laws, which derive from ancient esoteric teachings will show you that." She caught Lucinda's eye and said, "Don't worry I'll get to each one of them."

She walked back towards her seat and went on, "By fully understanding and practising these Universal Laws, one is able to experience a relationship with the Universe where nothing is separate. Thus, these Universal Laws inadvertently aid the transcendence of the ego and ultimately results in you being happy and attracting into your life all that your heart truly desires. Your pure heart I say and not your mind, your crazy monkey mind. For now, you are all dead – in transit – but dead. Still, you have a chance to learn."

"But I have learnt!" wailed Magnolia.

The Chair looked at her pathetically and said, "If you had learnt then you wouldn't be wailing like a street cat, dear. Let me ask you this? I just mentioned the Seven Universal Laws and you chose to complain rather than be open to the truth, which is, that you know nothing."

"I have a degree!"

"So, you can study. So, what? What about life lessons? What do you really know about anything beyond serving your own needs? I mentioned the Seven Universal Laws and you didn't even flinch – not even about the number Seven."

Tears welled up in Magnolia's eyes, and she sorrowfully said, "That was his lucky number."

"Still obsessed about him I see. Even now. Let me try to enlighten you further. The number seven is much more than just *his* lucky number. The number seven is recognised as a number of divinity. Esoteric traditions talk about the seven states of consciousness or seven stages of life. Some exoteric religions consider the number seven as holy and worship it. In the Bible, it is said that God created the world during six days. The seventh day, a day of rest, became a sacred day. There are some Christians who think that there are seven levels in hell. In contrast the Islam faith believe there are seven levels of Heaven. Hence the expression, "I'm in seventh heaven!"

"Wish I was," snorted Magnolia.

"Keep wishing, my dear, but do it silently and don't interrupt me. There are also seven days of the week, seven deadly sins, which I do believe you have fulfilled. There are seven notes in a music scale, seven Chakras..."

"Seven colours in a rainbow," shouted Lilly and clapped with excitement.

"Seven major metals," continued The Chair, "seven phases of the moon, compartments to the heart, natural divisions of the brain, major body organs. And then there is the seven-year itch, which you would know nothing about since you've never committed to anything."

"I am committed to my love."

The Chair laughed. "You were committed to an idea. He was never yours, Magnolia."

"I know he loved me once. He just, he just..." Magnolia stopped. Tears streamed down her face, and she shouted, "Fuck you all!"

Lucinda nervously shifted in her seat. It hurt her to see another person in so much pain at the hands of unrequited love. For a second she had compassion for Magnolia.

The Chair didn't share the same sentiments. Brushing Magnolia away with her hands, she ordered, "Take your seat. We do not have a family for you yet. Unless you wish to be born into one that you are now ready for. For if you return too early you will only carry on from where you left off; misery and madness will circumnavigate you from the very onset of your birth. Sit down Magnolia, you are lucky to be chosen to be here in transit now, so don't waste this opportunity and please..." The Chair paused before saying, "my dear, sit down."

The room softened as Magnolia walked back to her seat. It was rare for The Chair to take an appeasing tone, and it quietened and humbled the group at large.

Before sitting, Magnolia threw Lucinda a bitchy glare. Slightly perturbed, Lucinda looked down and felt her heart flutter as a faint image of Joseph entered her mind.

# Three

Lucinda and Joseph had met in Northern India, in Kilganga, a beautiful sacred mountain range on the tip of the Himalayas, where two of the revered Indian Gods, Parvathi and Shiva, were said to have consummated their partnership.

Within minutes of meeting, their relationship flourished. Before a word had been uttered, an explosion of magnetic chemistry burst forth, intertwining their forces and making it nearly impossible to fight the impulse to be together.

Just as Shiva had taken Parvathi, that very same evening Joseph took Lucinda under the watchful eye of the full moon; its lunar force exciting her resident madness.

Ferociously and lovingly they were taken to deeper levels neither of them were properly aware of. Each thrust, exhalation, and caress stripped away another layer, and the facade dropped, revealing the victim and perpetrator as they came head to head. Through gritted teeth and screams they spat out what had previously lain buried in the cemeteries of their hearts and through their desire had now been resurrected.

Their patterns fit as snugly and arbitrarily as beads in a kaleidoscope, and a union bred from years of karma wove itself into the core fabric of their souls, rewriting the script of many lifetimes.

From beginning to end, their relationship lasted nineteen months. The first few of which were like a heavenly honeymoon where they silently communicated through their hidden feelings and psychic connection; seeing the same room from completely different angles - feeling it in the same way.

#

There was one other person in the room who had no moral right to be there: Magnolia, Joseph's childhood friend.

That same year, she too had decided to go travelling. Unlike Joseph, her motivation hadn't been to explore the world but to hunt him down.

Her original plan had been to travel for a few months and get a catalogue of stories to impress him with, before she met him tanned, healthy and ready to seduce. But, by the time she was ready to face him he'd surprised her by first changing continent, and then cutting his travels short to return to a marketing project that was going to 'make him rich'.

Although Joseph was her primary target (and one she'd missed) the journey itself ended up being a refreshing experience, and she returned to the UK with, as she'd hoped, many interesting stories and a renewed power for life.

Whilst away, she'd also made up her mind to have Joseph forever and to finally lay her heart out. A part of her felt a strong urgency to do it quickly. On some level, she felt him slipping away and couldn't take the risk of losing him.

#

*Autumn 2006*

She decided to make her move on the same day that she returned from her travels, one month after him.

Once outside the airport she was greeted by a trail of black cabs parked up like cockroaches. This was England where things were done properly, and without being hassled by drivers all vying for her business, she got into the first cab and was finally on her way. 'Good. Things are on track,' she thought as one of her Grandmother's favourite songs, 'I'll Never Stop Loving You,' by Doris Day, played on the car radio.

The roads were clear, and within forty-five minutes she was in her neighbourhood. Joseph's flat was only a few miles from her own, and as she passed his street, she excitedly peered through the window to see if she could catch a glimpse of him. It occurred to her that if she hadn't looked so haggard from the long plane ride that she may have gone directly to his house. But, she decided that it was a blessing in disguise; it would be better to call him first.

She had no intention of laying it out all out over the phone. The initial 'Hi, I'm back,' conversation was just meant to be the entree to the main meal. The anticipation of which ruffled the nerves in her body. To comfort herself, she put her fingers to her mouth (an action she'd often done as a child) and was temporarily soothed by caressing the contour of her shapely lips. She held her finger over the beauty spot just above her lip on the left-hand side. It was Joseph's favourite part of her mouth, and so, became hers too. By the time she'd gotten home, she was in a much calmer state.

This peaceful feeling didn't last long. Seeing the interior of her untidy, overcrowded studio flat only brought back memories of Joseph. They'd fucked in every possible crevice of her room, and her nerves started jumping around like disobedient children.

She let her backpack slip onto a pile of dirty clothes but refused to fall with it. She had to get a grip and decided a hot bath was in order, with lots of bubbles and a big fat spliff. She remembered leaving a small stash in her weed box somewhere under her bed and rushed to find it, kicking away anything that got in her way.

After scrambling under her bed, she had the box in her hand. The weed had dried out a little and was of a mediocre quality; certainly, not as potent as what she'd been spoilt with in Thailand. But, it was still a welcoming sight, and the disobedient children calmed down now that they had the promise of a treat.

Feeling more relaxed, she stripped off her clothes and ran a bath before sitting down naked on the cool floor of the tiny bathroom to skin up. There were lots of seeds in this batch, and she muttered in annoyance as she first sought to pick these out.

Like most of her experiences in life, smoking was one she shared with Joseph. They had only been thirteen years old when they'd gotten high in the playground late at night and had had sex on the children's slide.

Remembering Joseph leaning against the slide, his hair messed up and trouser button still undone, aroused her. He'd looked like a young Marlboro Man. She was no match for him back then. It had taken her years to get used to inhaling those toxins. So, instead of exuding sensuality like her idol, Greta Garbo, she was more like

Thomas the Tank Engine, coughing and spluttering like an old train. Joseph was also the one who'd shown her how to roll. Most people developed their own style, but she never swayed from what he'd taught her.

Her reverie coincided with a stream of light shining through the gap of the partially closed curtain. Thinking the light was a good omen, she excitedly rose from her spot on the floor to let it in. Briskly pulling the curtains apart, the heavens opened, and the sun splashed an orange ray into the room. Her fears were on the down of the see-saw of her emotions and hope was at the top. She'd wished long enough. She'd waited, and now was her time to take what was rightfully hers.

As the water reached the rim of the bath, she leaned over to turn off the taps then sat down and picked up the spliff. She examined her work of art – perfect roach, perfect cone and perfect twist at the top. Everything was perfect. Well almost, she couldn't stop the sun setting and watched as the orange rays mysteriously dissolved. The thought of being alone in the dark frightened her. Being in a dark room with candles was as far as she would dare to go.

There were already a few half worn-out candles dotted around the bathroom from the last time she and Joseph had tried to have sex in the bath. It had turned out to be a shambles - drunk and stoned they'd slipped and tripped all over the place. She even had a small burn mark on her pubic area where her pubes had been singed by the flames. She lovingly touched that spot and rose to light the candles. Smiling, she thought that it wouldn't be too long before she would be with Joseph again.

To her utter dismay, the vision of them together wouldn't come to mind, and a wave of nausea flooded her like a river of corpses. She smelt the death of something.

Leaning over the bath, she opened the small window to let out the stench and heard the birds tweeting their autumn song. A cool breeze tickled her face, and the last few sun drops fell like tears from the sky; she imagined herself falling amongst them.

The see-saw swung the other way and dark thoughts emerged like the dead from the morgue. To drown them out, she abandoned lighting more candles and submerged herself into the near scalding water, resting her neck against a cushion of bubbles.

Reaching for the spliff, she sparked it up. Having timed it just right, the sky was on fire as the sun lay to rest, and she smoked her tension away.

#

She awoke in darkness with only the flicker of a dying candle flame to shed a little light into the room. The bath water was cold, and the roach of the spliff had fallen into the water and lay floating like a dead dream.

Magnolia felt doom.

She shuddered but put these dark feelings down to tiredness and eased herself out of the water. Nothing was going to get in the way of her mission.

To give herself some Dutch courage, she prepared for the phone call in the same way as she would a date, by washing and grooming herself into a beatific condition.

The inspiration to make herself up came from her Grandmother, who even in old age had managed to look elegant, fluidly reaching for the pearls or tenderly applying her foundation. Her every move was a musical note Magnolia swayed to as she watched in awe, unaware her brain was programming the events for her to imitate at a later date.

In a relaxed mood, she sat down in front of her beauty table as gracefully as her Grandmother used to. On the top right-hand side of the mirror was a picture of her and Joseph as children, with a red ribbon attached to it. They were about twelve-years-old. It had been a perfect time. Joseph had had nobody else but her back then.

Taking the picture off the mirror, she looked more closely at it. Her eyes were happier and his filled with stories he'd never told. She'd never pried. Joseph was a private boy - it was part of his allure.

The memory of their first time together pleasurably haunted her, and she felt once more how fear and desire had danced a tango within, until his warm breath melted them, and she was left only wanting him. She never stopped only wanting him. On that day not only had he taken her virginity but her heart too, and she never wanted it back. She liked being owned, and in return she rewarded him with her loyalty.

With each passing year, her love had hastened. As a result, she'd spent a lot of time and energy on him. In that way, he'd unknowingly groomed her. He was the reason she'd grown her hair long after he'd made a casual comment about liking girls with long hair. At the time, she'd just cut hers into a bob, and had felt devastated by that remark. There was no doubt that it had been directed at her.

From that day on, she grew her hair with him in mind, sitting each day at her dressing table, brushing it like Rapunzel. With each stroke of the brush she made a wish for them to be together. That was at least fifty wishes a day. She smiled as she worked out that fifty wishes a day for fifteen years, amounted to fifteen thousand wishes.

43

Surely, pure determination should warrant her wish being granted.

At twenty-seven-years-old her hair reached down to below her breasts, her nipples peeking through the strands of auburn like two chocolate buttons. Her radiant brown complexion meant that there was no need to apply any foundation; a little mascara was all that was required, and she scantily brushed her lashes.

The time had come. She was ready to face him, even if it was just on the phone. It was seven o'clock, Joseph's lucky number. Hopefully tonight, hers too. She sat naked on the edge of her bed, took a few deep breaths, and dialed.

After the ninth ring, and just as she was about to give up, she heard a girl say, "Hello."

She was shocked, and had not expected to hear a female's voice since none of Joseph's 'fucks' were permitted to answer the phone. "Erm, hello, who are you?" she blurted, then wished she hadn't.

"I'm Lucinda," replied the girl with a childish song in her voice.

"Not your name. I mean *who* are you?" she said unable to stop the violent tone of the words explode from her mouth.

Lucinda, slightly taken aback, obediently answered, "I'm Joseph's girlfriend," and giggled at the same time as Magnolia heard Joseph in the background.

The vibration of the voice she missed so much sent waves of anxiety to her stomach, and she churned with envy, imagining Lucinda naked on the bed with Joseph tickling her. Before the vile fantasy could grow, Joseph took the phone and asked, "Who's this?"

"It's me," said Magnolia shyly.

"Who?"

"Magnolia," she said as if her heart had just been ripped out.

"Hey, you're back," said Joseph, pausing to take a drag from a cigarette.

"Didn't you recognise my voice?"

"Give me a break. It's been ages since..."

"Yeah, yeah, ok," she said trying to reassure herself. Unable to catch the words running from her mouth, she teasingly asked, "And... who's that girl?"

"Ah, now that is the Lovely Lucinda."

She nervously guffawed. She hated Joseph's Delightful Dina, Perfect Pennie, and Beautiful Betty lines - pet names with condescending filaments to them. She took comfort in the fact that at no time had he called her, The Magnificent Magnolia. It set her apart and confirmed that she was different from the rest of the fucks, of which he had many.

She never tired of hearing about his sexual conquests with other women. His regurgitation of events delivered with detachment (like somebody walking away from their own vomit) only revealed his lack of respect for them.

His love life was like one of those Spanish soap operas she used to sit through with her Grandmother, where he was the main star. It gave her great pleasure to watch the twists and turns of his affairs become entangled like octopus' legs. But then something changed. Even though she had the privilege of being a spectator in the VIP box, there was a part of her that wanted to feel the strangulation of painful desire. To be a character burnt by his love. Magnolia the Martyr would have been happy to hang from the cross next to all his other lovers and sacrifice herself to love him. As long as she was his Mary Magdalene. His number one lady.

Deep down, she was sure of that. She was separate from the crowd; she was a constant companion to him.

Unlike Lucinda, who would be a person in transit - she was the final destination.

After reminding herself of that again, the shock of hearing Lucinda say, 'I'm Joseph's girlfriend' dissipated. Besides, there'd been plenty of women in the past, who'd also felt deserving of the title – one Joseph had never awarded them. Years of friendship had taught her that he never loved any of them.

She relaxed. Lucinda posed no threat to her. The image of her on the cross faded, and she quickly turned her attention back in time to hear Joseph ask, "So how about dinner tomorrow night then? There's someone I want to introduce you to."

"Not a girl, I hope," she said with a hint of a plea in her voice.

"Nah, this is a bloke. I know girls fight like bitches when I'm around."

"Ah, you're so full of yourself."

"I bet you'd like to be full of me," he said smugly.

Lucinda looked nervously at him. He winked at her and brushed his hand in the air as if it were an irrelevant comment and said, "I'm joking!"

Magnolia on the other hand was close to creaming herself. "Half-joking," she said believing him.

"See you tomorrow then?"

"Yeah, just send me the details. That is if you still have my number."

"Somewhere I guess," he said and took another pull from his cigarette.

Magnolia mouthed the word 'cunt'.

"Later skater," said Joseph and quickly put the phone down.

Magnolia sighed heavily. Something was off. She was only half relieved to have a date with him since it would've been better for them to be alone, but very quickly she decided that it didn't really matter if there was someone else present; she'd do anything to see him.

#

With the date set and conversation over with, Joseph threw the phone onto the bed. His stomach tightened. The weight of her desire wasn't unwelcome. He never turned away from those powerful feelings, but her nervousness had infiltrated him, and he was torn between fearing and loving her.

He rubbed his forehead, hoping to erase his creeping thoughts. But it was futile. Magnolia was back. She'd been the only one to ever touch his sensitivity. He was sure it wasn't real love, feeling assured that he wasn't capable of that. A deep pain in his gut contradicted this with a gnawing sensation that warned him that this was the start of something bad. Ignoring this feeling of doom, he stepped back onto an old path.

If only he'd walked away from her then. If only he'd turned to the woman by his side and given her his love. If only he'd trusted his inner voice that had warned him to leave - Magnolia - alone.

#

Lucinda waited a few minutes for Joseph to acknowledge her. The silence after the call was unsettling. He was rarely knocked off guard, and she wanted to know who was capable of doing this. Having already been disturbed by the aggressiveness of the girl on the phone she asked, "Who was that?"

Joseph was startled. He'd forgotten Lucinda was even in the room. Throwing on the cloak of denial, he quickly composed himself and calmly took her small face into the palm of his hand and confidently replied, "An old friend of mine," then walked away to mark an end to the conversation. Something in him knew not to reveal her name - that somewhere down the line, Magnolia would be trouble.

While she watched him strut off, Lucinda saw the first signs of deceit. On some level, she knew that by ignoring the warning, she had skidded onto a well-trodden path that laid the foundation of what was to come.

#

Seven miles away, Magnolia looked at herself in the mirror and shook off her jealousy about the Lovely Lucinda. Her intuition warned her to act quickly, and she began to think of ways that she could have Joseph forever.

# Four

That evening Magnolia dreamt of Joseph passionately making love to her. They were in a side alley, and she was dressed to the nines in a long, red dress with a slit on the left side. In the midst of their embrace Joseph tore the dress right open until it fell off her, and she was fully exposed. Then he walked away.

She woke up in a sweat. He hadn't even looked back. Bloody dreams, she thought to herself, fuck it, they're just my fears. It's not real and it won't be real. He'll be mine.

Her stomach churned and in her mind, she heard, will he? To shut up her thoughts she had to act, get moving, have a shower, make the bed, anything.

She got up and looked at the pile of clothes on the floor. They bored her, just like everything did after a while, well everything except Joseph. She missed him so much and couldn't wait to see him, couldn't wait for him to see her in, in - what? It had to be the red dress. It was gorgeous but was it a good omen or a bad one? Joseph hadn't been able to resist her in it, but then he'd walked away. She wanted to believe that he wanted her as much as she wanted him, and so of course it was much easier to focus on the fact that he couldn't resist her. Having made that rash decision, she hurriedly dressed and rushed out to the shops to find it.

Three hours and two hundred and eighty pounds later, she had her doppelganger dress in her hand: a red, figure hugging loaded weapon. She especially liked the low front, exposing the top of her breasts positioned like twin planets.

Standing proudly at the cash desk with the dress draped over her arm like a befallen lover, she wondered if it might be a little over the top. This didn't stop her from wanting it - from having it, and she paid for the dress and rushed home to prepare for the date.

All afternoon she tried out new hairstyles and chose a selection of possible accessories. Her room looked like the peak of a jumble sale, with even more clothes scattered in piles around the floor, and in between them a few dirty plates poking out like scared children.

Magnolia couldn't care less. She had only one focus, and it couldn't come soon enough.

Finally, the evening swarmed on her like a harem of fairy nymphs, and she admired the dress hanging on her bathroom door. Touching it with as much tenderness as if it were her own body, she held the hanger up in front of her and danced around the room, watching the satin drape to the floor and follow her like a shoal of salmon.

Before she broke out in a sweat and ruined her make-up, she glided into the dress that now appeared to have a mind of its own and obsessively clasped itself around her form. With one hand on her hip, she practised walking in her new skin, enjoying the way her body moved fluidly through the material. Just the tops of her legs lightly brushed past one-and-other, sending waves of pleasure through her body. She caught herself enjoying it, and her reflection in the mirror told her that tonight she had to use all that 'her mama gave her'. Magnolia had been blessed in that department – mama gave her so much in all the right places.

Knowing this, she slithered like a snake towards the mirror by her bed to push up her large bosoms and create the cleavage Joseph dribbled over. Her breasts were one of the favourite parts of her body, and she ran her fingers down the dip of her cleavage, imagining Joseph's tongue there instead. Vibrations of ecstasy rippled through her body, and she pulsated with pleasure. The temptation to touch herself was strong, but Joseph would do it better, and she told herself to wait.

For this evening, everything had to be perfect. She had to go to him hungry.

The last part of dressing up was choosing her shoes. The only one's worthy of the dress were the delicate, diamante heeled thongs that she'd bought for her wedding, 'one day'. In this instance, and given the person that she was trying to impress, she decided that it wouldn't hurt to give them a pre-wedding outing. She very carefully took them out of their box, held them to her chest to infect with a prayer and then slipped them on like Cinderella.

Just before stepping out of the door, she turned and blew herself a kiss in the mirror, which naturally kissed her back. She looked the bomb and couldn't wait to explode all over Joseph.

Earlier that day he'd sent a text message with the restaurant's location. It was in Islington, not too far from her home. A bus ride would have gotten her there in fifteen minutes, but that was out of the question. With no horse and carriage available, she took a minicab.

Islington was bustling with lots of new cafes and restaurants that had popped up whilst she'd been away. The one Joseph had suggested was a new trendy hot spot that 'you'll just love.' That's what the text had said, and as she read it again, she tried hard not to focus on that word 'love'. How loaded was it? It was much more than, 'Hi Love', and much less than, 'I love you'. The word 'love' and 'you' are in there, she thought. If only it were possible to get rid of a few other letters and...

"Here you are, love," said the taxi driver as the car pulled up outside the restaurant.

Right then, she thought, the taxi drivers just sorted that little problem out, and she fished around her purse to pay him. As a good luck measure, she tipped him far more than was necessary.

"Thank you, love," he said.

And there is was again, you and love. Never mind, she thought, it really wasn't necessary to read into everything so much.

She got out of the car and stood outside the restaurant admiring its swanky appearance. Joseph was making an effort. Happy with that, she walked in fashionably late, strutting like a model on a catwalk.

It wasn't difficult to find him. Of all the tables packed with young trendies, Joseph stood out. He was by far the most handsome man in the room. Even the way he sat, leaning back in his chair, arm casually swung over, was enough to make Magnolia's heart ache.

Before she reached the table, Joseph spotted her and stood up with a broad grin on his face. She slowed down her pace to savour the flow of attention. He knew what she was doing and gave it to her, mouthing, 'Wow,' for extra effect.

A dark haired fellow next to him also rose, but she had no idea what his initial reaction was, and she really didn't care.

When Joseph was within arms-reach, she flew into his embrace and tightly squeezed him.

After more than a reasonable amount of time had passed, he prised her off, and in an overly theatrical voice introduced her, "Dan, this is the Marvellous Magnolia."

Her stomach dropped, and her face turned the same colour as her dress. Desperately trying to smile through her shock, she held out her hand, which Dan gently took and put to his lips, not once taking his eyes off her. She liked that; it felt particularly good after the lashing from Joseph, whose words had devastated her.

She was aware that it was Dan, and not Joseph, who pulled out a chair for her to sit in, creating a triangle where she faced them both. To stave off the negative thoughts creeping into her mind, she looked for an immediate distraction, hoping that a little time would allow the pain from the comment to dissolve. Whatever happened, she couldn't allow it to solidify.

Since there was no alcohol in her immediate vicinity, she picked up the menu and looked at both men behind a mask of happiness. Dan looked hopefully at her as if he were in a commercial trying to sell himself. He wasn't bad looking, she thought, but being good looking wasn't enough. His even features and straight, dark hair bored her. There was no fire, no drama in his soul, and he had as much charisma as a dead rat. Now there were two things she needed to distract herself from.

"Oh, I am starving, let's order," she said quickly looking back down at her menu, not wanting Dan to think her critical gaze held any promise. It didn't matter how she looked at men, they always wanted her - for one night at least. Besides, the menu was the perfect veil. It hurt to look into Joseph's eyes, and Dan's were just scary, empty holes that she was afraid she might fall into.

Very quickly, she randomly picked something from the starter and main course sections. It didn't matter what she ordered, since the words, 'Marvellous Magnolia' strangling her insides like a rope had made food an impossibility. Just as her eyes were beginning to well with tears, a waiter arrived like the image of God himself and presented the table with a bottle of red wine. Before he had finished pouring the men's drinks, she downed her glass in one go.

Joseph laughed and said, "Steady on!"

"Ah, I'm just thirsty. Besides, you know I have a liver the size of an island." Turning to Dan, she teased, "I can handle my drink just as well as I can handle my men." She cringed inside at the sliminess of her remark.

In his own way, Joseph responded by lifting the corner of his mouth in a semi smile. He knew her well enough to know that that was *not* a Magnolia remark; she was normally way cooler than that. He put it down to nervousness, and although it was the right assumption, he was oblivious about the correct cause of it.

After another glass of wine, which had the desired effect of temporarily dissolving the double M words, Magnolia totally eased up and became the fun loving, charismatic, magnetic beauty that she was. Naturally, just as she'd expected, Dan was wooed off his feet.

To begin with, she had no intention of giving them equal recognition, but she felt the need to punish Joseph for his earlier comment. To her dismay, instead of feeling any jealousy, she sensed that Joseph liked the fact that she was being so attentive to Dan. He had after all wanted to introduce them, and she questioned if he had an ulterior motive. It annoyed her to think that Joseph was up to something, and more questions raced to the front of her mind like a gang of psychotic patients, fighting to be the first in line to toxify her thoughts. The winning question, Had Joseph not missed her at all? crossed the race line, and her face drained of blood. She hadn't really seen the relevance of bringing somebody else along at the time of the telephone conversation because she'd just been so overjoyed to have a date to see him. And she was sure that the evening would end up with just the two of them.

There at the restaurant, it all started to slip into place. Joseph was trying to pair her off, and to make matters worse, he was hardly paying any attention to her but was instead having a more intimate relationship with whomever it was he was texting; texts, which made him smile, and she was sure on one occasion, even made him blush.

After a while she began to tire of it and decided to intervene in his phone affair.

"You know," she said obnoxiously, "it's rude to be on your phone the whole time during dinner."

"Oh, and since when did you give a shit about those types of etiquettes?"

She seductively lifted the glass of wine to her lips and took a sip.

He ignored her flirtation and said, "Besides, they haven't even served the main course yet," and pointed at his appetizer, a spicy tortilla roll, before taking a large chunk out of it.

In an attempt to muscle in on the conversation, Dan made a fatal error by naively adding, "Oh, let him be, Magnolia... he's in love."

She almost choked on her wine and looked up at Joseph, who sat smiling as if he'd done no wrong. "Oh really, and with whom might that be?" she asked, trying to hide the quiver in her voice.

"Why, Lucinda, of course," said Dan jovially, raising his glass up towards Joseph.

"Oh yes, The Lovely Lucinda," she said, glaring at Joseph with an evil flicker in her eye, which Joseph caught and was disappointed but not surprised to see.

"Yes, Magnolia, Lucinda," Joseph firmly reiterated and raised his glass up to meet Dan's. Trying to be a bit softer, he added, "You know, the girl you spoke to on the phone yesterday."

"Ah yes, the giggler." This time she couldn't hide her contempt.

"How far gone is she now, Joseph? Three months?" asked Dan.

"Thereabouts," responded Joseph a little meekly, as he waited for a retaliation of some sorts from Magnolia.

There was none. She was gob smacked.

Her words backed up like a traffic jam in her throat, suffocating her with fumes that she had no desire to escape from. Instead, she decided to add to them by lighting a cigarette.

"A quarter of the way there Daddy-O," sung Dan and smiled at him.

"I can hardly believe it myself," said Joseph, avoiding contact with Magnolia's eyes.

"Neither can I. A little you on this planet – rascal mania." Dan affectionately slapped him on the back.

"Yeah… God help us all," said Joseph and laughed.

Seeing him happy whilst she was in such distress made Magnolia despise him, and the psychotic bandits rushed her mind with more questions: How could he smile like that? He must have known that this would knock her. If nothing else, wasn't she supposed to his best friend? How come Dan had all the info? Since when did Dan move into the fucking, Friendship Premier Division?

Her thoughts churned around her head, and she saw more clearly what this dinner was really about: Dan was Joseph's cushion as well as her date. A double whammy for Joseph, who didn't have the guts to tell her about Lucinda and this pregnancy when they were alone. A man with no backbone was the vilest specimen of them all. It surprised her that he had taken this stance.

Anger burnt through her flesh like acid, and she looked Dan over and internally cursed, And what the hell is he supposed to be? The fucking booby prize? She felt humiliated and bitter for not having seen this coming; after all, she was the queen manipulator. In actual fact, Joseph should have referred to her as 'The Manipulative Magnolia'. He, by no means a virgin to any drama, had kinged her in this stake. Defeated in the royal dethroning, she excused herself just as the waiter was about to serve the main meal.

The toilet break would only give her a few minutes. Still, it would be long enough. She just needed to look at herself in the mirror, to see her reflection, and allow it to guide her. She was sure that her friend, Narcissus would find a vengeful resolution to this problem.

To her dismay, when she looked in the mirror she was shocked to see not the beauty whom had earlier stood before her, but a desperate woman glaring back; a wild, crazy lady sneering at her. With an urge to smash her reflection, she slammed her fist on the sink. Her hand throbbed, and a wave of pleasure flooded her like melancholic tears dipped in ecstasy. Narcissus drew her back to her reflection and said, "Have faith. Get him back. Use Dan. Use Dan. Use Dan...."

For the remainder of the evening, she drunk an enormous amount and flirted with Dan. After discovering that he was a doctor, she made 'save me' jokes and stroked his ego, by saying things like, 'being a doctor is one of the most honourable professions.' Although she was going slightly over the top, she was impressed with doctors, and it made it just that bit easier to shower him with praise.

Initially, Joseph was pleased that Magnolia was hitting it off with Dan, but became a little wary of the cold looks that she would throw at him from time to time like a snowball. He knew she was up to something, but was feeling less responsible for her, and he moved (albeit only a little) more towards Lucinda.

# Five

"Joseph, Joseph my old chap, welcome back to the arena," said a man that Joseph thought looked an awful lot like a character from a Jane Austin novel. The man held out his arms and pulled him into his embrace.

Who is this? questioned Joseph, attempting to pull away from the man's grasp.

The man with the overly cheery tone seemed to read his mind and said, "Why, my dear fellow, don't be a stranger, you have known me many times before."

Joseph freed himself from the man and looked him up and down.

"I, as your beloved Bianca the Wanker," continued the man, "as your tortured puppy, and a century ago when it was not the done thing," he moved in closer and whispered, "I was your lover."

Upon hearing this Joseph stepped back to further examine him. He couldn't remember a man called Bianca The Wanker. Did he ever have a puppy? And as for the last comment about being his lover - he had no idea about that.

He stood dumbfounded, and the stranger filled the silence with his own words. "Ah, Joseph, you will come to remember. Now embrace me like a brother." The man opened his arms out again and smiled wickedly. Raising his eyebrow, he said, "For, next time, we may come back as twins, my dear fellow. But I do wonder who will take the other out first."

"Marcus, step aside!" bellowed a male voice from nowhere. "You know the rules: do not approach or inform the new attendee. They must work it out for themselves. Now leave. You have missed an opportunity to return."

Marcus' happy demeanor diminished, and he hit Joseph on the back of his head and spurted, "Yet again you manage to ruin me." Turning away, he disappeared in a blaze of fire.

The Formless Voice spoke again, "Enough shenanigans people and take your seats."

It suddenly occurred to Joseph that he might be dead and if the voice he'd just heard belonged to God. To his disbelief, he heard his own thoughts aloud, and the strange men in the room; his living room, roared with laughter.

"Oh dear," said The Formless Voice mockingly, "it seems we will have to turn the dial down. Shepard, please lower the screen so Joseph's thoughts appear in written form. Oh, and mute the universal speakers, so we may continue in semi-peace."

Joseph scanned the room to see who this Shepard character was. But, just as he heard The Formless Voice, who was indeed formless, Joseph was unable to see Shepard. All he saw was a crowd of men, of various ages huddled in his living room. To add to his growing distress, a large projector screen magically appeared on the right-hand side wall.

"Joseph," said The Formless Voice with a hint of a smile in his tone, "please sit down facing the screen, so you can see your thoughts in written form, just like the rest of us."

*"Oh fuck! My God! This can't be happening to me. Get me out of here. Help me,"* appeared on the screen, and the room exploded with laughter.

"Enough!" shouted The Formless Voice, "now, down to business."

"Business!?" screamed Joseph, "what the fuck is this place?"

The silent room echoed Joseph's voice in a mimicking tone, "Business!? What the fuck is this place?" and Joseph roared with fury. To his dismay his roar was echoed in the tone of a cat's meow. Dejected, he slumped into an empty chair.

"Hahaha, look at you? Feeling sorry for yourself? Hahaha," laughed a bald man in his early thirties, his face covered in scars. Jabbing his finger into Joseph's shoulder he continued to taunt him, "Oh my, aren't we the quiet one."

Joseph stood up and took in the whole room; chairs lined up in rows facing the front wall of his living room and sitting in them the weirdest, sickest, most vulgar looking men he had ever seen. "What the fuck?" he muttered in disgust.

All the men in the room mimicked in unison, "What the fuck?" repeatedly until they started to trail off into a bad chorus line.

"Fucking shut up, you morons!" Joseph kicked the chair in front of him, and the man sitting in it turned around.

"Temper, temper," he said, holding a doll with a knife stuck in its head. "Nothing to get so angry about...yet," he chided and licked the doll's face.

"Sicko," said Joseph with revulsion.

"Would you like a lick?" asked the man holding the doll out to Joseph. "She smells and tastes just like a Lilly."

Joseph moved back not wanting the doll or the man to get near enough to touch him. Just as he was about to shout obscenities again, he heard sexual grunts emanate from the walls and saw a semi-naked man holding his penis walk through the wall to his left. The man took a seat in the back and began to masturbate.

Joseph looked around in shock and shouted, "Is he fucking serious?" When he saw that nobody was going to do anything about it he yelled louder, "Oi! Stop that. Oi! perv! Cut it out."

The man ignored him as he reached a climax and came on the back of the head of a shabbily dressed homeless looking man, sitting in front of him. The homeless looking man didn't even flinch.

"Get out of my house scumbags. Get the fuck out!" screamed Joseph.

"Your house? said the man with the doll. "This is a room and only a room."

"My living room!"

"Err... no it isn't. Not anymore," said the scarred man stroking his mutilated face.

"That's my book case," said Joseph pointing towards it, "and that fat fuck is sitting in my sofa."

A fat man chomping on a heart smiled at Joseph, revealing a vein stuck between his teeth. Joseph shook his head in disbelief as he continued to scan the room. None of the men in there looked reasonable to him. He daren't think what their lives had been like, or what awful deeds they may have done. Even a man in a suit who looked like he might be a decent member of society was completely unaware of his surroundings, as he picked his nose and ate his snot.

"Joseph, give it up and sit down," said the Formless Voice, "all will become clear very soon."

"I'll make it all very clear now," said Joseph and stormed over to his front door. Just before he got there it turned into a wall. He ran to the window, and that too transformed into part of the wall.

He spun on the spot. Eyes wide with terror, he said, "This is hell. It's got to be hell."

"No, it's not Joseph. This is cushty compared to hell," said The Formless Voice.

"Cushty?!"

"Sit down, Joseph," said The Formless Voice in a measured tone, "sit down."

The Formless Voice had the effect of calming Joseph down a little. He felt that there really was no other choice for now except to see how things panned out. Moving away from the huddle of men, he walked to the end of the row he was in and sat down.

A young man in his twenties, sitting a few seats away from him, lit a spliff. The smell of the weed intoxicated the room and Joseph wished that he was positioned closer to the boy, so that he might be offered a toke. But he assessed, as quickly as any stoner might, that there were too many people in between them. Even if the boy (who had already taken his third drag and was blatantly not following the spliff rules) was willing to share, he was too far away to even get a tug at the roach. *Oh well*, he thought, as his words appeared on the screen, *I don't care what that invisible bloke just said. This really must be hell. Sniff it but don't smoke it. What next? Hot chicks but no fucking?*

He sighed loudly just as the smoker leaned over and asked, "Brother, do you want a pull?"

Joseph couldn't contain his smile as he reached for the spliff, clambering over the other non-desirables to get there. "I guess you read the screen," he said coyly, and took his first drag.

"Nah, I know you," replied the smoker, "I've been watching you from up here for some time now."

Joseph didn't want to believe that he was dead and pulled the next drag deeper into his lungs.

"You were just a kid though, I..."

The Formless Voice cut him off and said, "Jessy, let him work it out. Why don't you tell him your story? Let's see if he recognises himself."

Joseph racked his brain, trying to think, Jessy? Jessy? He didn't know any Jessy's.

This time, having read the screen, Jessy replied, "Oh brother, you never knew my name, in fact you hardly saw my face."

Holding out a DVD, he stood up and asked, "Do you mind if I begin somewhere in the middle and show you the film, rather than tell you the story?"

"As you wish, Jessy," replied The Formless Voice.

Jessy handed the DVD to a tall, faceless man in the front row. The man took the DVD and disappeared in a plume of electrical smoke. Simultaneously, a screen appeared on the other side of the room, and the film began.

#

INT. LIVINGROOM - DAY

Four males in their early twenties: KYLE, NED, JASON and RICHIE, are sitting around a table smoking WEED and snorting COCAINE that Ned is cutting up with a credit card. There is laughter as they chat amongst themselves.

SONG: Legalize It – Peter Tosh.

Kyle is moving his head rhythmically to the bass.

> KYLE
> Turn it up bro, this tune's
> the bollocks.

Ned leans back, reaching for the volume on the stereo, and turns up the music.

> RICHIE
> Ere, pass me the note.

Richie reaches for the rolled-up bank note from Jason.

> JASON
> My pleasure, bro.

> RICHIE
> Nice.

He takes the note.

LEXUS, late twenties, enters with a cigarette hanging from his mouth. His hands are full of drinks, and a packet of biscuits are under his arm.

There is a LOUD BANGING on the front window.

They all jump. Lexus drops the drinks.

> LEXUS
> Oh shit!

The banging is relentless, and Jason goes to have a look.

> JASON
> Who the fuck is that?

He pulls open the curtain.

> JASON (CONT.)
> Oh, my God!

The other boys look at each other - worried.

Jason rushes out.

The other boys get up and follow him.

INT. HALLWAY – CONTINUOUS

Jason opens the door and JESSY falls into his arms, his head and face covered in BLOOD.

> JASON (CONT.)
> Fucking hell!

> LEXUS
> Shit, man. Get him in.

Ned and Lexus pull Jessy into the house and lay him onto the floor.

Kyle closes the door.

> NED
> Jessy, what the….

                    LEXUS
              Oh, God. Oh, man!

Kyle runs up the stairs.

Jason, Lexus and Ned crouch down by Jessy's side.

Richie is standing back with a look of shock on his face.

                    RICHIE
              You all right, man?

Jason is covered in Jessy's blood.

                    JASON
              Of course, he's not all right you
              fucking idiot. He's got blood
              coming out of his fucking head!

Lexus leans in closer to Jessy's face.

                    LEXUS
              How did you get here?

Jessy holds up some CAR KEYS covered in blood.

                    NED
              Since when did you have a car?

Jessy COUGHS up blood.

                    JASON
              Hospital…We've got to get him
              to a hospital.

Kyle comes back with towels, sits by Jessy's head, and
presses a towel onto the gaping head wound.
Jessy tries to sit up.

> JESSY
> (crying)
> I just wanted her back. She's mine,
> man. I can't love anybody else.

Jessy looks up as if he is talking to 'God.'

> JESSY (CONT.)
> You hear me? She's mine!

> KYLE
> I told you not to stress over that
> little bitch. There's plenty more
> pussy out there.

Jessy grabs Kyle.

> JESSY
> Don't refer to her as pussy. I
> fucking loved her. I loved her.

He sobs relentlessly, spit and blood dripping out of his
mouth.

> LEXUS
> Get a grip, man. We'll sort this out.

> JESSY
> No! No! You can't. I did something
> really bad.

                    JASON
              Obviously! I hope the other
              guy is--

Jason stops as it slowly starts to dawn on him that it's
possible that the other guy is in a much worse state.

                    NED
              What's her new boyfriend's
              name?
                    KYLE
              Pierre! Pierre the fucking penis.

    Kyle strokes Jessy's face.

                    KYLE (CONT.)
              So what, he beat you. He'll get his
              share mate, don't worry.

                    JESSY
              Too late... too late.

The boys are really concerned now and look at each
other.

                    LEXUS
              Where is Pierre now, Jessy?

                    JESSY
              At the house. I fucking killed him...
              I killed them both.

                    KYLE
              You what?

JESSY
I killed my love. I killed her. That
fucking wanker ruined it all.

NED
Oh, Jessy.

JESSY
It's over... my life's over.

JASON
It will be if we don't take you to
get your head seen to.

Jessy GASPS and COUGHS up more blood.

JESSY
(breathless)
I can't go to the hospital.

LEXUS
Mate, there's no other option.

Ned starts to search over Jessy's body and notices a
BLOODY WOUND on the right-side of his upper
back.

NED
Shit Jessy! What's this? A fucking
gun-shot wound?

Jessy gets paler. His breathing becomes shorter, and his
eyes roll back. He tries to talk but is unable to.

Kyle tries to lift Jessy.

KYLE
Quick, get him in the car.

Jason opens the front door. Lexus, Ned and Kyle lift Jessy up.

They just about get him upright and put one of his arms over Kyle's shoulder and the other over Jason's.

Ned holds a fresh towel to Jessy's head wound.

They all walk out the front door.

EXT. HOUSE – CONTINUOUS

KYLE (CONT.)
(to Richie)
We'll take your car, it's the biggest.
You get in the back with him. I'll
drive. You've been drinking more
than me.

RICHIE
Fuck off man, it's my car. And
like alcohol is the least of our
worries. If I'm coming, then
I'm sitting in the front.

LEXUS
Do you mind having your
fucking gay row after we save
our mate from dying?

Richie throws Kyle his keys and gives him a dirty look.

                    LEXUS (CONT.)
              On second thoughts, you stay
              here. There's not enough room
              for everybody.

Richie backs up towards the door of the house.

I/E CAR – DAY

Ned gets into the back of the car and drags Jessy in.

Jason slides in next to him.

Kyle gets into the driver's seat and Lexus into the
passenger's seat.

Kyle turns on the ignition, and the radio automatically
starts to play a song - Lady Killer.

The car zooms off at high speed down the road.

Jessy starts to lose consciousness.

Ned slaps Jessy's face to keep him awake.

Jason holds the blood-drenched towel to his head.

                    JASON
              Hurry man, he's fucking bleeding
              to death.

Kyle speeds up and hits a KID that runs out into the
road.

The car SKIDS.

All SCREAM, as the Kid hits the windscreen. He is catapulted over the bonnet into the air and flung twenty meters behind.

Kyle's face hits the steering wheel. His nose is broken - blood everywhere.

Lexus' head slams against the side of the window - cracking it.

The SCREAMS stop.

There is a deathly silence.

Jessy takes one last gasp of breath before his eyes roll back and fall open.

> JASON
> He's gone. We lost him…
> Jessy's dead.

#

Jessy was right. Joseph had never seen his face. He had been hit at fifty miles an hour, and it was a miracle that he had survived at all.

#

In the Female Courtroom, Magnolia, resigned to staying, took her seat next to a girl with a gunshot wound to the head and a photo stuffed in her mouth.

At a slow, leisurely pace, the girl pulled out the crumpled, bloody photo that unraveled in her palm to reveal an image of her snuggled in a boy's arms. At the bottom right-hand corner, hand written, were the words: "Love Jessy."

#

Simultaneously, in the Male Courtroom the final scene when the car hit Joseph was shown in slow motion, and it was only then that he saw himself as he had been as a small boy.

The memory was so faint in his recollection that it was painful to remember himself as a five-year-old boy, who still had his mother. The early years of his life were the best, and yet like some awful twist of fate, he was not able to voluntarily access them.

As an infant, a higher part of his being sensed that he would not recall those precious memories when he grew up. So, at the time he told himself to cherish those moments; moments that from time to time were awakened in his adulthood by a smell, a picture, a woman with her small son, or some other obscure object, like the print of a dress.

One of those moments that regularly came to him in the form of a flashback, was his mother pushing him on the swings. Shared laughter rose from their bellies and left their mouths, joining in an embrace of love that he could see, feel, and fall into.

Other memorable times were when she tucked him in at night, her eyes warmly penetrating his, as he swam in the sea of her blue irises. He vividly remembered the sound of her sweet voice lulling him into sleep, carrying and rocking him gently to the shore of his dreams.

There were the blessed instances when he was honourably haunted by the vision of her sitting with him as he ate. Lovingly and adoringly she gazed at him, as he received each morsel of food as if it were a kiss; the food that touched his mouth was soaked in her love.

He adored everything about his mother and watched in awe her every move. The way she walked was sleek, gracefully attracting all the beauty in the universe. A universe he trusted so long as she was physically in it. He was safe in her arms and in her space. His world was beautiful with her, and he felt a part of the cycle of life.

However, he had never expected it to take her so soon and leave him falling down the black hole of despair, frantically grabbing the streams of light that slipped through his hands as he fell deeper and deeper into the great void - until he could no longer see her or feel her. It was then, with a thud, that Joseph aged just six-years-old, fell from his animated world of light into a harsh one filled with darkness.

Somehow, remembering the accident brought to the surface all the memories of his mother, unlocking a tomb filled with the sweet smell of her love, and the warm song of her voice. Whereupon, he saw her, and he saw the light; he felt her, and he felt the light.

She had died the year after his accident, and Joseph, betrayed by her departure, had never healed the wound. Instead, he constantly sought this love with a painful desire to destroy whoever gave it to him.

The effect of this realisation cut through him and released a clot from his past, allowing the tainted blood from his heart to run free. Peace came with this new insight and for a few moments he forgot where he was, as it didn't seem to matter, until he heard The Formless Voice.

"This room is filled with sins of malice and evilness. Well, that is what some would say but who is anybody else to judge? Good versus bad is the easy way out."

"You're doing my head in," said Joseph, reaching the end of his tether. "What the hell is going on?"

"Close Joseph, but, as I said before, not quite hell. Not yet."

"Who and where are you?"

"I'm everywhere and everything."

"What kind of bullshit answer is that?"

"The answer."

"For fuck's sake - hell's answer to The Riddle King."

"Haha, I like you Joseph. Quite the entertainer."

"Then give me a break, man and let me... Oh this is ridiculous. I'm listening to and talking to a voice."

"Oh, you'd be surprised how many people do."

"Why can't I see you?"

"For the same reason that no-one can really see themselves. The ego, old boy. The ego."

Joseph moved as far away from the men as possible and sat in the back.

"You really do think that you are better than this crowd, don't you?" jeered the Formless Voice. "None of you are in a better state than the other. You all made choices with consequences, and so you are all here."

"What choices!"

"Some are so obvious, others are not. Like the angels you encounter daily but perhaps do not even see."

"Angels? You're having a laugh aren't you. I don't believe in that shit."

"Then why have the Indian God, Hanuman, tattooed on your arm."

"Stoned, drunk, Indian mishap on acid - that's why."

"But for some reason you chose Hanuman when you could have had a fairy or metal banger or whatever else a stoned, drunk, acid head would have chosen. But you, my dear boy, chose Hanuman: The Superhero of Indian Gods."

"Well there's the answer."

"Also, a staunch celibate."

"Too bad for him."

"He is also the perfect symbol of bravery, perseverance and loyalty. Perhaps, you had a desire to acquire these qualities."

"Or maybe I was stoned, drunk and high on acid. Anyway, looks good." Joseph pulled up his sleeve and stroked his Hanuman tattoo.

# Six

Joseph had met Lucinda the day after getting the Hanuman tattoo done. It was her favourite Indian God, and so a good omen, she thought. He let her believe that and didn't tell her that it was an accident.

Having shagged copious amounts of women already, he naturally thought that Lucinda would just be another notch to his belt and had no idea that meeting her would transform his life.

There was something different about her though. Her unassuming nature and flighty childishness brought in a freshness he liked to be around, and for once his fascination with a woman lasted longer than his orgasm. She had an energy that fluctuated from benign to dangerous, layered with a mysterious power hidden beneath her delicate nature. And it was precisely this contradiction that excited him.

It was rare for him to stand being around anyone for so long. Magnolia had been the only other person who'd been awarded that privilege. But over the years, he'd seen all that she had to offer, and it was never quite enough.

She wasn't the one to unlock his unconscious desires. That fate fell onto Lucinda.

She was one of the best things to come out of the travelling trip. He was glad that he'd gone after initially worrying that it would damage his career by giving space for the underlings to rise to the top in his absence. Much to his pleasure he found the contrary to be true. His time away only reinforced his ambitious desires, and he returned full of adventure and passion in his heart, taking the company by storm again and knocking all those aiming to rise, right back down to the bottom.

Within six weeks of returning, he was promoted to Head of his Department in one of London's top Marketing Companies. He was falling for Lucinda more each day, and with Magnolia back, he now also had his faithful lover by his side again. Even though her bad behaviour the night before had been slightly disturbing, he put it down to shock. He had, after all, not told her about Lucinda's pregnancy. Still, he was sure that she would get over it and continue to respect the boundaries of their relationship, as she had done for many years.

The day after the dinner, he walked into the scheduled work meeting five minutes late, made no apologies, and sat down in the seat designated for him.

"Ah Joseph, welcome. We were hanging on for you," said Mr. Parsons.

Joseph smiled and nodded his head respectively; he had a way with the bosses. Had he not been superb in his job and made the company immense amounts of money, they may have been less tolerant of his avant-garde approach to work, for he knew the hours, but more or less came and went as he pleased. The general idea that geniuses should be given the space to be brilliant was advocated in his case.

Amongst his peers, Joseph was a 'love him' or 'hate him' character. More often than not it was the latter. The knack he had for his profession often jarred his peers, most of whom were graduates from top universities. Being a common-boy-made-good, he was different from them. His entry into the company was also unique. Unlike most of his well-bred, educated counterparts, Joseph had joined the company when he was just seventeen-years-old with no qualifications. They bore no relevance to his mentor Samual Parsons, who saw something special in him.

They were an unlikely pair from the start, on two opposite ends of the spectrum. Mr. Parsons, at the time an account executive, had never committed a crime, and Joseph an uneducated drop-out had a criminal record dating back to when he was ten-years-old.

Their paths fatefully crossed after Mr. Parsons had had a mid-life crisis and discovered that his ever-so-well-orchestrated-life lacked meaning. There was no purpose in anything. All activities were joyless, and he felt like he was dying.

He took a leave of absence, expecting to go into a major depression but was instead drawn to volunteer at a juvenile detention centre where he was already a patron. His hard-core work ethic meant that he had plenty of money, but now also had time. The juvenile detention centre board were very happy to accommodate their patron's wishes, and though they were a little concerned for his safety, nonetheless obliged.

From the onset, Mr. Parsons found something magical about the place. The grittiness that accompanied destitution resonated with the core essence of a hidden part of himself; the pulse of violence that beat through the boys, escaping through the windows of their eyes, mirrored his own; and the reflection burnt through the veil, freeing him. Finally, he could be himself in a place that was real. Unlike the plastic world and plastic people that he was normally exposed to.

The raw emotion pumped blood back into his veins, and in that place of depravity, he slowly came alive.

It was then that he met Joseph and took an instant liking to him.

He admired the boy's guts, his sharp wit, determination, and passion to succeed in whatever he put his mind to. Joseph had a strong potential to be somebody great – he was sure of that. The boy just needed the right opportunity, and he wanted to be the one to give it to him.

Strangely enough, Joseph gave him a purpose again, and with that gift Mr. Parsons returned to work with more vigour than before. Having hit rock bottom, he became more determined than ever to rise to the top – this time, joyfully. Within a few years, he was made CEO of his company, and for that he felt indebted to Joseph.

Whilst still at the juvenile detention centre, Joseph had been invited to Mr. Parson's house, where he saw the benefits of this man's profession: lots of money being the primary one, and power being the other. Over time, he got to see how the two were intrinsically linked.

Weeks later when Mr. Parsons invited him to the office, he saw the employees pander to him, rushing around like servants to please their king. It was then that he saw how respect was another attribute associated with this position, and though he had swung between forcefully demanding it and attracting it with his charm his whole life, it became clear that this profession was one where the title alone proceeded you. Respect was a given.

Finally, there were the ladies. Joseph observed how as Mr. Parsons walked through the corridors, every woman, each one seemingly more beautiful than the next, smiled coquettishly at him, honouring and respecting their leader. Their gazes held the promise of availability, whether that be of their time or body he had no idea, but he guessed that it was both.

After Joseph was released from the juvenile detention centre, Mr. Parsons took him into his home and workplace. Joseph worked hard at first, but as soon as he learnt the tricks of the trade, he found that he was a natural. It was easy for him. His character alone got him fifty percent of the way there, and his untamed creative force made up for the rest. What took other people hours to achieve, he found himself completing in minutes. He was the digital amongst the analogues.

#

The meeting on that day was to discuss a pitch. Joseph hoped to win them over with his idea and bring the meeting to a quick ending. Just as he was about to stand and do his spiel, he felt his phone vibrate in his pocket and was sure that it was Magnolia texting or calling him again.

Already that morning he'd received two texts from her. Years of Magnolia had taught him that if he didn't go to see her soon she would become irate.

After the dinner date, and despite all her hints, he'd not escorted her home but had left Dan to do that honour instead.

The first of the text messages that morning had been a sexy request for a lunch date at her house. When he didn't respond, the following text expressed her disdain at being dumped at the restaurant.

It normally turned him on when she got her knickers in a twist. However, that morning he'd already requested the assistance of his new co-worker on a very important personal project. And by the shy glances that she was throwing his way like handfuls of confetti, he guessed that she was more than looking forward to it.

Magnolia would have to wait her turn.

Being rich and successful brought him time and choices, both of which freed him to satisfy his needs. He didn't need love. He didn't want it. Or so he thought...

# Seven

*One Year Later (Autumn 2007)*

Joseph and Lucinda's love-making could be likened to a cannibal's feast, and that evening was no different than any other, as he ferociously took her pussy into his mouth and ate it like a starving animal. His unadulterated desire unlocked her darker passions, and she responded by tearing his flesh with her fingernails and licking the blood that dripped from under them.

The pain excited him, and he mounted her, pounding her with violent force. In return, she received every bite, pinch and slap with devilish pleasure; begging for more pain to match the rising tide of emotions that grew with the force of his hardening cock.

Their sexual positions changed as much as their wavering temperaments, and in his next move, he slipped out of her and lay on his back. His strong arms lifted her onto his face, and she parted her legs to feed the beast with her juice that dripped like morning dew onto his lips.

Savouring every drop, he buried his face deep into her, relishing in the pleasurable groans that escaped from her gut as she writhed on his mouth, his tongue flicking rhythmically like the engine of a motorbike that she rode on a path to nowhere. She wanted him more than anything, and he knew it.

Thrusting his fingers into her wet hole, she came with the cry of a crashing waterfall, and he sank his teeth deep into her flesh, drawing out her blood and ecstasy.

Her heart racing, she flopped to her side, and he pulled back her hair, twisting her onto all fours. With her hair wrapped tightly around his fist, he slammed her head onto the bed board. The moan from her throat not satisfying him, he pulled her head back and rammed it like a bull into the wall. This time the heart wrenching scream from her gut gave him the pleasure that he felt he deserved.

Penetrating her again, he jabbed his cock into her inviting hole, pumping her wildly and piercing her anus with his thumb, which pulsed around it like a heart valve.

She turned her head around to look at him and reached out to touch his face. He stopped her, grabbed her arm and pulled it behind her back like a police officer's grip, whereupon she wailed in discomfort and dripped harder onto his cock.

Her juice now trickling down his leg urged him to slam his truncheon more forcibly into her vagina, slamming against her uterus, until she felt the vibrations shake all the way through her. His panting and hot exhalation filled the room, and she longed to disappear into his breath and merge with the unseen force rising out of him.

The loss she would have to endure one day ripped like a photograph of the two of them in her mind, and she saw him walk away. Tears plunged out of her eyes, and she shook with the death of each one that rolled down her cheek.

With her free hand she reached under herself, to pull his balls. The harder she squeezed them, the tighter his grip became, and together they came in painful ecstasy. The King of the Jungle, he roared like a lion; and she, a subordinate species, screamed like an animal whose heart and body had been reluctantly taken.

The lion transformed back into Joseph, and finally he released his grip, and she fell like a feather onto her stomach; he tumbled down after her.

Covered in sweat, he laid on top of her, stroking her hair and tear-streaked face. In a quick motion, he twisted them both over so she now lay on him, fragile and wet.

The drops of sweat from their moist skins merged, their bodies stuck together, hearts beating in unison. For a silent, still second, they felt as if they were one, until Joseph moved his head, heavy with euphoria, and the blood from her wound dripped into his mouth.

#

"Oh, fucking hell, Joseph, not again," said Dan in disbelief, fighting every urge to not slam the phone down.

Joseph laughed and said, "Do you have to complain each time?"

"But Christ, man, it's not normal. You're going to kill her one day."

"Not if she kills me first," said Joseph winking at Lucinda.

"I'm not even at the hospital," said Dan defensively.

"Why not? You're always bitching that you never get a day off. Anyway, even better, you get to come over here."

"Night shift," said Dan yawning. "Oh fuck, I just don't believe you." He lazily pulled himself out of bed and said, "Let me see if I have some sutures." Shaking his head in dismay, he searched through the medical bag next to his bed.

"Ah, it's pretty deep Dan. I reckon you're going have to staple it again," said Joseph as he drew matching heart shapes with Lucinda's blood on each side of her face.

"Oh fuck," said Dan, more quietly to himself, and then in an irater tone added, "she's not bleeding to death, is she?"

Joseph's laughter on the other end of the line only infuriated him. He couldn't believe that his dearest friend was such a psycho. "One of these days, you're going to get me into trouble, Joseph," he said, unable to hide his frustration. Although he knew quite well Joseph never thought about things like that. A constant rule bender, he always found his way out of trouble.

There was a pause that Dan filled with a sigh before saying, "If she's losing a lot of blood, you'd better take her to the hospital, man. I can't have her dying in my arms."

"Whoa, compassionate doctor."

Dan rolled his eyes. "Oh God, all right, I'll come over." Both men knew that result was inevitable. Dan never refused Joseph. "But just so you know, mate," Dan went on, determined to have the last say, "I'm leaving behind a precious lady to come and clean up your psychotic, sexual mess." He shook his head and lovingly looked at the sleeping beauty snuggled under the duvet next to him.

He felt gutted. It was rare for them to wake up together due to the excessive number of hours he worked at the hospital. This morning was one of the few occasions when they could. Things had been strained between them recently, and he sensed with a feeling he pushed down that he needed to give her more time.

It didn't matter. The power of Joseph's words erased his own needs, and he quickly dressed, hoping she would still be in bed when he returned. In the event that she awoke before he got back, he scribbled a note to say he would be home in a couple of hours to make her a delicious brunch.

This morning would be perfect, he tried to assure himself. He'd make her happy again. Grabbing his doctor's bag, and with his shoulders stooped, he walked out of the door.

#

As soon as she heard the door shut, Magnolia opened her eyes. Having secretly listened to the conversation, she wished that she was the one leaving Dan in the bed to go over to Joseph's.

#

"Right," said Dan cheerily, "that's the last one in." Turning round to face Lucinda, he warmly asked, "You alright, Lucinda? You don't feel queasy or anything, do you?"

Lucinda smiled shyly and nodded to indicate a 'no,' and got up with her head feeling both heavy with pain and light with pleasure; a sensation she thoroughly enjoyed.

"Tea anyone?" she asked if it were a normal occasion.

"No. But I'll have a whisky," said Joseph.

"It's not even midday!" said Dan tapping his watch for extra effect.

Joseph shrugged and slapped Lucinda's backside as she picked up the baby monitor and left the room.

Once out of sight, Dan turned to Joseph and in a quiet warning tone said, "That was a nasty one. Be careful, I'm not even sure if she shouldn't go for an X-ray."

Joseph was in the process of pillaging Dan's medical bag and stood with a handful of gauzes and syringes, before smiling and walking away. His behaviour led Dan to just want to run out of the flat, away from the blood of his friends. But he couldn't. Something about the whole sordidness of the affair excited him in a way that he didn't like to acknowledge.

Joseph, on the other hand, satisfied with the morning's results, sat down on the sofa and reached for his box of supplies from the nearby coffee table and started to skin up.

From the corner of his eye he could see Dan standing rigidly with his hands on his hips. "Chill out Dan, you're so fucking straight man...but then again with that posture you're taking, I'd be more inclined to say that you look like a gay lord."

"Fuck off," said Dan dropping his hands by his side and trying to bite back the smile creeping up onto his face. He didn't want Joseph to think that this was a laughing matter and felt the need to convey the potential seriousness of this extreme sexual play by not succumbing to his charm.

On several occasions, he'd already said all there was to be said regarding this issue; his words, all of which had gone unheeded and lay like an unopened book in Joseph's library of ignored guidance. Even though he knew Joseph did what he wanted, he still felt compelled to reinforce at every opportunity that he didn't condone it. His worst fear was that one day Lucinda would die in his arms, or worse still, she would die from a fatal head wound, hours after he had tended to her.

Although he'd known Lucinda for a little over a year, their infrequent and only contact was for medical procedures. As any Doctor would to any patient, he advised Joseph, "Watch her for the next twenty-four hours."

Lucinda walked back into the room and placed a half empty baby bottle onto the table.

"Where's my whisky?" asked Joseph.

"Just give me a second, you big baby. I had to see to the little man first." She walked out shaking her head.

An awkward silence settled into the room and Dan asked, "How's it going?"

"Don't ask."

"Is she taking the meds?"

"Nope."

"This is serious, Joseph. Post-Partum..."

"Drop it Dan, will you."

"And this rough sex shit probably isn't helping either."

"She wants it."

"Since when did you give her everything that she wants."

Joseph unraveled a large bandage from the stolen stash. "Cool," he said, clearly impressed. "When did you get these new bandages? Nice for a tie up." He wrapped the bandage around his wrist.

"Do you even know where the main arteries are? Because one day you'll slice one of them, and she could have only minutes to live."

Joseph lit the spliff and took a deep drag. "Haven't you got enough on your plate with Miserable M?"

"Tit for tat, is it?"

"Tit for tit is more my style," he said and passed the spliff to Dan. "Save the lecture. Have a toke instead."

Dan reached for the spliff and seriously said, "Any headaches or sickness and you take her straight to the hospital. Do you hear me?"

Joseph remained silent, which should have been a warning for Dan to shut up. Instead, he raised his voice, "I'm telling you now, don't make me do this again." Softening his tone a little he added in almost a whisper, as if he didn't want Lucinda to hear, "Bruises, slight lacerations, I can deal with...barely. But you come to me with a head wound like that again, and I won't fucking deal with it."

Joseph stared harshly at Dan's finger, now pointed directly at him. The cold glare in his eyes reminded Dan who the alpha male was in their relationship, and he cautiously took his finger away.

Lucinda came back into the room holding a scrapbook and newspaper under one arm, and a glass of whisky in her other hand.

"That's my girl," said Joseph and took the whisky. He swigged it back taking a moment to enjoy the liquid flowing down his throat. Pursing his lips, he sucked in the air and said, "Oh, was that a Hennessey?"

"Of course, darling."

"Jesus, Joseph," said Dan totally exasperated.

"I quite like the sound of that, Jesus Joseph. Call me that from now on."

"Are you pissing money or something?" asked Dan, passing the spliff back to him.

Joseph took a big pull and said, "Been a good month I can tell you that much."

Lucinda sat on the sofa next to him, and he gently put his arm around her and placed the spliff to her lips. She sensually inhaled and put her scrapbook onto the table.

"More interesting news articles?" he asked.

"Just one," she replied.

"Darling, you should have been a journalist."

She blushed. "I just like collecting them," she said shyly, unable to accept the compliment.

Joseph put the spliff to her lips again; partly for her enjoyment and partly to shut her up. He wasn't that interested.

The ash from the spliff fell onto the newspaper article that was now resting on her lap. Dan bent down and brushed it away, pausing for a second to read the headline: *Homeless Man, claiming to be Jesus, saves infant from drowning in local pond.*

Lucinda noticed him eyeing it up and possessively covered it with a pillow.

"I guess I'd better be off," he said, slightly offended.

"Alright mate. And Thanks." Joseph winked at him.

Dan couldn't get out quick enough and slammed the door shut behind him.

"Oh no, I forgot to give this to him." Lucinda pulled out a heart-shaped, ruby stone from her pocket. "It's a ruby for Ruby."

Joseph sat upright in surprise and asked, "You're giving away your precious stone?"

"Well it felt right. Ever since the chillum broke it just sits on the bedside table. You know that if we'd had a girl I would have called her Ruby. Did Dan know that? He didn't steal our name, did he?"

"Don't be ridiculous," he said and leaned back into the sofa, no longer interested.

"You're right though, it is precious to me. And look, it's the same size and shape as the beauty spot on my thigh." She pulled up her dress and placed the stone over her beauty spot. It was an exact fit. "It really is as you said. Well what you said the French call it."

Joseph looked baffled.

"Don't you remember, silly? You're the one who told me that a beauty spot is called a beauty stone in French."

He sighed and casually asked, "Did I?"

She was hurt that he didn't remember.

"Well it certainly is beautiful," he said in a dead pan tone.

She managed a weak smile. "You used to love it."

"I still love it. Your beauty stone. Your beauty." He held his hand open for Lucinda to place the ruby into. "I'll give it to Dan next time I see him."

"Shame I can't give it to Magnolia myself. I'd love to meet her. I can't believe that…"

He took his hand away. "This again? Dan's working like a dog, and I hardly see Magnolia anymore. We were mates as kids. I set her up with Dan that's all. I told you before I don't do coupley shit."

"Ha! But you think swinging's alright."

"Oh, drop it Lucinda. One fucking suggestion once and you go all fucking catholic on me."

Lucinda looked down. "Really, I don't mind giving it away. It was second hand anyway. And besides, I got in India– land of non-attachment."

Coldly he said, "How apt that we should meet in the land of non-attachment."

# Eight

Joseph ran his fingers over his Hanuman Tattoo and said, "A staunch celibate eh? You plonker."

The Homeless Man from the newspaper article leant over to have closer look, "Very nice," he said and offered Joseph a chillum with a ruby stone imbedded in it.

Very naturally, Joseph took the chillum from the stranger's hand and said, "This hell malarkey's not so bad, there's weed everywhere."

"They turn a blind eye to it in prisons too – keeps the inmates calm, happily incarcerated in their own minds."

Joseph took a hit from the chillum and passed it back to The Homeless Man.

"So, you're saying this is like a prison?"

"Everything is a prison if you view it that way. Most people are imprisoned and don't even know it."

"What and you're not?"

"No. I'm a traveller. A creator. A craftsman, if you like." He pointed at the chillum. "I made this after been touched by a special girl called Ruby."

"Touched?" questioned Joseph suspiciously. "Was that a paedo's touch then? Or did you kill her?"

The Homeless Man laughed. "I'm not surprised that you would think I was a murderer, considering the calibre of the other men in the Courtroom. But no. I did not harm her in anyway."

"Why then are you here?" scoffed Joseph, "who did you rape, murder, torture or fuck up in some way?"

In a calm and happy manner, The Homeless Man turned to Joseph quite lovingly and placed his warm hand over his and said, "Joseph, I am not really here in the same way as you. I am just passing through. My teacher is calling me back. I must go soon. I just wanted to see if this place really existed and was as hideous as they say."

Joseph felt a heat from The Homeless Man's hand and was surprised at how his initial discomfort at being touched gently by a stranger was burnt through. In a soft tone he asked, "And is it? Is it as bad as they say? Compared to where you've been?" Although he didn't say it, he intuited that this man had just come down from heaven.

The Homeless Man smiled peacefully and answered, "You know heaven doesn't exist as a place like they say in some of those religious texts. There is no such thing as, 'The Garden of Eden' – unless you want there to be. It's a fantasy. But where I am going back to is just like the common image one has of heaven, or has had of heaven, created by what they have heard about it and formulated in their own minds. Joseph, whatever you envisage, you will one day find yourself in. My brother, both in life and death this is true. For in life you make mind – in death mind makes you."

Joseph looked blankly at him, and The Homeless Man offered him more, "So, whatever you create in your mind whilst alive is the same mind set you carry into death. It becomes your path in the afterlife.

"Oh shit, I'm fucked then."

"Something like that, Joseph," said The Homeless Man and smiled. "What did you think? That you would end up in a Heaven Harem of Women?"

Joseph tried not to look too pleased with this possibility.

"I said it is mind, not experience, that determines that path, dear brother," said The Homeless Man and took another hit from the chillum. He took another moment to enjoy it before saying, "The Universal Law of Mentalism states that The Universal Mind is a single intelligent consciousness from which all things manifest. It is called universal since it's also a means to understand mystical and psychic phenomena. There is only one mind but each individual due to them being an ego, creates their own egoic, separate reality through their mind. One of the easiest ways to try and understand this is to see the mind as a mirror. Everything is simply a reflection of your perception. So, your inner world: your thoughts, becomes your outer experience: your reality. And the result in death is the same, except the life you led determines your afterlife experience."

He looked lovingly at Joseph and said, "The place that I am returning to is beautiful. It's peaceful, it's full of growth and divinity. It's a place of magic; a limitless place of light."

"And what? They allow you to smoke there?"

"I only smoked to come down to you. You might not have noticed me if I were not holding a chillum. In my last incarnation, I was a Satlan, which means a stoner amongst Israelites. Still, I used my life well. Smoking, like most earthly pleasures, has its downfalls, but in my human incarnation it became a tool for me to connect with many people: smokers and non-smokers, travellers and natives. I lived how they did, and I experienced their lives with them. But I never did it solely for my pleasure.

I believe my purpose then was that of a messenger. If you look closely, each and every one of us is a messenger."

He paused to take a pull from the chillum and winked at Joseph, who just looked back at him with a mixture of admiration and envy.

"Another hit?" asked The Homeless Man, passing the chillum back to him.

Taking it, Joseph said, "It would be impolite to say, no, but then I don't get the rules around here anyway. I mean I thought that drugs and spirituality weren't supposed to go hand in hand. Isn't that like mixing God with the Devil?" He took a deep pull from the chillum.

"And what do you think the difference is? There is no difference. It's all energy. It just depends on how you use it."

Joseph held his forehead. This guy was messing with the simple notion of good versus bad. What did he mean that there was no difference? Of course there was. Wasn't there?

"Joseph, there are good things and bad things, behaviours, habits, and lifestyles. But too often in society, in our earthly lives, we are caught up on them, judging each other for them."

Joseph looked again at the chillum, and The Homeless Man laughed and said, "You really are stuck on this, aren't you?" He took the chillum from Joseph. "Let me explain to you. Ultimately, to reach higher states there is no need at all for any drugs of any kind. In fact, it is a hindrance, just another attachment, a distraction, an illusion. It's true that drugs can elicit alternate states of perception, and if not abused for solely pleasurable feelings, can encourage an individual to move towards a spiritual life by breaking out of the mould that societies have trapped people in, to control them. So, higher states of consciousness through drugs are only an illusion that can give people an insight into the Real Truth that there is more – much more than our limited existence, promoted by the current powers in rule, would like us to believe."

Joseph silently pondered this truth.

"I am not doing this out of a need, and I neither advocate nor support it. But there is no point in having any judgement about it."

"So, what do I have to do to get out of this place? It's driving me nuts! Look at them," he said, turning his head to gaze around the room, "freaks and loony bins."

"How you judge them, Joseph. Their deeds are heinous, but how do you compare? Really now." He looked tenderly at him. "It is possible that you will leave this place and be reborn, or you may move to another place outside of the earthly realm. I have seen many more dimensions. This one is the Narcissistic Afterlife and contains the Male Divine Courtroom. In this same room on another ether is the Female Divine Courtroom."

Joseph perked up. "Really? How do I get there?" Then he shook his head and regretfully said, "Actually, forget it if it's anything like this place, then I definitely don't want to be in a room full of crazy bitches, even if they are hot. Are they hot?"

The Homeless Man laughed and looked affectionately at him and said, "Ah Joseph, you are a character. First you want the women, then you don't want them crazy, then you might just consider it if they are smoking hot."

"Yeah something like that. But not so smoking that they set themselves on fire and shit like that. Would they?"

"Probably," joked The Homeless Man and winked at him. "To be honest I have no idea. I've never been to that ether, but I should imagine that it's probably not too dissimilar to this one. However, I have passed through many other dimensions. Some much more disturbing than this, and as frightening as the image of hell. Just like a horror film. Then there are others so filled with love that my heart exploded and felt the oneness of all."

Upon hearing this, Joseph was pleased to not be in the worst place. Still embodied in his earthly condition, it fed his ego to know that there were people more dreadful than himself out there. This made him feel happier about his ranking, and with a renewed enthusiasm, he asked, "Which was your favourite?"

"The one of the Yogis. The great men who have lived on earth as spiritual masters, teachers and guides - that place of Yogi Heaven. A new teacher arrives today. One they say is the highest of all realisers: a seventh stage realiser. I will join him. There is much work to be done." He paused and his face took on a grave expression as he felt the great task at hand: the world's future at stake, and the Masters furiously loving through it all.

He wanted to be back with the Yogis and knew that for this reason that his time with Joseph was running out. Swiftly, he continued to address him and convey the message that he had been bestowed to send. "But back to you, Joseph. You may not journey anymore in any of these other realms, and it is also possible that you will stay in this realm for many years. Many others have. Or you may be reborn directly after this hearing – somehow this process is drawing you into the phenomena of reincarnation. If you are reborn, you will not remember this time here. But I will pray for you to move on in your earthly life to advance through the limitations quicker, so that you do not come back to this realm ever again. You have, my brother, been here too many times before."

This all seemed rather far-fetched to Joseph. He had no idea what to believe anymore; so very little made any sense. One thing he was aware of was that time was running out. He could feel it rushing past him, and he felt an urgency to understand.

It too was time for The Homeless Man to move on. Just before he left, he offered one more verse. "I do not know what will become of you, Joseph, and that's the beauty of it all. Try not to know. Be guided instead by your feeling, a true feeling in your heart, free from limitation. Now I must go to this new teacher. He is giving a talk I want to hear, called, The Wound of Love. I hope that one day you will hear it too."

He stood up and put one hand on Joseph's shoulder. Touching the crown of his head with the other, he warmly said, "Perhaps, I will see you soon."

The message in those words cracked Joseph a little but didn't penetrate him as much as the warmth in The Homeless Man's eyes. The light in them looked so familiar. It felt like love in a fluid form seeping into his heart.

In a sudden flashback, he remembered where he'd seen those eyes before. It had been in a picture that had hung in the assembly hall of his school. This Homeless Man had eyes just like him - just like Jesus.

As quickly as he had appeared, The Homeless Man disappeared, and nothing but the ruby from his chillum remained. Joseph bent down to pick it up, and his heart ached. Then he remembered why: it had been Lucinda's favourite stone.

# Nine

The fear in Lucinda's eyes after hearing the non-attachment comment both empowered and softened Joseph, and he pulled her into his arms and kissed the wound on her head.

The heightened eroticism still lingering in the aftermath of the sexual storm that had raged hours before, now trickled like the gentle raindrops streaming outside their window. The wind's soft whistle called out to Lucinda, and she peeked through Joseph's embrace at the afternoon sun, circled by the heavy clouds, whose impending darkness preyed on the day with the looming promise of keeping it imprisoned. There was something safe about that, and she was excited by dusk drawing in early on that crisp, cold day. Excited in more ways than one, since cold afternoons outside, often meant moody afternoons of deep, gentle sex, inside.

Joseph felt it too and guided by the dark skies, proceeded to kiss her face and neck. She felt his love in the softness of his lips, in the lightning that struck, in the thunder that roared, and in the air that she breathed.

Everything was a mirror of his love. It's just that the mirror was so broken.

Cradling her in his arms, he carried her to the bedroom and delicately lay her on the bed and stood back to soak in her beauty: so still, so pure, so tortured, so very, very much his Lucinda. She was a light born out of darkness; a darkness born out of light. Lucinda, so aptly named, as she lucidly crossed both worlds.

He scanned her white skin shinning against the backdrop of the dark room and noticed that his heart was beating faster. Unable to resist her anymore, he reached for the cloth on the bedside table and covered her eyes. She was even more vulnerable now, and he softly caressed the side of her face with his fingertips.

The temptation to cover his own eyes was strong, but he knew the blackness would draw out the beast in him, and with his fowl already injured couldn't take that risk. Having reached a new limit, he didn't trust himself to go any further.

He questioned how far he would go; whether he would be able to stop and whether she would ever stop him. He even thought that she would like to be killed by him. He sensed that pathos was deep within her. He sensed it with his cock, he knew it with his mind, and he feared that he felt it with his heart. And he had to protect that - protect his closed heart from opening.

#

Nothing could have been more perfect for Lucinda. After falling asleep in his arms, she awoke with the feeling that he did indeed love her, that he would never leave her and how utterly wrong she'd been to ever doubt him. With her eyes still bound, she searched for him in the bed only to find a warm spot where he had previously lain.

Gently pulling off the cloth so as not to disturb the staples, which were now starting to throb in her head, she opened her eyes to the same blackness. Night had rolled in, and a sinking feeling filled her stomach. Tired of her instincts, she reluctantly rose to follow them as they guided her quietly across the room, asking her to be as silent and invisible as possible.

She tiptoed up to the door and hid in the shadows like a prisoner on the run and listened to his voice murmuring through the room next door. It was clear that he was on the phone, intentionally talking quietly so as not to wake her. Listening intently, she slowly grasped the gist of the conversation.

#

"Not tonight," he said quite firmly, as if it were something he had just repeated. There was a pause. "I told you why. You know the set up." He tiredly repeated yet another line that he had to use in every one of their conversations when he wasn't ready to jump to her command. "I just can't," he whispered loudly into the phone, "I'm running out of excuses."

He threw these words out, and the listener on the other end of the line knew it was a lie. Joseph had a magic tongue and could get out of anything.

"No! I'm not in love," he said indignantly knowing full well that that was her way to get to him. She knew him the best of all, and he knew every single one of her tricks. It got him though, and his anger became released with the fear of the possibility that he was indeed falling deeply in love with Lucinda.

Lucinda backed away, her heart thumping as loudly as a toddler repeatedly throwing himself against the floor. Those dreaded words that he did not love her only confirmed that it had to be a woman that he was talking to.

Blood drained from her face, and she felt faint with devotion. Stumbling, she heard Joseph end the conversation with, "Ok, I'll be there soon," and only imagined the broad smile on the faceless girl she never knew.

#

Magnolia ended the call, happy at not having lost her ability to have Joseph whenever she wanted. During every single one of his relationships, she'd been there on the side to make that he never committed to another. She couldn't have him for now, but that didn't stop her from trying. Besides, she consoled herself with the notion that there was something exciting about having secrets with Joseph; it's how they had bonded as children.

#

Lucinda crept away from the door and sat on the bed at the same time as Joseph quietly entered. With amazing artistry, he lovingly smiled at her, and like a true pro looked into her eyes and said, "I have to go out for a couple of hours."

She stared blankly at him, trying to hide the pain behind a veil of self-deceit. Why didn't she just leave? Why couldn't she just go? Trying her best to hide the quiver in her voice, she asked, "Where are you going?"

He looked at her and sternly said, "You know I don't like you asking me questions. It makes me feel as though you don't trust me."

She swallowed her cry, knowing full well that she was being manipulated. It made no difference, they'd been there before on numerous occasions and knew the script well enough to know that he would go, and she would pretend not to know.

Before he left the room, he bent down to kiss her on the lips. Sulkily, she moved her face away from his, and he ended up kissing a tear that fell onto her cheek. The sweet, salty drop seeped through the doors of his deceit, and he almost sat down by her side to stay. Then he heard Magnolia's accusatory voice in his head, say, *you falling in love with her?* Each one of her words was like a burning cinder trapped in the walls of his gut, as trapped as he felt by her demands, by Lucinda's tears and by his own need to be loved.

His eyes locked with Lucinda's, and he quickly averted his gaze from the sadness that oozed from them, and left.

The door that slammed shut behind him was like the top of a coffin falling onto her, and Lucinda, in the still breath of the moonless night, driven by a sadness and anger raging a war within her, touched her wounded head... and began to pick out her staples.

# Ten

Joseph got into his car, silently cursing under his breath. His phone bleeped, and he pulled it out of his pocket and looked at the screen. It was a message from Magnolia. He sighed heavily and said, "For fucks sake, what does she want now!" and opened the message. He read: 'Get some nappies 0-3 months. She's looking more like you every day.' Attached was a photo of Ruby, two months old.

He stared at the photo, at the same eyes staring back at him, and before he could feel anything, deleted both the photo and message. Throwing his phone onto the passenger seat, he solemnly said, "I don't want this shit anymore," and started the engine.

#

The journey in his new convertible BMW took only fifteen minutes. It took him that long to get the image of Lucinda, sitting forlorn on the bed, out of his head.

After driving well over the speed limit, he slowed down and turned into Magnolia's road. The thick, languid, sexual force from her being drenched the whole street, pulling him towards her house, and his stomach tightened in rebellion against the sexual meal that he was about to ingest. There were plenty of reasons to not go to her anymore, but he was afraid of the primary one: a pulsing sensation of love for Lucinda that he didn't want to acknowledge or feel.

He pulled up outside Magnolia's house, and felt the weight of her sticky lust spray all over him like child's snot. For years, he had contained the oppressive force of her desire; having always been in the lead position, he was in control. In the past few months things were changing - Magnolia was becoming uncontainable.

He stared at the pack of nappies on the passenger seat and said, "These bloody women."

The sound of someone banging loudly on the windscreen made him jump. He looked up and saw The Homeless Man with his face pushed up against the window and shouted, "FUCK OFF!"

The Homeless Man was unperturbed and said, "There's a h..."

"I haven't got no fucking money for tramps. Get lost! You're marking up my car."

The Homeless Man stepped back. Joseph was grateful. "Thank You," he said, calming down a little.

"Be careful of that hole on the ground as you step out."

"What?" Joseph opened his door and looked down at an open sewage hole, right where he would have put his foot.

"It's a metaphor for your life."

"What the hell do you know about my life?"

"Just that you've dug yourself into a right hole."

Joseph got out of the car and stepped over the hole. He looked around but couldn't see The Homeless Man anywhere. "Fucking weirdos everywhere," he said quietly to himself.

He took a few steps away from his car and walked towards Magnolia's house. Each step felt heavier, and he stopped and said, "Fuck it!" and walked back.

He got into his car and turned on the ignition. Just before driving off he looked towards the house and said, "Metaphor for my life? Nah, no way."

#

Magnolia peered through the window and saw Joseph's car zoom off. "Where are you going?" she quietly questioned, then consoled herself with the thought that he'd probably forgotten to get the nappies. She picked up her phone and dialed his number. It went to answerphone, and she suspiciously asked, "Where the hell did you go?" She paused as if waiting for an answer then ended the call. He'll be back, she thought. Surely, he'd come back. He'd never ditched her like this before.

She walked over to a plant by the window and picked up a faded vision board from under it that had cut out photos of a perfect two point four family: a Latino woman that resembled her, a handsome man that resembled Joseph, a large house, Range Rover, and scattered pictures of children. It all looked so idyllic. Nothing like the reality that she was living.

She threw the vision board down and flopped into a chair. Home alone again. She tried convincing herself that that's exactly how she liked it. The truth was that she didn't like to admit how lonely life had become. Once the initial interest from people after Ruby's birth had died down, nobody had come to visit her, and she had no-one special to go to. Although she'd been very popular at university and in her early twenties, she hadn't made strong bonds with people, choosing to keep her relationships more superficial.

The few close female friends she'd acquired over the years had disappeared because of her Joseph obsession. Against all her wishes there were many occasions when he'd found a way into her circle of female companions and ejaculated his charm, like semen-soaked dye, through the fabric of their bodies. Even the lesbians found him charming enough to be knocked off their guard.

Time and time again, Magnolia watched the females respond to him, and at the first sign of any flirtation, launched an attack. She was smart enough to not publicly trash any of the assailants, instead choosing a quiet moment to infect with bitter jealously.

One by one, each of her friends got a lashing of manipulative defamation and either began to tire of her and drift off, or were cut off by her, especially if they were pretty and, or single. She wasn't that bothered until her repertoire of male companions also started to disappear as they approached the 'settling down age' and their partners didn't want her seductive, flirtatious persona around.

She had little to do with her family; her father had re-married and had a new family. Her mother had also re-married and although didn't birth again, seemed to forget about the two sprogs she'd brought into the world.

Magnolia was the younger of the two siblings by eighteen months. Her older sister was working for a human rights charity in Africa; Magnolia didn't know which country, and neither cared nor had the impetus to find out. The sisters had never been close, and the increasing years spent apart slowly erased the years that they'd shared, until there was nothing to connect them at all.

She hated to admit that she was Magnolia-No-Mates, resigned to watching groups of children playfully passing her door. The only purpose their presence served in her life was an indication of what time of day it was. She didn't wear a watch and what with Ruby's erratic sleeping pattern, she'd lost all sense of time.

Her stomach grumbled. She hadn't eaten all day, desperate to lose the baby fat. Hunger and tiredness were her worst enemies, and she battled with them both, since Ruby's arrival also meant that sleep was a luxury she rarely got to enjoy.

Magnolia couldn't have been grumpier.

Having already finished a bottle of wine, she decided that a cup of tea would have to do.

Two weeks before when Dan's parents had made the dreaded visit, they'd brought round some Earl Grey. Magnolia was grateful that they'd only stayed for an hour, and the whole time had been disgusted at Dan's nervousness around them. Unbeknown to him, he dropped a few more ranks that day. Earl Grey was her least favourite tea; she resentfully made a brew.

Her quivering lips enveloped the rim of the cup, and she sipped in the liquid that warmed her mouth and brought back comforting memories of her university days. Life had been so easy then. She and her housemates had lazed around all day, often from a comedown, and sat drinking cups of tea. Always PG Tips.

History had a funny way of haunting her, and dark thoughts emerged like spirits telling her that she had no one anymore. Even her thoughts knew that Ruby didn't count.

The warm tea froze in her throat and dropped like ice into her stomach. She was so far from peace and happiness, left chasing a dream that grew further away until it faded just like her vision board.

110

She'd created the vision board during the second trimester of her pregnancy when her morning sickness had been replaced with happy hormones. Back then, everything was going just as planned. Joseph had not mentioned a thing to anyone, he was still coming over to make love to her and genuinely seemed concerned for her welfare. Was she eating right, not drinking, sleeping enough, comfortable enough? She longed to be taken care of and though Dan was doing a matron's job of that, it was the equivalent of being looked after by a stranger. Joseph was her family not Lucinda's, and she wasn't going to let her take him away.

It was after hearing about Lucinda's pregnancy that she'd made laborious plans to have his child thinking that surely, he'd leave Lucinda for her. Falling pregnant had been easy. She'd told Joseph that she used the cap, and indeed she did when she had sex with Dan.

To cover her tracks in the month that she was trying for Joseph's baby, she lied to Dan, telling him that she'd forgotten to put the cap in and suggested taking the morning after pill, knowing full well that he would talk her out of it, seeing this as his opportunity to not only become a father but to get the girl of his dreams to marry him.

Naturally, she allowed him to believe this and pretended to forget, as hers and Joseph's cells formed another being.

Even though things were going to plan, she wanted to do everything in her power to solidify her dreams. The vision board was a result of that.

It was on a Saturday morning after a long, brisk walk in the park that she'd decided to pass by the newsagents and pick up an array of magazine: Homes, Vogue, Mother and Baby, Cars, and Cosmo. Magazines she would never normally buy.

The walk was invigorating, exercising her mind and body. It was rare for her to exercise, but the subtle suggestion from Joseph to exercise after the baby weight began to pile on in the third month of her pregnancy had left her feeling insulted. The last thing she wanted was for him to find her unattractive, and as a result, religiously walked a minimum of four miles a day.

Dan wished that she'd let him accompany her on these long walks and had romantic visions of strolling hand in hand through the park with people looking over and smiling at the new life and adventure that awaited them.

Even though he respected her need as an expectant mother to have some time alone, whenever he was home, he sat at the window like a small child missing its mother and waiting for her to return.

That Saturday as soon as he saw her turn into the street, he rushed to the door to greet her.

"Darling, you shouldn't be carrying all these magazines," he said, taking them from her arms. "Why didn't you tell me to buy them for you?"

"Oh, don't fuss! It's just a few magazines. Honestly, you treat me like an invalid. I'm not one of your patients..."

"Yes, yes, quite right. I'm sorry. You know I just want the best for you and our little baby." He placed a hand onto her belly and smiled warmly. "Thank you for this beautiful gift. Thank you for being my wife."

"Not married."

"Oh, but we will be," he said expectantly.

His smile faded when Magnolia squeezed his arm,

pressing in a 'you wish' print and pushed passed him.

"I'm tired - going to lay down," she said, walking towards the bedroom.

"Ok. I've prepared a freshly-squeezed juice. Would you like me to bring it to you?" he called after her.

Magnolia climbed into the bed and shouted, "No thanks, I'll have it later," and threw the duvet over her head.

Ten minutes later Dan left to start his shift at the hospital, and she hopped like a bunny out of the bed and raced to the kitchen. The thought of a freshly-squeezed juice had nearly driven her insane for the past ten minutes, and she gulped down the pomegranate, grape, apple and orange juice in one hit like a shot.

"Thanks Dan," she said sarcastically, "you're such a good boy."

She grabbed the magazines from the kitchen table, knocking over the empty glass in the process and watched it roll along the counter, making no attempt to stop it crashing onto the ground.

Ignoring the mess, she walked into the living room and sat down on the floor to scour the magazines. How can people read this shit, she thought as she looked for her and Joseph's home? After finding the perfect one and sticking it on the board, she searched for the Ferrari he'd always dreamed of, and the family Range Rover for herself.

Very carefully she cut out the cars and stuck them on the board in the driveway of the large home. They would need a garden, and she found a huge one filled with swings for the children; she was sure that they would have more.

Today's models were all far too skinny, and she struggled to find a more voluptuous beauty like herself. The closest was a photo of Jennifer Lopez, but she didn't want to be based on a real star. Just as she was about to go back to the shop and buy more magazines, she came across an unheard of Latino beauty, who even had a beauty spot in the same place as her. She'll do, she thought, and hurriedly cut her out of the magazine and stuck her on the board.

Finding Joseph was the hardest task. No man was good looking enough, and if they were good looking, they were not sexy enough, cool enough, or dangerous enough. They all had that fire missing from their eyes.

In a fit of anger, she threw an armful of the magazines into the air. As fate would have it, an advert for a men's aftershave landed on her lap – she'd found her Joseph. The male model was a bit too pretty, but had the same cheek, charm, sexiness and sensuality as Joseph. Caressing the photo, she paused to take in the model's beauty before diligently cutting it out and sticking it on the board facing the cut out of her lookalike. They were the perfect match, and amazingly, their eyes locked.

Lastly, she found some pictures of some cute babies and children and inattentively scattered them around the board.

Later that evening Dan's eyes filled with tears when he saw the board. He was touched that she wanted more children. And the fact that she had gone to the effort of creating a vision board indicated her deep intentions of a 'forever.'

The cut out of her looked quite similar. For a millisecond, the kind of millisecond that is so quick that if you don't like what it reveals you can ignore it, he saw that the cut out of him looked nothing like him; in fact, it looked more like Joseph.

Dan had created a vision board in his head many years before, and not one millisecond, not even one with

114

the power of plutonium, was going to erase his vision.

Magnolia thought carefully about where to place the board. It needed to be in a position that would involuntarily catch her attention throughout the day. It also needed to be in a place that caught the light from outside. LA was her destination (as far away from Dan and Lucinda as possible) and it was always sunny there.

She eventually found a hotspot in her living room under the window by her large coleus plant. As soon as she placed it there, the sun burst forth and a ray hit the picture, illuminating her dream...

#

In time, the vision board faded under the heat of the sun. The distinguishing colours sunk into a morose dimness, and the board stood like an abandoned bride at the altar: lacklustre and sorrowful. The picture of her had creased like wrinkles, Joseph's eyes had lost their brightness, a part of the house was torn, a child's swing was half hanging off, and the once happy faces of the babies were faded in parts and looked like they were crying.

Magnolia kept the board in the same place to involuntarily catch her attention. Nine months on, and with the happy hormones on vacation, it was a reminder of a lost dream that she enjoyed passing each day.

Winter had drawn in, the sun seldom shone, and on the rare occasion when the light did come into the room, Magnolia drew the curtains.

# Eleven

The Chair stood by the Vision Board and said, "It was a good idea."

"Good Idea!" screeched Magnolia. "Useless piece of shit! Law of Attraction bollocks."

"Oh Magnolia, Magnolia. Did you really think that all you had to do was want something and make a board and then, POOF! like magic your dreams would come true?"

"Isn't that what's supposed to happen!"

"No dear. It's not that simple. You see the Law of Attraction is a part of The Law of Vibration, which states that everything in the Universe is pure energy vibrating at different frequencies. For this Law to come into effect you must have a real heart need and not just desire. There must be a great purpose. In order to attract what you need you must vibrate on that frequency. Simply put, a positive mental attitude attracts positive experiences and circumstances, while a negative mental attitude attracts those conditions that we deem negative or unwanted."

She looked piercingly at Lucinda. "Being miserable, sad and feeling sorry for yourself only attracts more of those negative emotions, and circumstances to support them."

"It wasn't my fault. Every single man cheated on me," cried Lucinda.

"This has nothing to do with anybody else. Know that by taking responsibility for your life, you also award yourself the power to change it. All of you, ask yourselves, have you taken responsibility for your lives?"

"All life wanted to do was punish me," whimpered Lucinda.

"There you go again. First it was their fault and now life? Lucinda, The Law of Vibration does not judge, punish or reward. It simply serves to bring like energy together. You and that Old Caww for example. And your previous partners of course."

"I loved each and every one of them so much."

"But you never grew. Nobody here really learnt to love."

Magnolia laughed maniacally and said, "Love is a feeling, you weird child - not something you learn."

"For once I agree with that woman. Who are you?" asked Lucinda

"Shut it stick insect. You'll learn soon enough."

"Ladies!" shouted the Chair, "or more appropriately, bitches! Both of you shut up!"

"Jesus Christ," said Magnolia and threw her arms up in despair.

"Oh, he can't help you now," mocked The Chair, "neither can all the other saints and prophets. The way to God is love. It is precisely this that should motivate you, guide you, and breathe you: true love, and not the kind of subordinate love that you would kill and die for."

She turned her attention to the whole room and said, "You all experienced love, and you all experienced loss.

How many of you though, were willing to lose that love for a higher love?" A silent pause permeated the room. "None of you..."

# Twelve

Joseph returned home slightly drunk and slipped into bed next to Lucinda. She was still wide-awake and smelt a concoction of cigarettes, alcohol and perfume on him; an orgy of sickening smells that turned her stomach. With tears streaming from her eyes, she fell asleep hating him and yearning for him to hold her.

After a restless night, she rose from the bed and saw a damp, red spot where her wound had dripped blood onto her pillow – ironically, in the shape of a heart. She chuckled sorely to herself and thought that everything about life was so cruel. The signs were everywhere, and they mocked her. Just like the lucid figures in her dreams.

Life was tormenting. Every waking and sleeping hour filled with pain and frustration. It would never end, she thought. Death might be the only time she could rest. Then she would be free.

She often thought about killing herself. The only reason she'd gone travelling had been to end her life on a remote island somewhere. But much to her surprise, she'd found the change of environment enlivening, and then she'd met Joseph.

She looked over at him now, peacefully asleep and resented every breath he took. He'd given her a second chance, and now, slowly, he was taking it away from her. She couldn't understand how he kept her alive and was at the same time killing her, like a drug she was addicted to.

She hated to think of herself like that, but she was addicted to him, and there was no way to cure herself. She knew of no support groups for this type of addiction. Besides what was she supposed to say, "Hi, my name is Lucinda and I'm a Joseph addict." It sounded ridiculous. Even so, it didn't take away the fact that it was true. She was always high on him. Whether it was pain or pleasure, it was always a hit. When she did withdraw, it was never long before he came dangling himself in front of her; a pusher of charm that she couldn't resist taking another hit from.

For now, he couldn't touch her. The drug was weak, and she slowly sat up in the bed and peeked her head into the cot and cooed, "Mummy's little sleeping angel."

Gently, she stood up, but the slightest movements made her feel dizzy, and she stumbled. She hadn't expected her head to feel like a lead statue, and had to stabilize herself with her hand against the wall. When she felt that it was safe to, she staggered into the bathroom and stood by the sink.

Swaying slightly, she looked in the mirror at her hazel eyes swollen from crying, and the front of her blonde hair stiffly slicked across her face, dyed with streaks of red by the coagulated blood that looked like a red gel.

The local hospital was only five minutes away by cab, and she made the quick decision to go and get cleaned up, hoping that by the time she got back Joseph would have left. She doubted very much that he would wait around to see if she was ok. Work always came first. She accepted that.

Throughout her life, she'd gotten used to being second, but had never gotten used to the pain this caused. Today was different. The pain in her head made up for the pain in her heart, and besides, the smell of another woman on his skin repelled her to the point where she had no desire to see or talk to him that morning.

#

She arrived at the hospital just before the morning rush. After registering herself, she sat down in the waiting area and rocked the pram back and forth with her foot. With nothing else to distract her from her thoughts, she picked up a magazine from the table in front of her and started to flick through it.

A goody-two-shoes type woman was sitting nearby, rocking a crying baby in her arms. She looked over at Lucinda and smiled sweetly, in the way that the cult of mother's do, and said, "I'm sorry, I hope it doesn't wake your little one."

"This little Boo Boo can sleep through a hurricane," replied Lucinda and put her hand into the pram.

"Lucky you. Mine's teething. Just a small fever but you can never be too careful. My first one."

A nurse stepped out of a room and called out, "Lucinda Roberts."

Lucinda raised her hand as if she was at school. Realising what she'd just done, she cautiously lowered it and got up from her seat. In a flustered state, she bent down to put the magazine back onto the table, but at the last second decided to slip it into the pram. The article advertised on the front cover about a cancer patient's bounce back from a near death experience was something that she wanted to read. One that she might even add to her scrapbook. Before the other mother could say another word, she hurriedly pushed the pram towards the nurse's room and entered.

The nurse, a large Afro Caribbean woman, looked at her and tutted before asking, "My dear child, what have you been up to?"

Lucinda explained that she'd fallen and bumped her head in the night but not thought it serious until she'd woken up and found blood on the pillow.

The nurse looked at her in disbelief and raised her eyebrows as if to say, 'Aherm, now sister, you expect me to believe that bull?' but didn't challenge her and proceeded to examine the wound.

After a few seconds, she gave her a new gauze to press against her head and asked her to take a seat in reception to wait for a doctor.

This time, and more slowly than before, she got up and pushed the pram back to her seat, feeling happy that nobody else had occupied it. Her possessiveness wasn't exclusive to Joseph. Anything she felt was hers, fell victim to this fate.

The Mother and screaming baby were not there, and she sat down and flicked open the magazine. She'd barely gotten through a paragraph of the article when Dan appeared, panic stricken, scanning the area, looking for her.

She saw him first and cursed. The last thing she needed was for him to go snitching on her.

It was too late. He spotted her, and the worried look on his face turned to anger, making it a huge struggle to hide his true feelings under the white cloak of professionalism. "Lucinda, please follow me," he said

122

leading her into a cubicle and shutting the door.

Once away from the public, he dropped the doctor persona and blurted, "What the hell happened? I thought I told you guys to take it easy di..."

She put up her hand to halt his rushing words and said, "This has nothing to do with Joseph. The staples just kind of got loose in the night and fell out."

"Lucinda, seriously... do you take me for a fool?" he asked, feeling insulted and folding his arms protectively across his chest.

She looked down in shame. There was something about Dan that was undignified. On paper, he had all the ingredients that should come together to create an idea of dignity. Still, something was lacking, and she wasn't quite sure what it was.

He was right to feel that she had no respect for him, and they both knew it.

Right then, he didn't have the time or patience to dwell on such matters and just wanted to get her out of there before anybody else saw that her wound had already been 'privately' tended to. And so, this time with an anesthetic, he numbed the area and re-inserted the staples.

All in all, she was in and out of the hospital within half an hour. Much quicker than she'd expected.

#

Dan watched her leave and rubbed his forehead. 'Thank God,' he thought to himself, 'that I'd been at the processing desk when the note came.' If another doctor had gotten there first and seen from the wound that it had already been stapled? They would have been sure to ask questions, and he didn't trust Lucinda to give the kind of answers that Joseph would have successfully given.

The kind of answers that provided enough information to not arouse suspicion.

Things were bad enough, and he really didn't need anything else to upset the already fragile situation at work. His dream job had turned into a nightmare. Though he'd been well prepared for the long shifts, and the sleep deprivation that came with that, he hadn't expected to be so insignificant in the eyes of his colleagues.

It was not a new phenomenon for him to be ignored. In school, he was never the most popular boy. In fact, he was terribly ordinary. Girls would say that he was nice, because there wasn't much else to say about him. He didn't lack wealth or good looks. He had both these things and much more, but also much less. Good looking but lacking charisma; intelligent but lacking wit; physically well-built but with no affinity to sports. In short, Dr. Dan Duffy was Mr. Average - likeable enough with no real reason to like him.

He was aware of his ordinary status. It was part of the reason that at the age of thirteen he'd made the decision to become a doctor; a profession that he was sure would afford him respect and admiration.

Patiently, he'd waited for the years to pass. It didn't make his adolescence any easier, but it made it more tolerable.

During his youth, in an attempt to be liked, he'd attended every birthday party, his arms full of gifts. He gave up on giving birthday parties for himself at the age of eleven when the only people that had turned up were family members, the boy next door, and the kid in class that no-body liked.

Years later a 'friend' suggested throwing a joint birthday party. His initial reluctance was overridden with the joy of somebody remembering his birthday, and he ignored the niggling feeling that this too would be a disaster.

As predicted, from his perspective it was a shambles. Ninety percent of the guests were the other boy's friends, and the only real conversation anybody had with him was something along the lines of, "Oh you're the other guy whose birthday it is! What was your name again?"

The warm birthday glow faded as he spent much of the night wandering through his birthday party like a gate-crasher. The only way to have gotten noticed would have been to make a scene, and that just wasn't his style.

The final straw came when he overheard the other birthday boy brag that the party was a freebee, and the penny dropped: he'd been used for his money.

Just as the party started to get really going, he left, drunk and on the verge of spewing his sorry-for-himself guts out.

He never bothered to celebrate his birthday again.

The pattern continued, and the issues he faced at work were also rooted in social problems, which began when one doctor took a dislike to him, and made it his mission to humiliate, annihilate and ridicule him, until the rest of the team repudiated him. Everybody liked to have a dog to kick, even if they didn't know it.

He certainly didn't need Lucinda coming into the casualty department to stir up any more trouble. The better he kept hidden, the more chances there were of having a peaceful, if gutless life. He was used to it.

# Thirteen

By the time Lucinda had gotten home it was nine, and as predicted, Joseph had already left. Most probably without questioning where she'd gone.

It disturbed her to think that she didn't occupy his thoughts in the same way that he occupied hers. She made every effort to know his movements. Not an easy task since he never kept to a schedule and had so-called meetings at the most inappropriate hours. Unlike herself, who was easy to track, if you wanted to.

She'd thought about having an affair once, just to trip him up. But there was no point, he was her everything. Besides, he'd already made it very clear one day that he wouldn't stand for it.

At the time, they'd been snuggled up on the sofa watching a film, when halfway through, the cosiness between them evaporated when the female character was caught being unfaithful to her lover.

Lucinda didn't even think Joseph had cared much for the film, as he'd been more preoccupied with stroking the mound between her legs. But when the male character didn't respond to the affair in what Joseph would term 'a manly way', he took it personally and incessantly cursed the man for taking the woman back. He was a loser, a 'seconds' man, a spineless, gutless, ball-less idiot.

He was so disgusted that he moved slightly away from Lucinda as if she'd been the adulteress, and said, "If a woman ever did that to me, I would never take her back." Even though he didn't take his eyes off the screen, she knew that remark had been made for her, and she believed him.

Putting Joseph to the back of her mind, she walked into the bathroom to examine her wound in the mirror. Her head still felt numb from the anesthetic, and when she prodded her scalp, the flesh felt like it belonged to somebody else. There were more staples in it this time, positioned closer together so they looked like a sheet of corrugated iron that she gently ran her finger over. This time, she thought, they would be much harder to pick out without taking a chunk of her scalp with it.

She remembered Dan's fretful face and the determination with which he'd reinserted the staples. It pleased her to think that there was somebody weaker than her, and she smugly walked into the bedroom and over to the baby's crib.

Her attention went straight to a framed photo attached to the hood of the crib, of her holding her baby hours after he'd been born. She stroked the photo and smiled. In the picture, she looked so radiant and full of joy. Standing next to her was Joseph, looking as if he should be in another photo - something apocalyptic. They reflected two contrasting emotions superimposed on print, like a work of art bridging the dichotomy of heaven and hell.

The more she stared at the photo, the more her smile retreated, giving way to a blank expression that became startled when her phone rang, shocking her out of her empty space. She quickly answered it before it woke the baby.

"Hello," she whispered into the phone.

"It's Caroline. How you doing?"

Lucinda walked into the kitchen. "Great thanks. Just got the little one off to sleep." She took an empty baby bottle out of the steriliser.

"Oh right. Of course. You know me I have no idea about nap times and things like that." Caroline cleared her throat.

"How are things at the Library?" asked Lucinda as she opened the cupboard and took out a milk formula.

"Same old. Actually, that's one of the reasons why I was calling you. Just wondering when you'd be coming back."

"Oh, Caroline I couldn't possibly come back yet. Lucas is far too small. But then you wouldn't know because some naughty friend hasn't been to visit," she teased and scooped some of the milk powder into the bottle.

"I'm sorry Lucinda, it's just been so bu..."

"I'm joking," lied Lucinda and poured some water into the bottle.

"I think it would be good for you to get out of the house for a bit. You know get back into a routine."

"I have a routine. A new routine," she said and put the bottle into the microwave.

"Just might be nice to get your mind off..."

"I don't know what everybody is so worried about. I've never been happier," she said.

"Okay. Just call me if you ever need to talk or anything."

"Come over whenever you like. Or are you waiting for his first birthday?" Lucinda laughed.

Caroline awkwardly responded, "Ha, no nothing like that. I better get back to work. Take care Lucinda."

"You too. Kisses."

"Kisses back. Say hi to Joseph."

Lucinda put the phone down. Her happiness waning, she mimicked, "Say hi to Joseph," and took the bottle out of the microwave. "Argh, why can't people understand I'm a mum now. Library shrybury! That was my old life." She tipped the bottle upside down to let a few drops of milk drip onto the back of her hand.

Satisfied with the temperature, she walked into the hallway and paused for a moment in front of a bookshelf.

On one of the shelves was a framed photo of her and Caroline smiling and holding ice cream cones. She stared at it. A caustic look spread over her eyes, and she turned the photo face down.

#

The work environment had been her domain - libraries were the place that she'd always gone to for solace, so it was no surprise that she chose to work in one. Unlike herself the library was stable, and she felt safe in the atmosphere of knowledge; safe enough to place her fragile emotions in the foundations of the books.

The books alone were just part of her love of libraries; the way in which they were housed was another. The dark corridors were like secret tunnels illuminated by streams of brightness that snuck through the windows at certain parts of the day; the high shelves that stood like skyscrapers, were like her skeleton, and the books that they housed, were like the flesh on her bones; the smell - more than anything, she loved the smell of history, of past lives, and the musty aroma of the book's souls that spoke loudly to her.

Most people liked going to the library for the peace and quiet. But not Lucinda. She enjoyed the space that the silence provided for the voices to seep from the books and wistfully waft in the air.

Including herself, there were five other employees at the library. Caroline was her only friend, and she liked to think of her as a sister. An only child herself, she'd always dreamt of having a sibling. Somebody who mimicked her movements, or spoke in the same soft voice as she did. Having a best friend was close enough.

They started working at the library at a similar time. Being the new girls, they stuck together, their biggest bond evolving out of a dislike they both shared for another colleague. In fact, eighty percent of their conversation was focused on ridiculing her. These moments in Lucinda's day, though morally unsavoury, brought a lightness that she escaped into from the darkness of her own thoughts.

She sensed Caroline was much lighter hearted about the teasing, and the resentment she felt about this resulted in her harbouring secret, negative feelings for her too.

As far as Lucinda was concerned there was a lot to be envious of. Caroline was beautiful, smart, peaceful, funny, and most of all, happy. Lucinda felt like she was none of those things. The only consolation was that on some level, she felt superior by having the ability to appear benign whilst on a deeper level envy boiled like bad blood inside of her.

None of it touched Caroline, who was full of hope, with the spirit of a newborn looking at the world in wonder. It's easy, thought Lucinda scornfully, for somebody who has never known pain or suffering to see everything as beautiful.

She only sensed a little of what she believed Caroline was living, and that was love. Caroline was in love. Ecstatically in love. With her boyfriend, her dog and her new flat. She woke up happy and went to bed happy. She only expected to be happy and she was. She was loved by her parents; balanced, fun people, and loved by life itself.

On several occasions, when they'd come to meet Caroline for lunch, Lucinda had secretly watched them with an eagerness that soon dissipated when she felt like an unpaid audience member forced to watch a live scene from a cheesy sitcom.

Each time it was the same: the mother delicately glided in like a spritely deer, beaming a smile of maternal pride and happiness. The father, equally handsome, followed suit and stood faithfully by the mother's side. The protector. The hero.

Then the perfect parents, would look overwhelmed with joy at the sight of their Caroline. They embraced her with such a loving force that a light surrounded them. Each time they came, Lucinda watched from the side line, like a sub that never got to play. She watched the light both carry and guide them out of the door.

Their disappearance, though anticipated, felt like an abandonment, and the mood changed. With their departure, they took all the beauty from the room, and Lucinda was left feeling dark. This darkness gave power to the evil forces, and the books began to gossip about her, by saying that nobody loved her, and how she was not worth it.

The last time Caroline's parents had visited, she'd asked Lucinda to join them for lunch. The embarrassment of never being asked before, over rid her joy at being asked at all, and she made an excuse. She couldn't bear the thought of sitting amongst the happy family, pretending to be happy herself. It would only make her feel worse. The distinction between her own family and theirs was so drastic that no matter what love Caroline and her family exuded, she would not be able to catch any of it. The disappointment would fill her with failure and drag her further into the dark world of depression that so eagerly awaited her arrival.

Caroline cocked her head to the side as if to say, 'are you sure?' then smiled and with a hop and a skip went out of the door and into her parent's affectionate arms.

Caroline had it all.

To make matters worse, her boyfriend, Freddie was also a frequent visitor to the library. A few days a week he came to collect her, his eyes sparkling with joy at the mere sight of her.

On Saturdays, he'd spend at least an hour in the company of the books, and if she was ever late, he patiently waited. They were cut from the same cloth, Caroline and Freddie; both happy and balanced; simple and respectful; loved and loving. Lucinda had never met his parents but already had an idea that they were probably not too dissimilar to Caroline's.

Lucinda believed some people were just lucky, and she was not one of them. Joseph had only come to the library once, and that was because he'd left his keys at work and needed to borrow hers.

He'd arrived towards the end of her shift, and when she'd seen him, her heart had leapt for joy. She approached him at the same time as he approached Caroline; his radar eye having found the most beautiful girl in the room. He got to his target first, and she slowed down her steps, sifting through the corridors to kill some time.

Caroline nervously smiled at Joseph. He liked them that way. She was as fragile as a bird, light and perky, immaculately dressed with preened nails, like filed beaks. He found her rather endearing and stimulating at the same time - a younger, more ambitious version of Lucinda.

Unable to take his eyes off her, he admired her beauty as if she were a piece of art in a gallery. And she, in return, faithfully stood there like a sculpture, allowing him to unveil her beauty.

The exhibit was not allowed to be touched - for that he would have to own her first. Until then, he fell into the canvas of her soft, white skin that contrasted against her pink rosy cheeks, streaking like a sunset across her face. He imagined stroking her sensual lips, pouting in discordance with the childish solitary dimple on the right side of her cheek that gave her the appeal of a 'Lolita'. Her delicate form inspired a desire to wrap his fingers around her long neck, slender like that of a swan. And the destructive force of an artist's creative mind, implored him to mess up her fine hair.

After a few minutes, he came out of the gallery and into reality. Taking a step closer to her, he smiled back. Not once did he take his eyes off her, and with each second she became redder. This was the power he'd been seeking. She was now a part of his collection.

#

Lucinda watched in the distance. She wanted to give them the opportunity to talk, so she could later ask Caroline, 'And... so... what did you think?' Another, more sinister part of her, wanted to catch them flirting.

After a few minutes, she walked over to them and saw Caroline was obviously wooed off her feet, shuffling in embarrassment, twirling her hair and blushing with pleasure. Lucinda tensed up with each step she made towards them, and just caught Joseph saying, "Well, you are quick-witted and smart, perhaps you should come for an interview. We're always looking for bright, new talent. I think you may have what it takes."

Lucinda assumed that Joseph was interested in much more than Caroline's working talent, and there was no way that she was going to allow Joseph to take her only friend away from her. Quickly butting in, she told an out-and-out lie by saying that there was a student in corridor four (Caroline's section) asking about a book. Caroline blushed again at being caught out for blushing in the first place and quickly excused herself, averting her gaze from Joseph and looking apologetically instead into Lucinda's static stare. Before Lucinda had time to say anything else, she practically ran to corridor four.

As adept as a politician, Joseph switched from charming to ordinary. "Can I have your keys?" he asked, "I forgot mine at work."

"Oh yes, sure, but you know, I'll be finished in fifteen minutes. If you want to wait we could go home together." She blushed. Seeing Joseph in her work environment, the place where she felt like a queen, embarrassed her, and she was immediately demoted to princess.

"Can't. Sorry," said Joseph brashly, scanning the bookshelf to the right of her. "I've got an important meeting tomorrow, and I want to get cracking on with the preparations."

Joseph still hadn't gotten used to being a couple. Even though at the time they'd just moved in together, he didn't like the idea of leaving her workplace together. It was too much of a public statement.

Lucinda felt herself drop another rank and went to get the keys from her bag, muttering to herself, "Fifteen minutes. Just bloody fifteen minutes." On her return, she saw Joseph eyeing up the aisles looking for Caroline, who darted between them trying to hide like a frightened gazelle.

Her stomach dropped. Once the queen, now the pauper, she handed her keys over to him. He smiled, his eyes softening for a second and said, "See you later...I'm sorry. You know, just want to miss the traffic." He did actually feel sorry. If Caroline hadn't been there he might have waited. But in this case, she was, and his identity was far more important to preserve than his relationship.

He left just as Caroline's boyfriend, Freddie, entered the library and took a seat in section four to wait patiently for her; his eyes, as always, sparkling with joy at the mere sight of her.

Under any other circumstance the suggestion from Joseph that night for them to go on a double date with Caroline and Freddie would have been met with enthusiasm. But she knew Joseph well enough to understand that he had an ulterior motive, and though she dearly trusted her friend, Joseph had a remarkable power and persistence that could turn a nun into a whore.

#

Lucinda entered the bedroom and turned down another photo of her and Caroline in a 'Forever Friends' frame with teddy bears and hearts all over it.

She walked over to the baby's wardrobe and placed the milk bottle on top and opened the drawer. Inside was an old raggedy doll wearing a dress with 'LILLY' embroidered on the front of it. She shoved it to the side and hunted around the array of neatly folded baby clothes until she found a cute baby grow. Turning towards the crib she cooed in a baby's voice, "You're going to be the most adorable little button there today.

# Fourteen

Magnolia paced up and down with the phone pinned between her ear and shoulder and Ruby swaddled under her arm. In her other hand was a glass of wine.

"Fucking voicemail again!" she shouted into the phone, "Joseph, stop being such a pussy and call me back."

Depression had sunk its ugly teeth further into her flesh, tearing her heart with each passing moment that went by without a phone call or visit from him.

His absence in her life was like a famine that left an empty space in her gut, creating a pool of hatred that she wanted to throw the rest of the world into. She was drowning from the inside out, weighed down with the last image of him that lay like a tombstone in her mind, engraved with the vile way that he'd looked towards her house. And it was this final look that she couldn't bear.

She blamed herself, as she always did when it came to him. Just as Dan did when he argued with her. Sweet karma as they were both the underdogs in the relationships that they were obsessed by, feebly barking their way through conditional existence, on a leash they

137

had the power to break free from, if only they had learnt what Real Love was.

Her self-love led her to believe that Joseph's most recent withdrawal was because she'd been too demanding. She berated herself for her persistent requests that now replaced his love with a smouldering rage; the smoke of which singed her eyes and burnt her throat, choking her as it slipped into her veins to blacken her heart.

By taking on all the responsibility, she deluded herself into believing that she could also turn it around and win him back. She would do anything to get that look of desire from him, including making the subordinate decision that if she couldn't have him as her partner, then she would have him, in whichever way he chose, so long as she had him in some way; and so long as he never stopped coming to see her.

Like a terminally ill patient being kept alive with medication, she could not live without Joseph, and was willing to accept the second prize with the hope that one day he would tire of Lucinda and come rushing back into her arms to present her with the winning trophy.

Her one advantage over Lucinda was years of friendship. Having seen all his cards, she had the upper hand. However, what she failed to recognise was that the Joker had been taken out of the pack. She was the Joker and Lucinda, The Queen of Hearts.

She dialed once more and got his answer phone again. In a state of frustration, she threw her phone on the floor. It landed by a flyer near the door, and she picked it up and read: Don't Be a Doormat! Fight for Women's Rights. There was a meeting at a local Community Centre for later that day. Maybe it would do her good, she thought, to get out for a bit. Even if it was to something lame like Women's Rights.

She checked the address and saw that the Community Centre was on the same street as her old school, just a thirty-minute drive away. The thought of being in her childhood area enlivened her a little, and she almost felt like a person again – somebody she could value, somebody of worth.

She looked down at what she was wearing: an old baggy tracksuit, and walked into the bedroom to change. Dumping Ruby onto the bed, she opened the cupboard to scan the array of clothes, sectioned off into pre-and post-pregnancy. None would do.

#

The last time she'd braved the stores, the sales had just started, and the shops were packed. She didn't see another pram or baby in sight, Ruby screamed the whole time, and she wasn't able to ignore her, as she usually did, in front of so many other people. Ninety-nine percent of the shoppers were women, some of whom smiled politely; others, mostly younger girls, smiled nervously, holding up their size four dresses with a look of 'Phew! Glad I am not that fat', on their faces; and a handful of women were just like she had once been, muttering annoyances under their breath like, 'Who would bring a baby to the sales!'

Magnolia told herself that she couldn't care less what people thought. This didn't stop her cursing, 'Ruby's big mouth', and the women who came over to love her.

In the past few months, things had changed so much. She wasn't a person anymore but a mother, invisible next to her child. During her pregnancy, she'd been awarded a lot of attention. On the public transport people gave up their seats for her, they let her by first, opened doors, and looked at her in awe. But since Ruby's birth, she'd been demoted. Everyone looked passed her, and she was not used to being second.

She'd traipsed around at least fifteen shops that day and, typically, couldn't find anything she liked. It was always the case: when she had the money, the shops didn't have the style, and when she was broke, it was like there was a fashion invasion. She hated to admit that this time the reason was different. Unlike on other occasions, on this day there were plenty of outfits she liked in a size ten, her size prior to pregnancy, but the same dress in her new size, fourteen, looked hideous. Determined not to walk around holding a tent, she grabbed the size twelve instead. Maybe she could just squeeze into it.

The changing rooms were packed, and though she hated waiting for anything, Ruby had momentarily fallen asleep, and she grabbed this fortuitous moment to do something, anything that she couldn't do whilst Ruby was screaming. Besides there was a small chance that the dress would fit.

After queueing for ten minutes, she got into the changing room cubicle and quickly stripped like a model in a rush to get onto the catwalk, all the while trying not to look in the mirror at the stranger looking back at her.

She took the satin, lycra dress off the hanger and stretched it to loosen it a little. The dress bounced back, and she cursed under her breath. Before her anger produced sweat, making an already difficult task even more difficult, she slipped the dress over her head and pulled it down like a sausage skin over her meaty shoulders. Just as she was about to become joyful, the tight material got stuck over her tits, pressing them down like a trigger, causing milk to shoot out like water from a water pistol. She held in her scream and struggled to pull the dress off amidst sprays of milk shooting onto the walls and mirror. The neck of the dress got caught on her wrist, and she swung it round before throwing it down onto the floor.

She was not about to give up yet. Being determined was one of her strong points, and she tried a new strategy by stepping into the dress instead. If the bottom fit, she could always alter the top and make it a bit looser by cutting a V shape in the front to accentuate her cleavage.

This time round, the dress went up easily as far as the top of her thighs. It got a bit more difficult after that, and she had to push the meat of her buttocks left and right to squeeze the dress over her backside. Success was imminent, until her jelly-belly hung like a power-crazed guard not allowing the dress up any further.

She'd been defeated.

In the pause that followed, Ruby woke up. To an enraged Magnolia, her screams sounded like laughter, further infuriating her; even her own child was mocking her weight and taking pleasure in the fact that she was the cause of it. With sweat now dripping off her sticky body and unable to bear any more humiliation, she ripped off the dress in anger and practically tore it in two.

She caught sight of her reflection in the mirror again - no longer a stranger looking back - she'd morphed with the image of the angry, overweight, mother and spat at her. Phlegm dripped down the mirror, and she gave herself the challenge of dressing before it hit the floor. So dreary was her existence that this new goal gave her a purpose, even if it was for just a few minutes. Winning the challenge, she stormed out of the store.

#

She ran her hand over the pre-pregnancy clothes and picked out the red dress that she'd worn on the disaster date with Joseph and Dan.

Holding it against her body, she glided towards the mirror in the same way that she'd done on the night when she was going to put it on for the first time. It wasn't quite the same. The sides of her body were a few inches wider than either side of the edges of the dress, and she knew that it would take a momentous feat to squeeze into; she daren't even try.

Sadly, she put it back amongst the pre-pregnancy collection and looked at her reflection and screamed, "You're a fat lump! A fat, disgusting lard-arse!"

Ruby wailed in unison and Magnolia stormed over to her, "This is your fault, you brat!" She grabbed her from the bed with the precision of a three-year-old and bundled her into the baby car seat. Grabbing her keys from the table, she picked up the car seat and practically flew out of the house.

Ignoring Ruby's cries, she strapped her into the passenger seat of the car. Sighing heavily herself, she got into the driver's seat and turned on the ignition. A radio station was playing a rock song, and though she hated rock music, it amused her to see Ruby's lips move to the same rhythm as the rock singer's scream. Small pleasures, she thought and turned up the volume and drove off.

Driving reminded her of how good it felt to be on the streets again amongst people going about their everyday business. It gave her a sense of belonging to something and being connected to the outside world – one she'd forgotten existed beyond her own turmoil and despair. Her desperate fight to have Joseph, the arrival of the baby, and her disdain of Dan had turned her home into a nomad's cave where she was the bear eating herself with madness. Once out of that zone, it dawned on her that for weeks she'd lived like a prisoner, and naturally she blamed Ruby for that.

After a life-enhancing ten-minute drive they arrived at their destination. Ruby was asleep and Magnolia peacefully parked up on the pleasant tree-lined road of the Community Centre.

She stepped out of the car onto mounds of leaves and for the first time noticed that autumn was in full swing. The changing seasons were always a fresh start, and she paused for a second under the leaves that rained down on her. The beautiful colours: yellow, red, orange, and brown streamed like a falling rainbow, and she felt happy. It amazed her to feel this good.

A ray of starlight fell like a splash of paint directly onto her face, and the warmness infiltrated her hardened skin, enhancing the beauty all around. She sighed deeply and breathed in the cool air, closed the car door and happily skipped away. Without looking back, she switched on the car alarm and the normal beep resonated like music. She was ready to dance in it, until she heard Ruby bawl and froze; she'd forgotten all about her.

In an instant, the sun disappeared and the cloud's weight increased. The pressure in the atmosphere began to eat up the oxygen, and she found it harder to breathe. The rainbow disappeared – the colours no more. All she saw was the bare tree, whose thin, finger-like branches were pointing at her in an incriminatory manner.

Dropping her shoulders in defeat, she walked back to the car, crunching her way through the dying leaves that lay randomly on top of each other like a pile of dead bodies.

143

Once there, she unlocked the door and yanked out the baby car seat. Ruby was screaming even louder, her scrunched-up red face, the only colour shining in the grey backdrop that had fallen like a sketch over everything. Magnolia had never hurt her baby before but couldn't stop herself from pinching her leg. It wouldn't stop Ruby crying, but it made her feel better.

With the car seat hooked under her arm, she trudged back through the leaves, kicking them up in the air so their fragile stems broke like bones.

She stopped when she was a few feet away from the sign that read, 'Community Center', and shuddered. It wasn't just on the same street as her old school, it was her old school; the one she and Joseph had terrorised in years before. The smell of stale leather wafted in the air, and she looked around for Bianca the Wanka. Of course, he wasn't there.

All of these 'memory lane' reminders brought Joseph to mind again, and she walked passed the door to a nearby bench. Maybe the school was a good omen, she thought and sat down, pulled out her phone and started to text.

#

At that moment, Lucinda was pushing a pram past the Community Centre. She checked her watch and said, "We have time for a walk in the park my little Boo Boo," and carried on walking, smiling at everything and everybody.

She stopped near the entrance of the park for a second to coo over Lucas. A woman on a nearby bench smiled sweetly at her.

"A spring baby?"

"Five months."

144

"Aww… I remember when mine were that small." The woman's phone rang, and she quickly answered it. "Well hello there Dr...give me an hour and I'm all yours...naturally." She got up and smiled at Lucinda and said, "Treasure these days."

"I will," replied Lucinda.

They shared a moment and the woman smiled again and peeked into the pram.

Her smile faded, and she briskly walked off.

Lucinda leaned into the pram and cooed, "Silly busy body."

# Fifteen

Dan zipped up his trousers and bent down to kiss the same woman that had been in the park earlier. He slipped his hands into her top to fondle her nipples and said, "Same time next week?"

She nodded and said, "My price is going up...all the girls are doing it. It's gonna cost you an extra thirty quid next time." Flashing her breast, she smiled and said, "But you know I'm worth it."

He gave a commando's salute, and in an authoritative voice, said, "Dress up as a policewoman next time," and left the room with a little piece of shame following him like a small child who'd just been told off.

He'd justified visiting prostitutes to himself many times before, but it never took away the guilt he felt after the event. Like an unwanted haunting, with the post-orgasm came the vision of Magnolia sitting angelically at home waiting for him.

It was with regret that every time he left the whorehouse for the drudgery of ordinary life, the cursing would begin: first of himself and then of Joseph.

#

*Two months previously*

Dan knew that had it not been for his dear friend than it would never have occurred to him to indulge in such extra curricula activities.

Joseph was the one to suggest it and to egg him on even, by telling him that it wasn't seedy, and if you knew where to go then it was like being in a five-star resort with some of the most beautiful girls at your disposal.

This came as a surprise to Dan. Not because Joseph had a girlfriend, and he shouldn't cheat. No, he knew his friend well enough to know that made no difference. But because Joseph already had so many beautiful women at his disposal, without having to pay for them.

This perplexed him for some time, and a few days later when he was at Joseph's house on one of those nights when Magnolia, in a fit of anger, had thrown him out, he asked, "Why use prostitutes, then?"

Joseph laughed at this question. He had a niggling feeling that ever since he'd mentioned the whoring to Dan that it had been eating away at him like a man starving for pussy. He guessed Dan's preoccupation with it meant that almost anything triggered the dilemma to arise, and for now concluded that the current trigger was the violent, video console game that they were playing.

"Why prossies? Well, I'll tell you why, mate... There's no such thing as just a fuck with a woman. The first time maybe, but when you go back for seconds and thirds, their expectations start to rise. Most of the time I can deal with it, but then there are the occasions where I think 'fuck it,' I just want a good round with a hot lady who looks like this..." Joseph pointed into the air at nothing in

147

particular. Dan got the picture. "Easy peasy, lemon squeezy - no emotion....here's your dough, now get on the floor and roll. Besides, it's sexy to pay for it. You know, the whole power thing." In the voice of an Italian boss, and with added exaggerated hand gestures he said, "Now you are mine, bitch, for at least an hour." Resorting back to his natural voice, he carried on, "And you get her to do what you want...hard or soft...slow or fast."

Dan wasn't sold on the idea, and shook his head. "I don't know man, you can get a woman to do all that stuff, anyway."

"Yeah, yeah, I know that, and they do. But you know, she's got her own agenda too, whether you like it or not. Now with prossies you haven't got that shit to deal with."

Dan could see his point. Picking up on this, Joseph decided to kill two birds with one stone by first virtually shooting him in the head, before overloading him with information like a foray of bullets.

"I mean, look at it this way. This shit's been going on for years, and now with the new internet generation it's even more accessible; everything's at your fingertips, like a frigging games console." Joseph held up the control pad. "You have the control, and you get to be any fantasy character you want."

He smiled and winked at Dan, who blushed at this suggestion. Joseph took this as a sign and knew that he was onto something. 'So, my little friend likes the whole dirty role-play thing, ha?' With the belief that he'd found Dan's weak spot, he went in for the kill. "Men need that shit. Like I said, since time began they've been going to whores. Mate, can you see that everything we have today has been created from that same need: power....and power over women has been there from the start. No matter what laws they pass, we have the cocks, and we do the penetration. They're always going be the ones getting fucked."

He laughed at his own words. He'd never thought about it so much before, but there it was before him. Women take it and men give it. This mere acknowledgement empowered him, and on a roll, he continued to educate Dan. "It's in our power, and why? Cause it's in our make-up, dude. All this hippy talk and lesbian crap about equal rights, is shit. Men and women are different. So, you can't have the same fucking rules when there are different needs. Now, I'm not saying men should go around and abuse that power. Don't get me wrong, I'm not a complete psycho."

"Well, thank fuck for that," said Dan and laughed nervously, only half-believing him.

"Nah mate, what I'm saying is, in all this modern talk, people are forgetting some basic facts." He paused to take a long drag from the spliff. "Listen, you go to a club now, and you see a few sexy women on the dance floor, all touching each other up and loving it. They do that shit even if men aren't there. Girls with girls, like a bunch of pussy munching sluts in a harem. I mean, mate, you're not likely to get you and me on the dance floor feeling each other up and slapping each other's arses, are you? One big difference here is that women on women is more natural, and why? No givers. No cocks. No penetration. No power. Just sublime harmlessness, touchy, touchy, gentle and free. Unless a girl knocks another out with her large kaboobies, no-one's getting hurt. Now, you have two men together and one could get his arse ripped before the night is done."

He winked at Dan, who looked away in embarrassment. Not only was he losing terribly at the game, but now, with the added shame of what that win from Joseph suggested, he began to get frustrated with both the conversation, which he felt had gone off target, and with his shooting, which was well out of range. Deciding to take a stand, he put down his control pad in the hope of it being a clear indication that he'd had enough of the game. Joseph didn't even notice.

"Have you been doing charlie?" asked Dan, "because you're talking a load of bollocks."

Joseph laughed again and put the control pad back into Dan's hand. "I wish. Nah straight up, this is how it goes. Women hang around together, talk about periods, stick their fingers in each other's cunts to pull out their babies, squeeze each other's zits et cetera, et cetera. And why? Cause they're women, and they look after everyone. Mate, they're the nurturers."

Dan showed no signs of swinging either way and reluctantly listened whilst dying in the game; Joseph was relentless both on and off the screen.

"Another thing is polarity. The woman needs the man. She's the one that carries the sprog and has to care for it. It's fucking hard doing all that shit on your own. That's why the social security system is fucked. All these selfish, single mothers letting the state pay for their irresponsibility."

"Oh Joseph, hang on, you're taking it a bit far now. What's that got to do with whoring? Also, what about the man's responsibility?"

"Hang on, hang on, Dr. Dan, let me get to my point."

Dan winced. He hated it when Joseph condescendingly referred to him as Dr. Dan.

This little subtlety of Joseph's character was a nuance of his retaliation. His way of marking his spot and rising up the rank. It wasn't too dissimilar to the reasons why he had pet names for his girls. A nuance that didn't bother Dan in the same way that it jarred Magnolia.

Joseph was too caught up in his monologue to notice the silent, hurt response from his friend, and carried on with his sexual sermon. "Now in those countries where there's no social security system, you've got to have a tight cultural tradition to keep that shit together. Either you have the man/woman marriage shit going on, where she tolerates his affairs as she doesn't really have any other choice, unless of course she's loaded, then she fucks around too; or it's a whole community that looks after each other like the musketeers: one for all and all for one."

"Joseph, you're so old school, man, it's not like that now. Yeah, maybe in the developing world, but not where we're living. Women are educated, respected as equals in the workplace, or at least respected enough to be given jobs and hold their own."

Joseph's silence and focus on the game didn't deter Dan from having his say. "I mean, I know that men are still the fat cats in the boardroom. You don't see that many ethnic minorities either for that matter, but that'll change over time too."

"Yes! Another bitch is dead," screamed Joseph after shooting a female assailant in the head.

Dan ignored the outburst and carried on, eager to make a point and stand up for women all around the world. "Another thing is, women these days are actually choosing to have their babies alone. You know what Magnolia told me?" Upon hearing her name, Joseph's ears pricked up. "She told me a friend of hers goes out with this dude, lies, saying she's on the pill, then gets knocked up intentionally and fucking dumps him. Can you believe it?" Joseph bit down on his jaw and shook his head. He was not surprised. "Apparently," continued Dan, pleased to have evoked a reaction from Joseph, "the

151

girl got what she needed! Said the bloke had good genes, money to help if he wants, but if he doesn't want to be involved then she doesn't need him. Allegedly, this cunning lady had been saving so that she could afford to take a year off work."

He looked over at Joseph to see whether this remark had also incited a reaction. It was unusual for him to be so antagonistic, but the game had fired up his testosterone to a level that invited a challenge. "You know that's a law now? They've got to keep your position open for a year."

Joseph was pleased to have sucked Dan into his corner but not so pleased with the angle that he'd taken. With his eyes focused on the screen, he shook his head resolutely before saying, "Yeah man, if I had my own business, I definitely wouldn't want to give a woman a position of authority. Too fucking costly, mate. Got to get a replacement, train'em, and all this on top of the fact that we already have to put up with their fucking PMT. Don't give a shit what anyone says, once a month, for at least a week, they're psycho."

"Yeah, yeah that exists. PMT, I mean. It's medically proven but with differing levels..."

Sensing that Dan was about to go into some medical spiel, Joseph interrupted him. "They are a liability in the workplace, man. I'm telling you. Anyway, as I was saying, polarity - women around the world need men."

"Or a good social security," said Dan, lightening up further.

"And men need to find a good, trustable woman to have their kid," said Joseph, now in tandem with Dan, grateful that they were finally on the same side.

"Yeah, I'm lucky, I guess, in that respect," said Dan, genuinely pleased with his family.

"Exactly mate, you and Magnolia. She'll look after your sprog…"

"Baby," added Dan firmly. It always bothered him that Joseph showed such little interest in the baby about to be born.

"…And you pay for it," continued Joseph, ignoring Dan's tone.

Joseph knew Dan had no idea how much he was paying for it. Paying for *his* genes to develop.

Dan was starting to lose Joseph's thread completely and wondered if the conversation would ever lead anywhere. "The point, Joseph. The point," he said impatiently.

"So, my point is…" Joseph went on, as if Dan had never spoken. Then paused, wondering what his point had been.

Dan was reaching the end of his tether and tried to hurry him along. "Men and women need each other….yeah?"

"Yes, exactly," said Joseph as the scores of the game came up, and he was announced the winner.

Dan sighed with relief - not only was the game over, but so was the pointless conversation.

Joseph hadn't yet finished and went on and up a level. Picking up the controls, he carried on with the game. Nudging Dan to join in, he said, "Women are fucking up the world by trying to change the rules. You can't change natural design, man. You can educate, and not tolerate abuse, but aside from that, it's all biology. Emotion, desire, all that shit is down to our hormones. Men give off millions of those in sperm, whilst women have limited eggs that only pop out once a month. Dan, my point is that men are supposed to be fucking around. It's the male design, and women are supposed to find the best sperm and birth it. Can't change that," he said victoriously, happy at having some point to relate his whole speech to.

"I can't imagine any woman these days accepting that," said Dan.

"They already do, mate. Besides, it's not something you go bragging about to them. Deep down, they know it. No need to throw it in their faces like acid now, is there? Dan, you've got to keep the ladies sweet. Too much conflict leaves a nasty taste in one's mouth."

Dan knew about this; his mouth had been bitter for months. "Yeah, can you imagine if I said something like that to Magnolia?"

Joseph sidestepped the last comment. He didn't want to bring her into the conversation. Instead, he felt a comradeship with Dan and perversely wanted to give him a little advice. "Having said that, conflict is no good, but a little tension works wonders. Best way to get that is not be too available. Even the nicest girl will bitch-slap a lap-dog."

Dan whimpered and retaliated by going on a shooting spree and killing anyone in sight.

"Mate you're not supposed to be firing at me," said Joseph, playfully kicking him.

"I read somewhere that ejaculation is degenerative."

"Oh, fuck off. I suppose you're going tell me that you're a vegan now, or hang on, even worse, doing a raw food diet. How fucking ridiculous is that? Who the hell would want to eat uncooked food and live off spinach and broccoli their whole life?" Joseph grimaced and said, "It's got to be disgusting, man."

Dan, doing better at the game, perked up a little and with more confidence challenged Joseph. "Seriously, just because men have the potential to germinate doesn't mean that they should. That's a ridiculous argument. It's like saying just because a man has the power..."

"Not just power! It's need. It's need that feeds a man. You strip a man of his need to fuck around, and that's when you strip him of his power. His God given right to exercise that power sexually." Sighing, he continued in a tone as if he were addressing a fourteen-year-old about the real facts of life. "Women don't need it. They need you to listen to'em, treat'em like princesses, fuck'em good, buy'em shit, tell'em they're beautiful, that you love'em, be there emotionally for them, whatever the fuck that means. They only fuck around if they are bored, drunk, or want to get out of the relationship. For men, it's simply like a sexual menu. The man has his favourite main dish: Magnolia in your case, Lucinda in mine, and he always wants to have that. The man doesn't want anything to change that, but he also wants a few extra side dishes from time to time. Eh.. eh? And if he's a real man he'll want to eat some meat, something fishy perhaps?" Joseph nudged Dan and smiled.

Viscerally, Dan felt what Joseph was saying, but he didn't want to see himself as so primal and raw. There had to be another level of sophistication behind this, something more evolved. Frustrated and not able to think straight whilst his adrenaline raged, he shot more of the people that he was supposed to be saving in the game. His hormones had taken over as if they were a separate entity of their own, behaving independently to his moral and ethical beliefs, and driving him into Joseph's psyche.

"Listen, as a mate I'm telling you to get some different pussy down you, or you're going start to lose your balls." Joseph grabbed Dan's balls and said, "Woah, get a load of that!"

"Get lost," said Dan, moving Joseph's hand away from his growing penis. "It's disloyal," he murmured regretfully, "what about Love?"

155

"I don't want to sound like Tina-Gorgeous-Fucking-Legs-Turner, but seriously 'What's Love got to do with it?' I can love one woman and fuck another. What planet are you on, mate?"

"The one where men face up to their responsibilities," said Dan defensively, as if he were being directly attacked.

"Mate, unless you're going to suck on a carrot forever and not fuck..."

"I didn't say not fuck. There's something called a regenerative orgasm. Some kind of yogic practice."

"Oh, my God, I've heard it all now," said Joseph shaking his head and chuckling to himself. "Ok, give up your cock to God then, I'd rather get mine sucked by two beautiful ladies...at the same time."

The thought of two ladies sucking him off made him want to bring an end to the conversation and make that fantasy come true. He didn't. For some reason, he felt passionate about changing Dan's view and said, "Can't you see, Dan? Cocks are power. Why do you think that nutter...oh what's her name...Bobbitt! That's it...Yeah, why do you think that she went and cut off her husband's cock? She knew, just like deep down they all know, we've got the cocks, and we've got the power."

"Looks as if she took control in the end," said Dan, a smile creeping up onto his face. He was starting to enjoy the conversation and Joseph's passionate banter.

For a change, Joseph's buttons were pushed bringing to the surface his worst fear, of one day waking up with his penis severed. Even before he'd heard about the Bobbitt incident, the awful sight of a cockless man had plagued his dreams for years.

"She was a psycho!" shouted Joseph. "Not likely to become an epidemic, is it? Like I said, they're doing it in less subtle ways now by fucking with your head. No woman is going take my power away. When I'm ready, I'll fuck any woman I want, when I want. And my dear friend, if you don't want any extra drama, then that's when you go to whores."

# Sixteen

Joseph felt exhausted with all the drama, and as the Courtroom took a brief recess, he quickly tried to work out what was going on. It occurred to him that although he had no recollection of actual events prior to being there, he still felt a sense of himself. His thoughts and beliefs were still intact; his identity was clear. Perhaps, he thought that he was neither fully dead nor alive. But then what and where was he?

Unbeknownst to Joseph, his detective skills were limited by his conditional state, and he failed to realise that unconscious forces had driven him to the afterlife. "I just don't get it," he muttered to himself.

"Had it not been for your lover, then you wouldn't be here now," said the Formless Voice.

Joseph rubbed his forehead as, '*Which one?*' appeared on the screen."

The Formless Voice laughed and said, "It doesn't really matter now, does it?"

Joseph was silent, as a catalogue of women flicked through the pages of his mind.

"Initially you were headed for another afterlife," said The Formless Voice, "The Reunited Souls."

"What? This place gets crazier," said Joseph and got up from his seat.

"Oh, Joseph do stop feeling sorry for yourself. I can see now, why you were heading there. You missed her when she died. But then you were so young."

An image of Joseph's mother appeared on the screen.

In an attempt to fight back his tears, he squeezed his brow with his fingers and widened his eyes. It was futile - a few teardrops fell silently into his palm.

His sorrow turned to anger and with nothing else to lash out at he turned on himself. *C'mon man think. What did you learn in physics…science is the only proof…this must be a dream.*

"Joseph please do not try to work this out," said The Formless Voice, "if you must have a conceptual construct, then see this place as one where you are in transit."

Joseph was surprised at first, but then he remembered, and the word, *'Shit'* appeared on the screen. He'd forgotten all about that *'fucking stupid screen.'* He waited for the roars of laughter from the imbecile's but the crowd was calm having already lost interest in their newcomer. This somehow offended him since he'd always been a central character and theme in peoples' lives, it was a novel experience for him to be of no importance.

Throughout his life, women in particular had made him their focus. He was an expert at that by first drawing them in with his charm, keeping them there with marathon sex, and then just when they thought that they couldn't live without him, he starved them of affection so that they desired and wanted him even more. He knew the line, and when they could take no more, he would throw them a cracker of devotion which they scrambled for, frantically stuffing every last crumb into their mouths.

Joseph's strategy was infallible.

With men, his success in the professional field had won him as many admirers as it had enemies. Either way, he was known by many and their mere preoccupation with him made him feel special.

The last thing he felt in that room was special.

Just as he was about to feel sorry for himself again, he heard The Formless Voice hum a tune that he didn't recognise at first, until the crowd excitedly started to fill in the words to Elvis Presley's, 'A Little Less Satisfaction.'

Every man in the room became infected by the melody. Their eyes filled with mischievousness as they clapped un-rhythmically like a horde of hyenas, until it all ended in a mesh of horrible screams and shouts.

*'Fucking loony bin,'* appeared on the screen and The Formless Voice said nothing with his words, but drew his response on the screen in the form of a *raised eyebrow*.

The crowd hushed immediately, with just a few gasps from some of the men. What had just occurred before their very eyes had been a first. The Formless Voice offered an explanation, "I have many forms that you have the power to reveal. Joseph somehow did that."

Joseph smiled broadly – he was back in the centre again.

After a small pause The Formless Voice went on, "But enough of that, the Court is in progress, and I wish the man, who knows that song is for him to stand."

*A smile* appeared on the screen and Joseph couldn't help but smile back.

"C'mon Mr. Musical Man," beckoned The Formless Voice in a mocking tone, "you wished your life to be a

160

song and dance, but you didn't expect it to end so cruelly. Do tell those here your tale."

A man rose from the back of the crowd and slowly approached the front of the room, dragging his feet and staring at the ground. His whole posture and demeanour represented a man on the verge of giving up: physically worn out and exhausted in every way.

Joseph only had a side view of him but could see something large swinging around his neck, weighing him down. When the man finally turned to face the front, he saw that the object was a large erect penis with a chain around the severed root of it.

"Not bad," said The Formless Voice, "it only took you five minutes and thirty seconds this time to walk to the front. I see, though, that your cock has grown and you are stooping more and more."

The Formless Voice paused, and from the ridiculing tone in his voice it was clear that he enjoyed addressing the man. "Tell me," he asked, "how is the pain, my little musical friend? My never-made-it-to-the-top-rock-star. Let's hear your response in your musical tune. You believe you're Elvis, you ridiculous loon."

"Fucking awful sir," blurted the man, "I beg you not to allow me to suffer no more. Already you see I wear my cock ripped from its core."

"Now, now Mr. Cock, you know that it's not I that makes you suffer," said The Formless Voice. "Though I do see that you still live with the musician identity.... so, I will rhyme with you, Mr. Weird Entity."

The room lit up with the laughter of the men, who sat eagerly in their seats awaiting the show.

"My story sir, is plain to see, I paid my penance for my awful deeds. And yes, I will tell what those were. But I pray to you for forgiveness, sir."

161

"Hahaha! I am not God and this is not a church! Your prayers mean nowt my son, when you live life as a search. But do go on, we want to hear your story, since you stand there before us in all of your glory."

The men in the room burst out into laughter again.

Mr. Cock had intended to try to trick those before him and appear humble. But being ridiculed in his suffering further debilitated his ability to be anything but real, and hastily he spat out his truths. "I cheated on her because she was a fool. She made me angry when I was so cool." He proceeded to do an impersonation of Elvis by curling his lips. Unlike the real star, he was far from cool or sexy, and the bad impersonation led the room to break out into humiliating laughter again. But this time he was unaware as he continued to rhyme. "She took it all and never fought back. How can I respect a woman who takes all that? Her sex was sloppy, her housekeeping a mess; her need to please me and give me her caress; her desperate attempts to find the love in me, made me want to destroy.... ahhh why can't you see?"

"Oh Mr. Cock we can, but can you? Pray do tell us something new," jeered The Formless Voice.

"You want to know what I have learnt? After all these years how I've been burnt? By carrying my cock like a medallion around my neck, for all those years of marriage she did wreck. And every time I take the stand my cock gets bigger, and I beg for a rifle and for you to pull the trigger." Mr. Cock simulated a gun to his head with his finger.

The mere action of what his only salvation would be had the effect of further distressing him. Wearily, he put his hands over his face as if he was about to break out into sobs, but instead managed to compose himself and shook his head in self-pity and said, "What I have come to in this realm of whatever place, because of that bitch,

162

that fucking nut case. Her mind is mincemeat, a scrambled mess, for thinking of this revengefulness." Mimicking a woman's voice, he continued with his theatrical performance. "I know, I'll wait, she says through gritted teeth, and then I'll find a way to get my piece." Mr. Cock bitterly pointed to his severed penis. "And good as her word, she sets me to sleep, all naive and sweet like Little Bo Peep. The pills took effect like a poisoned wine. I caught her smile, which should have been a sign. I became the lamb for her merciless slaughter, and then she went next door to murder our daughter."

Mr. Cock paused, waiting to hear gasps from the crowd, who he was sure would be outraged with a murdering mother.

Unsatisfied with the lack of response, he continued with his story. This time with a little more agitation in his voice, he looked the men dead in the eye to convey to them the horrors of what he was about to reveal.

"Although I was out, I was not totally unaware, so when the knife touched my cock I thought, 'No, she wouldn't dare?' Unable to move, I sensed only a little pain, but felt the squirts of blood that throbbed out of my vein. With my severed cock, erect in her hand, she opened up my eyes and made a hissing sound." Mr. Cock grabbed his penis and hissed like a mad cobra. His eyes bulged out of his head and saliva dribbled down his chin. Ignoring the slimy mess, he stopped hissing and continued to rhyme in an irater tone than before.

"She ripped my medallion from around my neck, tied my cock on the chain, bent down and gave me a peck. My eyes peeled open and the last thing I saw, was her leaving the room to enter our daughter's door." Mr. Cock stood, his eyes blazing with anger, feeling the resentment of the vile act that he had fallen victim to.

"Are you angry, Mr. Cock, for what Mrs. Prim did to you?"

"Of course, I am angry, you fucking fool."

"Are you sorry, Mr. Cock, for treating her so bad? Do you have any remorse? Do you even feel sad?"

"Sad? Are you mad? Have you lost your mind? You're as crazy as that bitch! Dear God, hear my rhyme."

The Formless Voice ignored the insult from Mr. Cock and continued to rile him with more questions. "Do you not accept that you had a part to play, in this drama of tragedy? What do you say?"

Mr. Cock paced the floor. "I say yes, I was angry with her, trapped in a life I wished to deter. I say she brought out the beast in me, during a time of my life when I was too young to see. I say I have learnt to hate, rather than to love. I say this easily to the man above."

"I must interject there is no God separate in human form. No man exists in this or any other room."

Mr. Cock was beyond hearing any more truths from The Formless Voice and impatiently said, "If you may allow me to go on with my tale, I say that every man should be allowed to fail. I say I loved her once for a short period of time and that love became twisted, instead of matured like wine. I say she deserved every little hit, because she lacked intelligence, beauty and wit. I say she enjoyed suffering in her way of life. It gave her a reason to pick up that knife. I say it was destined, and I had no part to play, in this tragic drama... That I will say."

Mr. Cock slammed his fist onto a nearby chair to signify the finality of his rhyming tale and stood as proud as a cock with the courage he displayed.

The Formless Voice was unimpressed and dryly responded, "Mr. Cock, alas, you have failed to impress. You started quite well, but you do not pass the test. Yes, she enjoyed suffering as she did. She was used to it and

164

behind your violence she hid. Yes, she was dumb; she was a simple homely lady that you chose for your wife, and together had a baby. Yes, she surprised you right at the end, when she found the devil in her and became his friend. But no Mr. Cock, it's not entirely her fault. You destroyed a growing flower with your heinous thoughts. You saw something so kind and beautiful in her. It made you aware of the cock, you are, sir."

*A smile* appeared on the screen, and with the exception of Mr. Cock, every man smiled back.

"I say now you are not ready to leave; may your cock grow bigger and forever shall you heave."

A sudden gust of wind blew into the Courtroom, deafening the scream that shot out from Mr. Cock's mouth but not silencing the words from The Formless Voice, which rose in the air above all the noise. "Your cock, it's growing now and.... bang! There is the sound of your fall, Mr. Cock, as you land on the ground."

Joseph zoned out of the rest of what was said, and watched in disbelief as Mr. Cock's penis grew four times in size until it was half the size of him. To be able to carry the weight of it, the chain around Mr. Cock's neck also thickened. Mr. Cock was still screaming as he tried to stand, but due to the heavy weight was unable to and stayed sobbing on the ground.

"Now, take your tears and your cock and go back to your seat," said The Formless Voice condescendingly.

Joseph watched in horror as Mr. Cock crawled with his engorged penis lagging behind him like a ball and chain. With each motion forward, he had to resort to turning around to pull the chain, and like this he pathetically went to the back of the room.

This time it took him ten minutes and twenty-five seconds, which to Joseph felt like an eternity.

165

Joseph's heart was thumping so hard that he thought it might break out of his body. He couldn't believe what he'd just witnessed. Before he even had time to question, consider, or wallow in his thoughts, an angelic looking image of Lucinda appeared on the screen.

"Whatever happened to her?" he asked.

"You have the cheek to ask that question!" shouted The Formless Voice

"All I remember is that she was a mess!"

"Oh yes, she came with her bundle, her mess, as you call it, of emotions, dramas and twisted patterns, but you took her on, and then slowly pulled that bundle apart. Not out of love, but out of your need to possess but not truly love her."

"I did love her," he said resentfully, "but she turned out to be a nutter."

"So, you left a sinking ship. How admirable of you, Hanuman."

"Fuck off! What was I supposed to do? And I didn't leave her. I wanted to though. Tell me, what the hell was I supposed to do?"

"Not cheat on her for a start."

"What's the big deal? Men are supposed to put it about."

"Not if it breaks their lover's heart. You were not born in the dark ages, Joseph. Society and relationships of your era have different expectations and people have different responsibilities to one and other, especially in the Western culture from which you were born into. So, you played your part. You set the course of events. The Law of Cause and Effect tells us that every cause has its effect; every effect has its cause. Simply put - what goes around, comes around. We reap what we sow. Nothing happens by chance. Every single one of our thoughts and actions, even feelings, creates a chain of events that are

166

transmitted into the Universe and eventually comes back to us. Perhaps not in the same lifetime, but it does come back."

"So, how in God's name did I get here? Couldn't have been a car accident, or something like that otherwise I wouldn't be surrounded by so much scum. I know for a fact that *I* didn't kill anyone."

"Didn't you?"

"Did I"

"Did you?"

Joseph held his head in his hands and said, "Dude, you're doing my fucking head in. Now I do feel like killing myself."

"Hahaha! Now that is not possible."

"Yeah you're right. I'd never do a Hara-kiri."

"Not quite what I meant, Joseph. But no, you would not be honourable enough to do a Japanese Samurai Suicide."

"I didn't know it was linked to Japanese Samurai's."

"It is the ritual suicide of a Samurai, where he chooses to die in honour rather than shame, and so kills himself through cutting his stomach and disemboweling himself."

"That's fucking insane."

"I don't think that you're in a position to question sanity. Some would argue that waking up at seven am and being a slave to a system six days a week is insane."

"Anyway, Samurai or not."

"Not."

"Whatever. I wouldn't do myself in."

"No, you wouldn't. Alas, Lucinda would."

"Did she top herself?"

"Oh yes. And as the Law of Cause and Effect would have it, your own thoughts and actions led to the result of your own death."

"And I guess you're still not going to answer my question about that. But her, what happened to her?"

"Her? Oh her? As you got to find out in the end, she was by no means whiter than white."

"Find out what?"

"So, she didn't really love you. You know that, don't you? She claimed to love you. She said she felt you, but she felt only herself and her own needs, which she resented you for not filling."

Joseph was finally satisfied that something negative about Lucinda had come to light and blurted, "Yes! That's just how it was. She was never satisfied."

"And why should she be, Joseph? You are a cheat and a liar! An egoistic, pussy hunting predator, who enjoyed the attention of all women!"

"What man doesn't!"

"The man who knows how to truly love. You enjoyed withdrawing from Lucinda, as it made her need you. She, in return, thrived off this drama and rejection; her own sick addiction to pain. You see, your patterns fit perfectly. Thus, Joseph there are no victims or perpetrators in this case. She may have been the one to murder you..."

"What?"

"But you murdered her heart."

"Hang on - rewind. Murder me?" It hits him. "Oh, my God, she killed me. That fucking bitch murdered me!"

"Oh, don't be so shocked. You wrote the script a long time ago and had many opportunities to change it."

"No! No! I didn't!"

"You have to own responsibility for your actions and the consequences of them. You killed Mr. Bianca."

Joseph remembers. "I did, yes I did kill that wanker. And I have no remorse about it!"

168

"In an earthly court of law, you would have been deemed a murderer. But then karma so adequately worked everything out and you were murdered. So, in effect, you are also a victim. However, in this realm, we do not focus on whether you are a perpetrator or a victim. There are no victims, no good or bad - just choices with consequences.

# Seventeen

Despite a good effort, Dan had not won the game.

Joseph rose triumphantly and grabbed the bulge in his trousers and victoriously shouted, "Cock Power, Dan." He looked at him and sincerely added, "Get some action and maybe you'll start to win."

Dan winced, it wasn't just the game he was talking about.

"Nobody likes a loser," said Joseph and playfully slapped him across the face.

"Oi, that hurt."

"Oi, that hurt," mimicked Joseph. "You little pussy."

Dan rubbed his cheek as Joseph walked over to his cupboard and pulled out a small tray with four fat lines of cocaine neatly lined up on it.

"Hey! I thought you said that you didn't do any charlie tonight," said Dan.

"Oh well, I lied," said Joseph and passed him a rolled up twenty-pound note. "Want a line?"

Dan took the note and said, "You fucking deception demon. You're good at that."

"What?" asked Joseph innocently and rubbed a little of the charlie onto his gums.

"Lying," replied Dan as he bent down to snort a line.

Joseph just looked at him with a mischievous grin on his face, and Dan was grateful that he was only a friend, pitying any woman who was crazy enough to ever get involved with him.

#

Joseph had given it a good go and pretty much (even in his coke-induced state) ironed out a lot of Dan's doubts.

Despite this, Dan was left with much pussy talk to chew on and silently broached the questions that evolved out of the conversation. Were the internet, games consoles, and pornography really all toys for men to exercise their need for power? And if so, were women not just the start of all those creative endeavors'? The need for power, the need for pleasure and the need to have it now? In that case, were these boy's toys then just becoming replacements for the real deal? Were men's powers being stripped from them by, as what Joseph called it, 'hippy talk and lesbian crap?'

Dan was well aware that it was no longer acceptable for a man to be unfaithful, like it once used to be, when women would say with a resigned acceptance, 'Oh well, he is a man,' and 'Boys will be boys'. That old attitude certainly wasn't tolerated anymore. As Joseph had quite rightly pointed out, women were cutting off men's dicks for being unfaithful. Was it really a man's right, though? It seemed a little absurd, but Dan had a sneaking suspicion, propelled by his own desire that maybe Joseph had a point.

He liked the idea of having power. He knew that in his own relationship she held the reigns of power. In his job, he was mediocre. Yes - he definitely liked the idea of being powerful. He liked it enough to try it at least once, justifying to himself that he was a man therefore, wasn't it his right? Besides, didn't women care more about the emotional connection a man had with another woman rather than the sexual act? Wasn't sex with a prostitute then less of a crime than enjoying a flirtatious meal with a female friend?

It had been ages since he'd last had sex. Ever since Magnolia had gotten pregnant, she'd all but forsaken that 'wifely' duty and his efforts to seduce her had rapidly turned into begging frenzies and humiliating rejections that made him feel even more powerless.

The more he mulled over the conversation, the more he started to think that Joseph really was onto something. And he wanted to tap into the power he'd always felt slipping out of his grasp.

He didn't have the guts to go alone and asked Joseph to go with him. Naturally, Joseph could not have been happier.

It wasn't the only time that they were going to share a sexual experience. The first time had been much more personal, but neither of them ever talked about that.

#

Joseph and Dan had known each other for ten years. Dan was Mr. Parson's nephew, and whenever Joseph was invited to family events, their paths crossed. Though they acknowledged each other, there was no real connection; the boys felt worlds apart.

It was only after the fourth event that the boys bonded. It had been on a beautiful summer's day at Mr. Parson's Silver Wedding Anniversary party, held at his summer house in Somerset.

Joseph was kitted out in a tailor-made suit that Mr. Parsons had very kindly bought for his seventeenth birthday. The last time that he'd worn a suit had been at his Mother's funeral - quite a different occasion.

The day that he'd picked up his suit, with Mr. Parsons' by his side, he'd thought how different things were compared to when he was a small child, standing at the graveside, numb with sadness and imagining his mother floating up to heaven whilst the cheap suit made his skin itch like hell.

This new suit was classy, softly stroking his skin and dancing like a sexy lady over his body. He liked the feel of it so much that even though it was hot, he didn't want to spoil his look by taking off his jacket, preferring instead to stylishly suffer the heat. The event was salubrious, and Joseph could smell money in the air. He enjoyed being a part of this new world of wealth and decadence.

After eating, and drinking some good wine, he wandered off to the back of the garden for an uninterrupted cigarette. Before he got to his normal spot, he smelt weed. Following his nose, he found Dan sitting behind a tree, chugging his lungs out. The missing connection had been found. Drugs bridged the gap between their two worlds, and they found that they were on the same planet.

They were event friends for six years before they started hanging out together. By then Joseph was working for Mr. Parsons, and Dan had finished medical school. With both boys released from their respective institutions, they were now free to move in any direction they chose.

Dan applied to internships in London and was pleased to be accepted by the hospital he most wanted. The only catch was he needed to start immediately. Not wanting to move back into his parent's home, and with no time to look for his own flat, he called Joseph to ask if he could crash at his place for a few weeks. Joseph was more than pleased to accommodate him and thought it would make a nice change to have Dan around.

Although he'd always loved the solitude of being alone, years of being in the juvenile detention centre had had two contrasting effects on him: on the one hand, the luxury of his own space soothed him, and on another, it disturbed him. In those first years after his release, he found himself torn between feeling peaceful and feeling lonely. Dan would be a distraction if nothing else.

Neither boy foresaw what lay ahead.

On their first night together, they planned to go out, get high and pull some chicks. Instead, they got stuck in, snorting charlie and dropping pills. They talked bollocks and then started touching each other's, eventually falling asleep in the wee hours of the morning.

Like hard-core ravers they woke up at sunset with banging headaches - standard. But what wasn't were the residual sensations left over from the night's soiree, of sore anuses and random love bites in the groin areas.

Joseph woke up earlier than Dan and was already smoking his second spliff and sipping a beverage when Dan wearily walked into the lounge. "Bloody hell mate, you snore like an engine," was all Joseph said.

Dan was relieved, and took that very normal comment to indicate that it had all been a bad dream. "Oh yeah, sorry about that."

"That's all right, mate. Here, have a toke and a swig of this. Hair of the dog, you know." Dan reached for the spliff and the coffee-laced whisky. In his hungover state, he put them both to his mouth. "Steady on, one at a time," said Joseph, "but then, you are a bit of a goer."

And there it was: the insinuation Dan was dreading. "Er, yeah, about that, I'm not, erm, I mean, do you...."

Joseph laughed and said, "Dan, chill it's all right. No need to have a fucking Oprah Winfrey discussion about it." Quite seriously, he added, "It's done. It's over. History. Mate, it never happened." He got up from his chair, ruffled Dan's hair and stepped into the shower. That was the last time they ever spoke about it.

Out of respect, Dan stayed another night at Joseph's, but was so ashamed by the previous night's activities that he made the rash decision to move into the hospital student's dorm.

They only saw each other on two more occasions after that. Each time Dan felt uncomfortable and made an excuse to leave before midnight. Joseph wasn't offended; in some way, he felt flattered.

Six months later, Dan moved out of London after being allocated a second internship in Nottingham. With the distance between them, he found a way to lay a new foundation. So, when he returned a few years later, he could pretend that it had never happened.

Not long after rekindling their friendship, Joseph introduced him to Magnolia.

#

In the car on the way to the whorehouse they talked about normal everyday things: the footie, work, the traffic and the new series of Top Gear. Dan became so relaxed, that he almost forgot that he was going to a whorehouse to be unfaithful to his partner. That was, until they arrived and his stomach twisted into the asanas from the Kama Sutra.

"Ready?" asked Joseph and smiled broadly. The worried look on Dan's face made him laugh, and he shook his head and said, "Gonna be the best day of your God damn life."

Dan eased himself out of the car and could barely stand up straight, in contrast to Joseph who flew out like a superhero and raced ahead.

He was only halfway up the path when Joseph rang the doorbell. Within seconds, the door was opened by a beautiful woman who welcomed him in like a prince. She didn't notice Dan as he rushed to get to the door before it shut in his face.

Once in, he desperately tried to stand up straight in defiance of Kama Sutra position number sixty-nine, which now took the stage in his gut. After much effort, he achieved the mission of adjusting his position slightly so that he no longer stood like Quasimodo.

A foot taller and with his head above chest level, he perused his environment. At first, he wasn't quite sure what to make of it. The entrance was kitted out in regal decor, and the centrepiece in the hallway had a large intimate chandelier that hung like a circle of dancing ladies in the centre of the ceiling. It was far from seedy and even bordered on being a bit extravagant. Still, he preferred being in a place that was over the top to one that resembled a crack house.

Before any more thoughts had time to pollute his mind, Joseph stepped in and began to give a quiet, running commentary of events as they unfolded. He enjoyed the role he had taken on of chaperoning his novice friend and whispered to him, 'who was who and what was what.'

He started by explaining that the lady who had opened the door was not one of 'those ladies' but something more like a maid, who of course, to fit the theme, was dressed in a sexy outfit that revealed her butt and bust.

Dan looked her over and wondered if this was like any other organisation where you had to work your way up the ladder. And if so, whether the maid had what it took to eventually make it to prostitute level. He lightened up a little as it occurred to him that the promotion would quite literally fit the phrase, 'fucking your way to the top.'

Within a few seconds another girl came to greet them, take their coats and guide them to bar. Joseph explained that she, too, was not one of 'those ladies.' Dan nodded as if he cared about the whorehouse commentary and followed Joseph like a lamb to the slaughter.

The bar was empty except for a man dressed like an Elvis wannabe that Joseph had seen in there before. He acknowledged him with a nod and the man turned his back to them. "What a cock," said Joseph and walked up to the bar.

Dan perused his surroundings and thought that Joseph had been right again; this place wasn't at all scummy. On the contrary, it was quite plush, like a private member's bar that smelt of decadence: a mixture of money, expensive liquor, coffee, and cigars.

The lasciviousness spread from his nose to his eyes and after scrutinising the area further, he saw that the floor was covered in white rugs. With his meticulous doctor's eye, he checked them over for any cum stains, of which there were none. Like a private detective, he continued to scan the room and saw large leather chairs upholstered to the highest standard. To the left of where he stood, there was a bookshelf with leather-bound books and next to that, a fireplace. He discerned that much time and energy had been dedicated to creating an opulent atmosphere, where all the furnishings seemed to have been chosen to complement the large bar table made from the finest wood.

The mood was sensual, with soft lighting from the lamps and a few candles to accompany the warm fire from the fireplace. This all pleased Dan, who was starting to feel aroused by the mellow, yet erotic surroundings, wrapped in an intellectual quality that reminded him of his university Dean's room; a man he'd greatly admired.

All was going well, and even his stomach relaxed into a post-orgasmic state of calm, until he tuned into the soft, sexy music and heard, 'Tu Es Partout' by Edith Piaf - his mother's favourite. To think of his mother when he was about to do something illicit and sexual opened the gates for guilt to absorb him, and his erection, which had been slowly rising like a contender sure to be announced the winner, slumped back into his pants in defeat.

Joseph was already standing at the bar. The timing couldn't have been more perfect, as Dan, with his flaccid penis and guilt-ridden head, needed a stiff drink.

He took the glass passed to him by Joseph and downed it. He hadn't expected it to be a straight whisky and had to control himself from gagging. Wiping his mouth gently with the back of his hand he looked at Joseph leaning against the bar, emanating the suaveness of James Bond and thought, God, he looks handsome.

Joseph smiled in response to the silent words and signaled to one of the ladies at the bar to bring another round of drinks. Dan blushed and took a step back.

The girl from the bar handed them both a glass of whisky. Joseph raised his glass to Dan and knocked it back before placing it into the girl's hand. The girl waited for a second to see if Dan would follow suit. When he nervously took a sip, she smiled endearingly at him, turned, and seductively walked away. Both men watched as the cheeks of her buttocks took turns rising and falling like two bouncy-balls.

A few drops of sweat dripped down the side of Dan's face, and he unbuttoned the top button of his shirt. Joseph coolly flipped a cigarette into his mouth and lit it. Taking a deep pull, he walked off through the smoke that swirled out of his mouth and sat down in one of the chairs, all the while hoping that his coolness would rub off on Dan.

When he got a glimpse of him he saw that there was no such luck. Dan was in the flight mode of the 'fight/flight' response and looked as if he was ready to run out of that place and into the comfort of his hideously orchestrated, mundane life. His discomfort clearly visible in the way that his eyes nervously jerked around in their sockets, trying to dissect every little detail. Before Joseph could distract him, Dan was by his side versing his worries.

"Ah, not again Dan," said Joseph with annoyance.

"It's just, I feel bad about this. I know I shouldn't. I mean, a man needs this, right? Sex, I mean, and she doesn't have sex with me anymore."

Joseph's inner voice that chanted, 'I know, mate, that's because she's fucking me,' was so loud that he feared it might resonate outside of his mind.

"I mean, I know she's eight months pregnant and tired..."

Joseph's inner voice silently bitched, 'Not too tired to fuck me.'

"But even before then, she wasn't mad for it. As soon as she got pregnant, she didn't want to have sex anymore."

Joseph's silent voice tauntingly sung, 'Not with you...'

Worried this inner voice might suddenly grow vocal chords and be heard, he did his best to silence it. He didn't want to lose Dan and studied his face for any signs that he might know something. It was clear from the way

179

that he was still jabbering on, trying to reason with himself that he hadn't tuned into a thing.

"Her excuses for putting things off for later were just like the reasons for not getting married; manana, manana were the words that trailed from her mouth. What's the rush? she'd say...."

Joseph cut Dan's sentence short by pulling his arm to alert him to the two stunning ladies walking directly towards them.

"Well, well," said the taller of the two beauties, who Dan thought looked like the epitome of an Arabian Princess, "if it isn't the lovely Joseph." She stopped a foot away from them and with a naughty smile on her face added, "And he has brought a friend, a handsome friend. And there I was thinking that I would have to share you," she cooed, running her long slender finger along the side of his face.

Joseph became as regal as the environment he was in, and eloquently responded, "My dear, you have me all to yourself."

Taking her arm, he walked away with her as if they were going down the aisle. All Dan could do was watch in amazement as they disappeared out of the room.

With Joseph gone, he was left not knowing what to do. In all his nervousness, he hadn't even looked at the girl standing before him now. The Arabian beauty had all but won him over. But Joseph had her - of course he did.

He had to do something, but felt like a fourteen-year-old asking a girl out on a date for the first time. He cursed himself for being so cowardly and meekly said, "Hi," as he shyly lifted his gaze from his shiny shoes.

To his relief, the girl fluidly launched at him like a wave washing him with her coolness and pressed her smooth, pale cheek to his, before brushing her thick, full lips across his thin dry ones. His heart beat erratically, and his penis suddenly hopped back to life like a man jumping out of a coffin and yelling, "Aha, I'm not really dead!"

Although physiologically he was ready for this new adventure, psychologically he battled with himself, and his thoughts turned to all the horror stories of his medical training: sudden heart attack through shock, syphilis, AIDS and leprosy.

The prostitute stroked his face so gently, her touch effaced these illnesses like an eraser, and his penis continued to harden. She moved her other hand over his growing bulge and stroked it through his trousers whilst looking him straight in the eye.

He tried to speak, but the blonde beauty put her soft, feminine finger to his lips to quieten him and said, "Let me do the talking for now. I just want to hear you groan."

She took her finger away and seductively put the tip of it between her teeth. Then let it slip over her bottom lip and said, "Now come with me. I am going to eat every bit of that young, delicious body."

The prostitute's desire put him at ease, and he became affected by her allure. He noticed that she had a captivating, husky voice, and her near perfect English accent led him to believe that she'd lived in London for a while, although he deciphered that she was most probably Eastern European and had the look of a Czech beauty.

Her body was exquisite, perfectly formed with medium-sized, pert breasts that danced through the silk of her top. Her confidence was so attractive, and her desire to please him, coupled with the indication that she could, would, and was only there to do so, made him want to grab her and enter her there on the spot.

He felt alive and was grateful to Joseph for opening up his world. Truly believing that this was a man's right, he followed his cock to the room with the prostitute and had one of the best sex sessions of his life.

He didn't go again for another month. He could justify it the once, as a means of experiencing something new. But upon leaving, the guilt ate him up with the ferocity of a thousand nagging women.

To relieve himself of his guilt, he doted more and more on Magnolia, who only despised his pathetic addresses to her whims. A man that did everything to please her only brought out more of the bitch, and she couldn't stop herself from being nasty.

Nothing he did was good enough. She always put him down, snapped at him, addressed him condescendingly and had no respect at all for her loving partner. She liked the bastards, and Dan was such a good boy. He, in turn took all that she dished out, as a kind of penance for the sin he'd committed.

Then, Ruby was born and Magnolia stopped being a bitch and just ignored him. He longed to be seen, touched, or even acknowledged. This longing was fulfilled in his dreams, and that one day of passionate sex with the prostitute haunted him with frightening pleasure.

Finally, he was unable to bear the loneliness eating through his flesh like deadly bacteria, and he decided to go back. Magnolia hardly noticed him in the house, and that woman (whom he didn't like to think of as a prostitute) made him feel so good. In fact, he thought, she made him feel like a man.

Perhaps, there really was some truth to what Joseph had said, Dan convinced himself as he drove to the whorehouse for a second time; perhaps Magnolia had ripped off his balls. He didn't feel worthy in her company and yet with that 'other' woman, he felt like a king.

The second visit was even better, and he felt his peacock feathers get brighter. Over time, his sessions became longer and more erotic. He tried different women: black, white, Chinese, brown-skinned, voluptuous, skinny, young, and old. The sex went from being one-on-ones to group sex, from straight to anal, to dressing-up and role play. He also went as far as experimenting with sadomasochism. It wasn't something he terribly enjoyed, as he couldn't relax in case his skin got marked. Plus, he wasn't as brave as Joseph and never wanted to get hurt or carry the responsibility of hurting another.

To his surprise, within a month, he no longer felt guilty. Overall, he felt better about everything. His new sexual excursions were a distraction from his normal life, and he cared less for the way Magnolia treated him. The added bonus was that he also became less obsessed with her.

#

He never told Joseph that he went back. He didn't want to share everything with him. And so, on that day when he'd been with the 'nurse' he almost passed out on the spot when he spotted Joseph at the end of the path standing by his car.

"Just the one time eh?" said Joseph, raising his eyebrows.

"Oh Shit."

"Chill out. It's not like I'm going fucking grass you up is it?" said Joseph as he got into his car, chuckling. He watched Dan smile faintly and scurry off in another direction. Shaking his head, he thought, That man needs to grow some balls.

Just as he was about to start the engine his phone bleeped. He looked at it and sighed as he read: Ruby is sick. Dan is out. I need you here. "Oh, for fucks sake," he said and threw his phone onto the dashboard and started the engine.

# Eighteen

Magnolia was still staring at her phone when Ruby started screaming. She reluctantly got up from the bench and waited a few more seconds for a reply. When she didn't get one, she stuffed her phone into her pocket and haughtily walked into the Community Centre.

A group of women were huddled in the lobby and Magnolia's entrance accompanied by Ruby's screams, got her instant attention. Much to her dismay the women rushed over like groupies to hover over the crying baby.

A chubby woman pushed to the front and took charge. "Hello love, I'm Jane," she said. "Are you here for the baby group? Just it doesn't start for another hour."

"No, I'm here for this," said Magnolia, holding up the flyer.

"Then you're right on time," said Jane and looked lovingly at Ruby. "Mine are old enough to have their own. I wish they'd get a move on. I miss holding little ones."

"Be my guest," said Magnolia and practically dumped the baby car seat into Jane's arms.

Before being able to enjoy the freedom of having her body to herself again, she became aware that her breasts were streaming milk like tears through her top. Jane quickly ushered her into a more private room so she could breastfeed.

Ruby had stopped crying by now, and looked serene. Magnolia took her out of the car seat and surprised herself with having the urge to stroke her baby's small face. In that rare moment, she thought that she looked beautiful. It was only to be a moment, for as she eased her nipple into Ruby's mouth she remembered that she was stuck with her and took her gentle touch away. Ruby was famished and chomped so heartily on her mother's teat that it wore her out, and she fell asleep.

Grateful for some peace and quiet, Magnolia walked back into the main room with Ruby tucked into her car seat. The crowd of women had now positioned themselves in chairs, set up in a semi-circle. Magnolia found an empty seat and sat down.

It hadn't occurred to her what type of women would be there, and she was surprised by the variety. Scanning their faces, she saw each adult as they had been as a child, easily identifying the bullies, the bullied, the do-gooders, the snitches, the whiners and the bitches.

Her perceptive ability to spot the child within the adult was not, as she would have liked to have believed, something to do with a higher sensitivity or psychic ability, but more based on her own dysfunctional psychological reaction: she herself was stuck as a twelve-year-old. The same age she'd been when they'd murdered Mr. Bianca.

After assessing the clan, Magnolia took an immediate liking to a girl in her late teens who was talking about her recent essay on Women's Rights. Magnolia conjectured that the girl had been untouched by real life, and as a result needed to get involved in another drama. She pitied her in a way for not being able to create her own.

Magnolia liked this girl because she stood out. Physically, she was very tall with blue streaks in her hair and random piercings over her face. On a more interpersonal level, there was a seriousness about her that exceeded her years. Even though she was the youngest in the group this didn't affect her confidence, as she fiercely conversed with one of the other women about a new government policy. Mostly though, Magnolia liked her because she had not the slightest bit of interest in Ruby. Anybody who shared this common interest, or non-interest in this case, was worthy of her appreciation.

Magnolia moved on from this girl and was drawn to look at Jane who was now rushing around trying to get cups of tea and biscuits to everybody and was panicking that there weren't enough mugs. The person that she guessed was the leader, since she sat in the comfiest of chairs in the middle of the semi-circle, grew impatient and shuffled her papers to indicate that she wanted to get things started. This only flustered Jane further, and she dropped the sugar all over the floor.

Magnolia enjoyed this change of environment and the opportunity to size up people. A private, critical viewing of the events played in her mind, and she speculated that busy-body Jane probably attended a few different groups a week so that she could be a part of something and do her hostess service. She was most likely a mother whose children had left home, probably as soon as they could, and now having spent her whole life looking after other people didn't know what else to do except find surrogate families to continue feeling like she had a place in this world.

Just before she moved on to critically view the next candidate, she was struck with an eerie feeling. There was something about the way that they were all sat in a semi-circular fashion that seemed vaguely familiar to her. In that instant, she had a Deja Vu moment. The past or future (she had no idea which one) flashed before her. Those kinds of moments always felt powerful, and she was pleased to feel a part of the source. This outing was already giving her much more than she'd expected. In the past twenty minutes, she'd felt more alive than she had done in months, and not once had Joseph entered her mind.

The leader cleared her throat and sarcastically said, "Now that we all have enough tea and biscuits -" she looked at Jane whose round face turned as red as a tomato - "shall we get on with the meeting for which we have all convened." She shuffled her papers again, and the meeting finally began.

Five minutes into it and Magnolia struggled to look interested. It was the interaction between the women that had excited her more than the topic, and she shifted her focus there. It didn't take too long for her to see that her previous observations were right; the bullies, the bullied, the do-gooders, the snitches, the whiners, and the bitches all revealed themselves.

After an hour, and on cue, Ruby woke up. Much to the horror of Magnolia, she watched the women shower her with love again. Like a nervous performer jumping onto the stage, Ruby suddenly turned from a desperate, crying, soiled baby into a shining flower, sucking in the rays of love from her admirers. It annoyed Magnolia to see Ruby so happy and felt waves of superiority smugly exude from her. In some way, that small being was raging a war with her, just as she believed everybody else was.

With the hope that it would somehow benefit her in the long-run, she let the ladies coo over Ruby for a few more minutes before making the announcement that she had to leave. The women pulled sad faces, and she mimicked them in an attempt to look bothered, until she was by the door and let her face drop back into static state of chronic suffering; her eyes glazed with acrimony.

Before stepping out, she briefly scanned an information board with a variety of advertisements and flyers. None were of any interest to her. Just as she was about to walk away, one flyer caught her attention, advertising a one-off visit from a renowned medium, Catherine Monika Fleming.

The week before, she'd seen her on a TV show and had been impressed by her abilities. The flyer explained that because she was only available for one day, a lottery system would decide who was read. Anyone wishing to enter should fill out the attached form and drop it into the Psychic Centre. Before anybody else got a chance to see the flyer she stuffed it into her pocket and walked out.

The warm autumn caress had turned to an icy slap, and she shuddered. Even so, she didn't want to go home - not with Ruby. She looked from the baby car seat to a trash bin, and sorely said, "I wish it were that easy."

# Nineteen

Ruby's birth certificate spontaneously appeared in Magnolia's hand. She crumpled it up and threw it into the trash bin and said, "Cancerous fucking tumor. Am I never going be separate from you?"

"There is no separation. There is only light, and no separation in that," said The Chair walking towards her.

"Oh, for crying out loud!"

The Chair, not at all fazed by her outburst, stood in front of her and said, "The Law of Correspondence states that there is no separation since everything in the Universe, including you, originates from the One Source. There is harmony, agreement and correspondence between the physical, mental and spiritual realms. All is One."

"If that's the case then how come we don't feel this oneness, this non-separateness?" shouted Lucinda from the back of the room.

"The sense of separation we experience in the world is a result of the way we perceive the vibration of energy through our five senses. But the truth is that you are one with Consciousness.

"Prove it!" spat The Old Caww.

"You my dear are the proof of it. By creating your reality based on your limited ego perceptions, you don't see the full picture. Everybody here sees the room from one point of view. But how many of you see the room as it really is?" She looked around the room and said, "You can't. If you did, then you would know that there is no separation in anything. Just light."

"If this is true then how come nobody has done it?" asked Lucinda.

The Chair casually walked towards her and said, "How do you know that they haven't?"

"You'd just be called mad."

The Chair stopped in front of her and looked straight into her eyes and said, "Tell me Lucinda, what is madder? This world humans live in filled with suffering because of un-love, war, destruction, greed and capitalism gone haywire? Or an acknowledgment of a deeper understanding of what we have yet to realise?"

Lucinda shook her head and said, "I don't know. It's all so confusing."

"Let me explain in another way," said The Chair, "since this Law has many levels of explanation, I'll elaborate in day to day terms." She walked away from Lucinda and weaved in between the other ladies. "If you really want to understand people, then look at what they do." She stopped in front of the Old Caww. "There is no separation in that either." The Old Caww stuck out her furry, white, tongue - rock n roll style. The Chair screwed up her face in disgust and continued weaving through the ladies. "Their behaviour in one circumstance, or towards one person will be repeated in another circumstance or another person." She stopped in front of Mrs. Primm. "For example, if your lover treats his mother badly, the chances are that one day he will treat you badly. If your lover cheated on his previous partner, then the chances are that he will cheat on you."

She slowly strolled back to her chair and spoke in a slow, measured pace, "If your boss acts without integrity towards an employee, then the chances are they will act the same way towards you one day. And if not you, then it will repeat itself somewhere down the line. The key is to watch and be aware of how people behave in all their relationships. When you spot something unsavoury, become aware that the same behaviour may come your way."

"I saw it all time but had hoped that I was different and that those people wouldn't do those things to me," cried Lucinda.

The Chair swung round and said, "What makes you so special? What separates you from the others? You should have walked away from those people and circumstances that were hurting you, instead of staying and allowing yourself to be a victim."

"I couldn't. I couldn't walk away from the people I loved. And so, I couldn't live in the world."

The Chair sat down and said, "So, you ran away from life."

"Yes, and now I can't live, die whatever, be here."

"And so, you want to run away from here too?"

"Yes, but I have nowhere to go."

The Chair leaned forward, arms rested on the table and said, "That's because, my dear, there is nowhere to go. Everything is here and now. Your whole life, whilst you've been running away, you've actually been running on the spot..."

# Twenty

Lucinda was running down the street in a flustered state, pushing the pram and muttering in annoyance, "Oh! Silly Mummy, I should never have dropped that form in now. Boo Boo we're going to be late again."

She arrived at the Community Centre and rushed in, bedraggled and out of breath. The hallway was packed with mums holding babies, and/or chasing toddlers. A few women smiled nervously at her, other's whispered to each other. You could cut the atmosphere with a knife.

Jane walked up to her and said, "Hello love. Lovely to see you again." She looked pathetically at her head. "I see you've had another fall. You must be more careful, love. Look after yourself."

Lucinda touched her wound and said, "Oh, it's nothing. I'm Little Miss Accident Prone. You know that."

A little boy came running over and said, "I want to play too."

Mesmerised by his beauty, Lucinda gently touched his face. The boy's mother rushed over and snatched him away.

Lucinda was deeply offended and bit back. "Looks like someone forgot to take their Prozac today."

"Ha! You're one to talk. A mental ca..."

Jane quickly provided a distraction and called out to the group, "Let's begin everyone. Kiddiewinks and mummywinks, get in your boats." She pretended to row towards a room and sung, "Row, row, row your boats gently down the stream. Merrily, merrily, merrily, merrily, life is but a dream."

The mothers and toddlers mimicked her actions and piled into the room behind her, singing along.

Lucinda silently followed them.

#

Before going home, Magnolia popped into the Psychic Centre and put her completed form into the designated box on the reception desk. It slipped in nicely, and sat on top of the form handed in by Lucinda not more than one hour before.

There were only seven slots that day and both Magnolia and Lucinda were lucky, or fated, enough to win one.

# Twenty-one

The Psychic Centre had been established in 1887 and since then thousands of people had visited to make contact with their loved ones. As well as psychic readers, the centre also ran courses on psychic mediumships, spiritual healing, meditation, dreams and the study of life.

Catherine Monika Fleming was one of the oldest psychics at the centre, and one of the most respected in her field.

A seer for as long she could remember, her earliest memory had been when she was four-years-old of her newly deceased family cat, Gertrude. Nobody believed her when she told them that Gertrude came to play with her. In fact, her mother accused *her* of bringing dead birds and mice into the house.

Other people's disbelief in her abilities only empowered them, but despite this, she knew from that day on to keep her clairvoyance a secret and didn't share her gift with anyone again until she was in her late teens.

Catherine was a very bright, young lady and became one of the few women in the early twentieth century to attend university. And it was here during her second year that she revealed her gift to another.

Mr. Saunders was one of her favourite lecturers who during the second semester had lost his mother to old age. He'd been very distraught at not being by her side when she'd died and took a leave of absence to grieve. During that time Catherine felt an overwhelming urge to comfort him and tell him what it was that Mr. Saunders' mother was pestering for her to communicate. Patiently, she waited for his return.

A week later, Mr. Saunders returned to work. Still in mourning, he conducted his lecture to the best of his abilities, unaware that his mother was also sitting in the room, knitting, and not understanding a word of what was being said.

At the end of the lecture and under the watchful eye of Mr. Saunders' mother, Catherine took Mr. Saunders to one side and gently held his hand. In a voice that he thought sounded a lot like his mother's, she told him that his mother loved him and for this reason hadn't wanted him to see her on her last legs. She emphasised that even though his mother had chosen to go before he could see her alive, she wanted him to know that she'd left a note in the bottom drawer of her cupboard in a small box that he'd made for her when he was a child.

Mr. Saunders was amazed by this revelation and quickly left to go his mother's house, fifty miles away.

The next day when Mr. Saunders came into the lecture hall, it was clear that the grief had been washed away. Before the lesson began, he approached Catherine and warmly thanked her. When she saw the positive change and the happiness that her communicated words had brought, she swore to always use her gift to help others.

Catherine had never met anyone else with the same gift but desperately wanted to. No longer ashamed of her psychic abilities, she conducted research on other people who understood this phenomenon. It was then that she found the Psychic Centre. At the age of nineteen, she was finally amongst her own kind, and although she was one of the youngest attendees, she was no less competent than her counterparts.

Over the years, she fine-tuned her psychic abilities and earnt a name for herself. The police called upon her services and with her help solved twenty unsolved murder cases.

One thing she stayed away from was possession. She was capable of challenging those spirits of malice and stand her ground, but it wasn't her 'cup of tea,' as she explained in one interview. There were other mediums who liked that work and since there was plenty of paranormal activity, there was enough for everyone to have their fix. She let them have it.

Working so much with the police hardly gave her any time for other mediumship work. But twice a year, without fail, she gave readings to large gatherings of people. Despite this, in recent weeks she'd felt a strong need to offer her counsel. She had no idea to whom and only knew that they were calling her. After contacting the Psychic Centre, a date was arranged, and she was quite excited about what the day would hold.

#

Magnolia was pleased that her appointment with Catherine was on the same day as the Women's group, so that she could leave Ruby to Jane.

Her slot with the psychic was in the morning, giving her the perfect opportunity to take advantage of Jane's kindness and have an extended lunch afterwards without Ruby's presence.

She arrived at the Psychic Centre five minutes before her appointment and was disappointed to hear that the medium was late. Like a moody teenager, she flopped down onto one of the sofas in the library that adjoined the reception area, and sifted through some magazines on the table.

They were all boring, repetitive psychic journals and new age magazines. She had a copy of the new *Hello* magazine in her bag, and despite feeling like a traitor, sneakily pulled it out with as much precision as a pickpocket and flicked straight to the horoscopes.

Quickly scanning her sun and rising signs, she looked up, unimpressed, and saw that the only other person in the library was a pretty, young girl walking up and down, her hand brushing the spine of the books as if she were strolling through a closet of silk and cashmere.

Magnolia thought that she was probably a student and envied the girl's free time and space. There was no way that this girl had a child to tie her down.

Just the thought of her life prior to Ruby, brought up feelings of entrapment, and she felt inferior with just a magazine in her hand. There had to be something else worth reading, she thought, and turned to look at the bookshelf to her right. The first book to catch her eye was, 'Fatal Attraction – The Planet Saturn's Role.' Naturally, she was drawn to the title and took the book off the shelf. She opened it and began to read.

Just when she'd gotten to an interesting part about the karmic nature of the planet Saturn, the receptionist called out, "Magnolia."

"Yes, I'm coming," she tiredly announced and closed the book. The pretty, slim girl smiled at her and Magnolia stared back - emotionless, and the girl quickly looked away. To her relief, Magnolia got up and left the room.

#

Lucinda walked into the reception area and joyfully said, "Hi, I have an appointment with Catherine at..."

Without looking up, the receptionist curtly asked, "Name?"

"Lucinda Roberts."

The receptionist looked disconcertedly at her and dryly said, "You're early – half an hour early."

"Oh, I know, I'm just late for everything these days and I..."

"Wait in there." The receptionist pointed to the adjoining library, then looked towards the pram and said, "I hope he, she, whatever it is - so difficult to tell with babies, will stay quiet."

"Oh, don't worry, he hardly ever makes a sound."

Having lost interest, the receptionist looked back down and said, "I'll call you when Catherine is ready for you."

Lucinda smiled nervously and pushed the pram into the library. It was her first time at the Psychic Centre, even though she'd passed it often, she'd been afraid to go in, afraid of what she might feel. Besides, she needed a reason to go. The seer Catherine was a good enough one, and she felt blessed to have been chosen. It made her feel important, as if the Gods had helped her in some way.

No sooner had she walked in, the books called out to her. The small library wasn't devoid of psychic activity and Lucinda expected nothing less. Since there were no traditional religious texts there, she felt at ease with the voices.

The first book demanding her attention was called, 'Children from the Spirit World.' She held the book in her hands and felt groups of children pass through her, eating sweets, playing sports, reading books, giggling and laughing. It warmed her to feel their presence; she belonged with them in their place of nowhere.

After a while she felt the happy voices of the children dissolve into cries that overwhelmed her. Their sadness, loss, and loneliness, reflected her own suffering, and she put the book back onto the shelf. Those children were trapped in that book; for a second, she'd released them.

She walked away from the spirit section of the library, walking away from the tiny hands that reached out to her, and stopped in front of a section called, 'Past Lives.' Curious to know about her own past lives, she ran her hand across the spines of the books and was pulled to one in particular. She picked it out, and the book flipped open. She gasped. Her head began to spin, and she was transported into a trance where she was aware of her current surroundings on some level, but also involved in another world; one where the whole scene was seen through her own eyes and felt with her heart.

The sound of panting and little feet running belonged to her - a little her that was running along a dusty path. She stopped when she reached an open, green plain and looked down at her feet and was surprised to see that they were a child's. Very quickly, she looked at her hands and saw that they too were olive-skinned, children's fingers. She touched her face and felt full, soft lips, a bumpy nose and long eyelashes that tickled her fingers. Her clothing was simply a shabby dress. It was clear that she was a child, and a poor one at that.

With no warning, the green plain disappeared, and she found herself at the front door of a house in a foreign land that looked Middle-Eastern. A man's chastising voice thundered out of the house, and her mood changed from joyous to fearful. The little girl she embodied was courageous and despite her terror, stepped into the house.

The scene blacked out, and Lucinda looked down and saw her feet again, this time larger. She was wearing a black gown partially covering her face, like those Muslim women she'd seen on TV. Before there was time to dwell on who she was, she found herself walking through a busy market place. Her hand reached under her black gown, and she pressed a button.

The sounds of screams penetrated the air and slowly faded out. She looked around but couldn't see anything. The place was very dark, pitch black, in fact. It was an absurd thought, but she didn't feel as though she had a body.

In the distance, two lights approached, and as they got nearer, she saw that they were a pair of scared eyes. They stopped about a foot away from her and just stared. The eyes were dark brown, and even though hers were hazel, she knew the soul behind them was her own, having once been inside the body of this past life being.

# Twenty-two

Knowing full well that Lucinda wouldn't be able to resist, The Chair asked, "Would you like to see a past incarnation of yourself?"

"Yes!" said Lucinda, unable contain her excitement.

"Then look behind me," said The Chair, moving away so that Lucinda could see.

Lucinda cautiously took her eyes off the Chair and looked towards the space that had been created. There was nothing extraordinary about it at first. Then out of nowhere she was hit with a vile smell, before being welcomed with the sight of blood and pieces of charred flesh. The awful scene turned her stomach like a mincer, and she turned her head away and vomited, holding out her hand in defiance against what she'd seen.

"Lucinda!" shouted The Chair, "look at the human bloody debris!

Lucinda wiped the vomit from around her mouth with the back of her hand and slowly turned her head to face the front. Placing her other hand over her eyes, she spread her fingers and peered through the slits.

The Chair, satisfied with having her request met, commanded, "Now ask it to tell you its story."

Lucinda's eagerness to find out about her past life completely vanished, but she knew by now that it made no difference, and weakly mumbled, "Tell us who you are and what you have done."

At Lucinda's request, the bits of flesh and bones came together, like a pixilated animation, to form a young girl of about eighteen, wearing a black burqa.

Lucinda had always been curious about those Middle Eastern women, and the whole burqa concept. A part of her was outraged by what she felt was a male chauvinist stripping of a woman's rights, and yet another part liked the idea of being covered up, especially with a burqa that only revealed one's eyes.

How odd, she thought, to be able see the world through a slit. To see the expansiveness of the world, and at the same time, feel your own hot breath inside the dark material cage, which depending on your disposition was either a haven or a prison.

For a wounded bird under attack from a cat the cage was lifesaving, but to a healthy bird that wanted to fly it was a place of incarceration.

She shrugged off this idea and instead welcomed the mysteriousness of wearing a burqa. It was easier for her to have a fantasised image, rather than to admit that she was a wounded bird afraid of what the cats might do to her.

This fear led her to believe that to see but not be seen held a power to it, an advantage that would evolve into another: the feeling of being at ease from the pressure of being really known. She treasured the parts of herself that she kept hidden in relationships. Unfortunately, what she failed to learn was that her fear of men really knowing her prevented the truth in herself from actualizing.

The natural burqa - the invisible mask she wore - became her cage in a prison that most of humanity occupied. If the wounded bird loved through its pain, then perhaps it would realise that there was in fact no cat at all.

Lucinda watched as the girl opened a part of her burqa to reveal her face. Seeing it was like unwrapping a present that didn't belong to you - the surprise behind the paper lasted a few seconds, and then meant very little at all.

She studied the girl with deep interest, and with every passing second was drawn more to her beauty, soaked in a pathos that seeped deep into her. The girl's dark, delicate features, illuminated by the light, created shadows on her face. Her eyes, which had shone through the slit like a bird of prey's in the night, drew out Lucinda's passion for destruction, and in an instant, she felt connected to her, as the shadows of her own face fluttered their wings.

In her hand, the girl held a large wall clock, set at four fifty-nine. As soon as it struck five, she began to speak. "I awoke in the darkness, but nonetheless had a warm feeling of the sun on my face. I imagined heaven to be just like this: warm and bright, drawing me to its centre. It wouldn't be long before I was in that place. It wouldn't be long before I served my race and faith with the love of self-destruction.

"How shocked they will be! All those people who thought I would amount to nothing - that I would remain invisible my whole life. Soon the whole world will know about me. I will die for my God, for the true religion of the world, and for justice. My life will not have been for nothing, and though I spent the best part of it in solitude, I will not be alone for much longer.

"That morning, as I slipped out of my bed like a baby from a womb, I felt born again. Today was going to be a beautiful day. The sun was about to rise and many people would be getting ready for their morning prayer. Today I will sit and pray with them, too."

The girl froze like a statue for a second whilst the clock hand swung to six-thirty, whereupon she was freed to move again.

"I watched the sun pop up over the horizon and wink at me through the low, solitary cloud that wavered passed it. The pasture's sparkle so green, and the flowers so bright, pulsed with the life of eternal struggle. Yes, today is a wonderful day to die for my belief, my faith, my God, and for the love of God.

"My death will save many in the future, that I believe. My death will awaken those veiled people to the struggle and the fight of all those from my faith. My death will change things. I will be remembered, and I will be honoured. Like the sun, I shall shine forever in people's hearts as the one whose life was not in vain."

The girl paced up and down the room with such vigour and confidence that Lucinda wanted to rise and follow her.

"Of course, there will be those who oppose this victory. They will be the ones who do not understand. The dramatic exit of my life, and the taking of many others will be deemed barbaric in many an eye. But no more barbaric than the political games of those wearing the suits and pushing the buttons from their infantile high chairs."

The girl looked around the room, pleased with the descriptive quality with which she was expressing herself.

"Many will die. Yes, that is true, but not as many as already have. Many will be injured. Yes! But not as many as will be. This end to my life, and end to many others, is just a tiny proportion of the mass destruction that the political powers kill each day.'"

Sitting down on the table, she paused for a moment before saying, "My family will be shocked to discover that I have made my own choice and not succumbed to the pre-planned life laid out for me. 'You will make a good housewife if you can learn to wash, clean, cook properly and obey your husband,' my grandmother had told me, just as hers had told her. 'Men don't expect too much from you,' my mother had said, 'be a faithful, obedient wife and you shall have a happy marriage.'"

The girl rose from the table and with an agitation in her walk, mockingly added, "Her marriage was less than happy. Her children brought her joy, and her female friends, companionship. Her husband brought home the money, he laid out the rules, and occasionally, he serviced her with his male organ. From time to time, he also serviced her with the back of his hand."

Her agitation increased as she remembered these scenes from her childhood. "As a small child, I challenged her to stand up to him and demand to be an equal in that home, adding that if I were her, I would!"

The girl chuckled as the vision arose in her mind of her mother's worried face. "Oh, you should have seen it. My mother nearly died on the spot when she heard me speak in such a way. 'How will we ever marry you?' she'd said, 'learn this and learn this now. Women are not the head of the family. You must give your husband his right to rule in his own home.'"

The girl's chuckle dried up as sudden as a blast, and she was overcome with disgust. "She sickened me. And he! Ha, he was pathetic. My father was a weak man amongst other men. The feeblest of them all. So, when I saw him exert his power over my mother and our family at large, it repulsed me. A pathetic bully, just like my brother was destined to be. Yet they spoke of him, my younger brother that is, as if he had the opportunities of a king, and they treated him as such, saying things like, 'Your brother can be a lawyer, a doctor, an engineer…' But I knew that he lacked the intelligence or courage to do anything of substance with his life. I would. I wasn't going to be second best anymore. I was going to be better than them all."

The girl paced up and down more quickly. "I barely fit in with my family. I was like a handbag to the familial outfit: a minor accessory, which they left empty. With a desire to be full, I prayed to God every night to present me with an opportunity, to be somebody of importance - to become visible."

The girl stopped, mesmerised by a holy force, and gazed ahead as if a light was drawing her in. Her eyes had a faraway look to them, shining with brightness and filling her face with hope. Smiling gently, and with thanks, she calmly went on. "Eventually my prayers were answered, and I found people who believed in me; who welcomed me with open arms, weapons, and artillery. They saw the fighter behind the burqa. They said it was in my eyes, and as soon as they recognised it, I saw it too. I knew then my life could be different. Yes, my prayers had been answered. After being so tired of being a nobody, with no identity, I was given one, and finally I belonged to something that respected and gave me a purpose."

Lucinda was amazed at how quickly the girl's emotions changed and how many different ones she had in such a short space of time. She wanted to believe that she was not like that but the more she watched, the more she feared that she was. This girl just exhibited and fed the expression of her feelings where Lucinda only knew how to starve her own.

The girl stood with a perfect posture and forcefully moved her arms in a victorious sweep and said, "My new family was strong. They were to be feared and were actively doing something in this world. I too decided that I would not live for nothing, and I would show them all. I realised very quickly when they took me in, and I was made to feel powerful, how humiliating my life had been. But they assured me that would not be the case for much longer." The girl smiled broadly for the first time and was filled with pride, remembering the unity she'd felt within her new family.

"My parents were totally unaware of what lay in store for me. They were pacifists who believed that change would come eventually, and violence was not the way. Even when a bomb killed my cousin, they said it was a tragedy. I told them it was murder, and though they knew it was true, it hurt them to admit it. I felt the humiliation of the weakness of my people, my parents in particular. 'Stand up and fight!' I wanted to shout, but my mouth was sealed in female fake-ness, as the lion in me roared to be free."

The girl suddenly stopped, as if something new had occurred to her. After a few seconds, she paced the floor again, this time more slowly. "It would kill them to know that they had pushed me to this. Their own weakness fed the strength in me to fight what they feared and to be a part of the war that they turned away from. Just being in their company made me feel helpless, and that helplessness and sense of hopelessness made my life feel unnecessary. I saw no point to a miserable existence, trapped in feelings of worthlessness. My blood family reinforced it, but my new family broke me out of the trappings of a worn-out script, where there was no room for innovation."

Lucinda saw it there. The creative spirit in this girl that had been given no positive space to be challenged or grow. She understood what it was to have her own creative spirit bound and held hostage in her heart and felt a connection with this girl: a kind of sisterhood.

"My new family gave me worth," said the girl, "there were lots of brothers and sisters." She smiled at Lucinda and then continued to address them all, "and they gave me the words of God to fill the cracks in my identity. This has grown a power in me to be what I am today. What I am about to be.

"It was like a revelation when I discovered that I had been taught the wrong interpretation of the holy text. My new family unveiled the true meaning, and it sunk its truth straight into my gut. Adrenaline rushed through me like the blood of many victims, and my heart beat for the new meaning behind the old text I was given.

"Initially, I had thought it odd that something I had studied for years could take on a whole new meaning. However, the new interpretation matched the raging fire inside of me, and I decided to follow that path. So, the words of God from the holy text confirmed any doubt that would creep up into my mind, which, I was told, was due to my prior conditioning.

"Daily, my new teachers read from the holy book; we chanted, we prayed, and I became filled with Godly desire. I was being trained to do God's wish, and I was an agent for him.

"Of course, I kept my meetings with my new family a secret. It gave me a sense of power to have something hidden from my parents, who saw me as weak and mediocre. They had no idea about my competence, and the great things I was destined for.

"Over time, I detached myself from them, their values and ideals, and allowed my new family to nurture me into a new way of life. I had a powerful identity within the group, which resonated with the true image I wanted for myself; I wasn't weak, or stupid, or a second-class citizen just because I was a girl.

"The group's respect for me grew, and last night at my farewell party I was treated like a queen. Back in the home where I grew up, I longed to be my father's princess instead of his servant. I got to live that fairy-tale during my last night of life, in the arms of true warriors, gallant princes, and kings to be."

The girl swayed from side to side, romantically remembering the feast of the previous evening's ceremonious sending-off.

The clock struck nine.

"Ah, my last night was superb, and this morning as the sun shines, I happily dress in silence, internally praying over and over for all to go as planned.

"Wearing as little as possible under my burqa, I go to leave the house, turning only to kiss my dog goodbye. My beloved dog with his tail between his legs and big sad eyes that foretell of the horror about to be unleashed. As I head for the door, he runs in front of me, and stands like a guard preventing me from leaving. Gently, I take his collar and pull him to the side, whilst he whimpers for the many lives about to end.

"Briskly walking out the door I head for the main house, where the leader, Yusuf…" she paused and looked at Lucinda, "known in the West as Joseph, greets me. His warm smile soaks up the fear gurgling in my gut, and he takes my head into his hands and kisses my forehead. He blesses me, saying how proud he is and looks deeply into my eyes, telling me how lucky my father is, adding if only I had been born to be his daughter. His words wet me like sweet dewdrops from a flower, and I blossom under his radiant charm.

210

"He holds my hand and leads me to a room where a strong, feisty lady is sitting down at a table surrounded in my favourite flowers, Magnolias. Some of the petals have fallen onto the special jacket that I am about to wear. Excitement fires like a thousand nails through me, and I tingle at the thought of the blast.

"Finally, it is happening; the day of reckoning has come. The men will think I am as powerful as them. My father will recognise my strength, and with God's will, he will love and be proud of me."

The clock struck ten, and the girl smiled. "I put on the jacket under my burqa and set out for the market, knowing that within an hour I will be with God."

The girl placed the clock onto the table, and Lucinda watched in horror as it turned into a bomb. The clock hands were still visible and turned rapidly until they struck eleven, whereupon there was a sudden explosion.

The smell of burning flesh hit the air in a blast of smoke. Blood dripped from the ceiling and congealed bits of human meat covered everybody in the Courtroom.

Lucinda gagged as slithers of flesh dribbled like fat all over her skin. Inside her head, she heard the screams of victims, and with her eyes, she saw parts of human bodies scattered around the floor like disembodied dolls pulled apart by two rival sisters.

After what seemed like her whole life, the blood dried up, and the flesh disappeared with the smoke and smell of corpses. Within a few minutes, the room was back to normal.

"That was never me!" screamed Lucinda in horror. "Never would I do such a thing…"

"Hahaha," laughed The Chair. "When you come back next time, and we show you what you did to your beloved this time," The Chair mimicked a lover's pose, "then I am sure you will say the same thing."

"What did I do that was so bad?" cried Lucinda.

"How many people suffered because of your deed? Friends, family, the ambulance men, and even the policemen who had to scrape your body off the ground."

Lucinda looked puzzled, but then slowly the pieces started to come together, just like the pieces of the girl's flesh had done moments before, and she saw the scene replayed in her head: the gun at Joseph's face and her leaping from the window – yes, she remembered.

"No! No! No!" she screamed and crumpled to the ground "How could I? How could I?" she murmured repeatedly. "Why didn't God stop me?"

"God? This was your choice just like your past incarnation had a choice - but you both chose murder and suicide."

The Chair looked across the Courtroom at the variety of different faces, and saw that most, even those who had been there many times before, hadn't quite got the lesson. Her mission was to help them. "By being aware of the Universal Laws you can begin to move beyond the ego. But, remember my dears, the ego cannot transcend the ego. It is only in relationship to God, the Universal Consciousness that one can grow beyond the ego. This is the function of the Universal Laws. And whatever connects you to that force that you already are, is where you should be putting your attention. Love is what you should learn."

The Chair looked at Lucinda and saw a look of struggle wrapped around her face like competing ivy and said, "The bad only brings you bad. But some people like to feel that. Most people, to a degree, like to feel this darkness. You could argue that it's just part of our being."

The competing ivy slowly disappeared. Lucinda understood more about darkness than light. The Chair was endeavouring to change that.

"We are all boring human beings," she said, "and yet we have the potential to live and experience life so differently. It's all about choices. It has nothing to do with God as a separate force answering prayers. It's what you pull to you. Everything in your life is your own creation. Even things you think you don't want, you create by a mere design of your being. But you can move beyond that design. Some do, many want to, the majority feel like it's unobtainable. Let me tell you something," The Chair moved forward and whispered aloud for the crowd, "it's already here."

Opening her small hand, she revealed an empty palm and though nothing could be seen with the naked eye, Lucinda felt a force. Still, like many, she felt herself as separate from it.

# Twenty-three

Lucinda's heart was racing, and her hand shaking as she attempted to put the book back into the correct place on the shelf. For a second, she was grateful for the miserable life she was leading.

She stepped away from the books and sat down, tired of her psychic adventures. Near her, she saw a book simply entitled, 'Reincarnation.' She didn't think that she had the strength to go another round but picked it up anyway and closed her eyes expecting to see something like she'd done moments before. Nothing happened. Just as she was about to put the book down, she heard an old woman's voice bitterly spit out, "Can you hurry up and get 'ere...I've been waiting blooming ages for you to die. Get a move on will ya!"

Lucinda was shocked and slammed the book shut. It appalled her to think that somebody was waiting for her to die, and an old hag at that. How could she be connected to somebody so foul?

"Lucinda... Lucindaaaaaa..." Lucinda jumped. The receptionist was practically standing in front of her with a fake smile covering her frustration. "Catherine will be ready for you in a few minutes," she said and walked back to the reception desk.

"Oh sorry, I was miles away…sure yes, erm, which way?"

The receptionist pointed at the door and said, "The second room on your right."

Lucinda got up, smiling sheepishly, and pushed the pram towards the room. Standing outside, she noticed the reincarnation book was still in her hand. Not wanting to make a habit of taking things from public places, she thought about leaving it on the chair but couldn't resist learning more about what connection she had to this old hag. Telling herself that it wouldn't hurt to borrow it, she quickly knelt down and put the book in her bag, just as Magnolia came haughtily out of the room and stepped over her.

Neither woman saw each other.

#

Magnolia wasn't at all happy with her reading. From the moment she'd entered the room she'd taken an immediate dislike to Catherine. She looked too intense for her liking with small, black, slanty eyes and loose skin that hung like a hen's neck off her skeletal face.

She wondered if this woman had ever been pretty and thought that somebody so ugly had probably never married or had children and was most likely a witch. Magnolia's self-critical voice chanted back, 'Takes one to know one.'

"Hello," said Catherine. Her warm welcome cracked the tension, and she rose from behind her desk, holding out her hand for Magnolia to shake.

Magnolia was shocked to hear that Catherine sounded a lot like her grandmother and was softened enough to take the hand offered to her.

"Please, sit down," requested Catherine.

Magnolia let go of her hand and did as she was told.

Catherine sat down too and asked, "Do you have a piece of jewellery that I can hold?"

Magnolia hesitated. She wanted to say that she didn't, except her sparkling gold bracelet shone like a beacon, lighting up the room. Damn it, she thought. There was no reason to trust this woman. Maybe she'll put a curse on me.

Catherine read Magnolia's mind and smiled sweetly. "Don't worry, it just helps me to feel you better," she said reassuringly.

Magnolia took off the bracelet and handed it over. Catherine closed her eyes and fondled the bracelet as visions of Magnolia's deepest thoughts and experiences crossed her mind.

Magnolia was an open book; a bitter young woman, beautiful in appearance, but ugly in intentions. She even felt that Magnolia hated her. But then again, she hated almost everyone, including her own child.

Catherine felt Ruby's terror and desperation and knew that she had to help that soul. The present situation was bleak, but the future – disastrous. Because of Magnolia's paranoia and more recent post-natal depression, she would have to use her words carefully. Somehow, she had to get Magnolia to warm to her.

Magnolia's grandmother appeared just in time.

"Your grandmother is here," said Catherine warmly.

"Oh really," scoffed Magnolia in disbelief, "describe her."

"I can't see her image so clearly, but she is a woman not too dissimilar to yourself."

216

Magnolia let out a guffaw. How original. What a cop out!

Catherine ignored Magnolia's rude response and continued to describe the grandmother. "Not just in appearance. She, too, was a woman that didn't trust easily. A woman who had a strong and passionate heart. A courageous woman with an eternal fire to succeed in whatever she put her mind to. She could be stubborn and determined. And if need be, this was at the expense of another. She did not enjoy motherhood particularly, although she enjoyed being a grandparent, as she was once removed from that responsibility. She keeps singing 'I'll Never Stop Loving You' – says you'll understand?"

Magnolia was pleased that Catherine's eyes were shut so that she couldn't see her mouth, wide open in shock - or so she thought.

"She loved a man terribly but made the safer choice instead. I think that was her one big regret in life. But, you see, it kept her alive." She paused for a second to let Magnolia absorb the words. Then continued, "Sometimes the things we really want are not the best things for us. Love can be disguised at times. If it is pure, it is crystal clear, but when it is twisted, it is cloudy. The love twists a person into knots. It ruins them." Catherine opened her eyes and looked at Magnolia, whose olive skin had turned a shade lighter.

Magnolia knew Catherine was talking about her. "Sometimes people need to grow into it," she responded sharply.

"That too is true, but only if they want to. You cannot force it. Surrender is the biggest gift we can offer ourselves. It takes a very courageous person to honour that gift and to let go." Catherine had to get through to her - for Ruby's sake. Magnolia's obsessive and unrequited love was killing them both. "You have a baby.

She needs you, but you feel like you don't need her. You do. She will be the one to bring light into your life, if you let her."

In her head, Magnolia saw Ruby's scrunched-up, crying face and felt nothing but disdain. How could that little shit ever make her happy if she didn't have Joseph?

"Take the time to be with her in a beautiful space," advised Catherine. Go swimming together. Go for walks in the park, join a mother and baby group. You will find support there. You deserve to not be alone."

This hit a nerve with Magnolia. She hadn't expected to feel lonely and was embarrassed to admit it herself, let only for Catherine to recognise it too.

"It is very hard to be a mother for the first time," sympathised Catherine and softly said, "it's a myth that it comes naturally. Some people do find it easier, but most of all it is an adaptation and a process of learning. Be kind to yourself."

Magnolia was tired of hearing about Ruby and changed the tone of the conversation. "Is there a man that loves me?"

Catherine paused and looked severely at her. Hadn't this girl taken in any of this wisdom? "Yes, there are two," she replied sadly.

Magnolia smiled to herself.

"One is somebody you live with, your partner. He loves you deeply," said Catherine looking pleadingly into her eyes.

C'mon c'mon, Magnolia wanted to shout out, she hadn't come to this reading to hear about Dan's useless love for her.

Catherine heard Magnolia's thoughts and quietly said, "The other is a man from the past."

Magnolia sighed with relief. The psychic had finally moved onto Joseph.

Catherine felt the need to take a tough tone with Magnolia and more firmly explained, "He is a man who is very vital, charismatic, and powerful. A karmic love – one to acknowledge, respect and move away from. Your time with him is up. You must let him go. You came together to do whatever it was you were meant to do in this lifetime, and now, for both your growth, you need to move on."

Magnolia's face flushed with anger. "No way! I cannot and will not leave him. He is mine. That love, Cathy, is crystal clear," she said, desperately trying to hold in her tears.

Catherine ignored her outburst and calmly continued to read her. "Another woman, his partner, is drawing him away from you." She saw an image of Lucinda in her mind, but felt her much closer.

The tone of the session had turned ugly, and Catherine changed the subject. "You have a spirit guide, a girl of about twelve-years-old ...a leader, a feminine energy that is strong and unique."

Magnolia didn't believe in such things, and was about to explode with frustration. "Spirit guide?" she snapped, "What a load of rubbish! I've never seen or felt such a force in my life."

"Maybe you will in your death."

"So, what, when I die I'm supposed to look out for this twelve-year-old leader who, what was it you said? Is feminine energy?"

"Strong and unique," finished Catherine.

"Oh whatever," Magnolia shook her head in disbelief and stood up, abruptly pushing back the chair with her legs. A civil nod of the head was all she could offer Catherine as a farewell before turning and leaving with as much attitude as Miss Piggy from the Muppet Show.

Magnolia was in such a rush to leave that room, that building, that she nearly tripped over Lucinda kneeling on the floor outside, and just managed to step over her instead.

#

Lucinda walked into the room and rushed over to Catherine as if she were trying to compensate lateness and overzealously shook her hand.

O' Lord, thought Catherine. She smelt death in the air. But it was too late; Magnolia was on a path of destruction and was going to take Lucinda down with her.

That was one of the hardest things about being a psychic - knowing when something was doomed and not having the power to stop it. She comforted herself with the fact that it wasn't her place to. Death, like life, was a natural event, and one she could only affect as much as the participants were willing and open to being affected.

# Twenty-four

Unfortunately, in this case, neither of the women were open to being affected at a transformative level. Lucinda left with more ammunition to be a victim, and Magnolia left with no intention of giving up Joseph.

The mere thought of a life without him turned her child-free, fantasy lunch into a brutal feast. Playing over the reading in her mind, she angrily stuffed food into her mouth, pausing in-between bites to gulp down red wine. She couldn't believe half of the reading had been about Ruby and cursed Catherine as somebody who didn't have her own children and so obsessed about others; a woman who wasted too much time with the dead to know about real life.

By the time she'd gotten onto her second bottle of wine, the room started to sway, and she drunkenly muttered, "As if I have time for baby groups with a bunch of boring housewives."

The happy couple at the next table looked warily at her. With her mouth full of chocolate soufflé, she maliciously grinned back at them.

The male part of the couple quietly said, "Look away, Rose, darling. She's obviously unwell."

"Yes, that's right, look away Rose, darling," sneered Magnolia, "happy now...but he'll let you down. He'll let you the fuck down." Just as she about to say something else, her phone bleeped, and she hastily grabbed it. She downed her wine and opened the message. Smiling, she said, "Fucking hallelujah. At last."

#

Even though Joseph had the keys to Magnolia and Dan's house, he waited for her to open the door, knowing full well that this would annoy her. It was his childish way of getting her back, and he was an expert at punishing people. Besides, if there was anyone that deserved punishing it was her. All those constant messages and threats were out of line. He was so tired of her and was only going to see her to keep her sweet, to give her a little fix, to get her off his back.

After almost a minute of waiting, his patience started to wear thin and just as he was about to take out his keys, the outline of her long, dark hair appeared through the frosted glass pane. Her voluptuous shape moved with the slithery deception of a snake, and her large bosoms, as full and ripe as all the apples Adam ate, bounced with the same beat as his heart. Even the nipples of her breasts could be seen through the glass of the door as they stuck out like the eyes of a seductive cyclops, watching his every move and teasing him with their hardness.

Her body was quite different to the slender Lucinda's, whose small frame and delicate bones brought out a desire in him to both protect and hurt her. Still, he couldn't help but feel something for Magnolia, even if it was lust, and that's what he hated more than anything.

After a small pause, Magnolia opened the door, and without saying a word, he followed her to the bedroom.

The sex wasn't nearly as rough but no less passionate than with Lucinda. He moved more slowly with Magnolia, pressing his fingers into the moulds of her flesh, which wrapped themselves around his digits like a cobra its prey. Like most women he knew, she liked to be on top. That was fine by him as he got to see more of their bodies, and hers was particularly tantalizing.

Clasping her large breasts, he pulled her down to bury his face into them. The motherly mounds flopped all over him, and he relished in her juice, vociferously licking the milk that oozed out of her chocolate nipples.

Her buttocks were like larger versions of her breasts: firm and well-formed, and he grasped them like a mountaineer. Turning her over, he took her from behind. But he didn't hurt Magnolia. Instead, he gently massaged her back, stroking her long hair and leaning forward to kiss her neck.

Her deep desire released in her groans and murmurs warned him of her imminent orgasm, and he prepared himself. Holding tightly onto her breasts, he increased the tempo and rhythmically moved in her. Thrusting harder and faster, he held one hand over her mouth as she groaned louder and louder, reaching a climatic crescendo. There was nothing he found sexier than a woman being pleased by him, and he came within a few seconds of her.

Having casually thought about it several times he'd concluded that the reason why the sex was more tender with her was because they shared nothing else. He reluctantly had intense emotions for Lucinda. There was something deep about their connection that drew out the rawness of his being; unlike the relationship with Magnolia, which never penetrated beyond the ego. With her it was just the simpler pleasure of sex, food, and drinks with an old friend. It was visceral and not emotional - not for him anyway.

The notion of things being simple between them evaporated with the sound of Ruby's cry. She'd fallen asleep soon after he'd arrived but the loud groans of pleasure from her parents had woken her.

Magnolia reluctantly separated herself from Joseph and reached for the glass of wine on the bedside table. She took a large swig to prepare herself for the task at hand.

Joseph didn't want her to bring the baby into the room, and pulled her back and said, "Leave her, crying's good for her lungs."

Magnolia's face twisted with anger, and she threw her glass down. It shattered into pieces, and the red liquid splayed like blood onto the floor. Pulling her arm away from him, she snarled, "What's the matter with you? That's our daughter in there. Do you have no feelings for her whatsoever?" Although she had no bond with their child, hearing that he didn't either only reinforced that they were not the loving family that she was so desperately trying to enact.

Joseph knew that he'd been tricked and side-stepped any guilt that she was attempting to chain him to. "She may be my flesh and blood, but that's not my daughter Magnolia, it's Dan's. You'd better get used to that," he said, aware that he'd raised his voice. But unable to control his temper, he shouted louder, "You have me, isn't that enough?"

Magnolia scoffed and said, "Ha, I notice an air of resentment about that. You'd better get used to the fact that we have each other, and we have a baby together."

"And we have marriages," he said and sat up in the bed.

"Marriages!" Her words shot our like bullets.

224

"Marriages!" she repeated again, "neither of us are married!"

Having only just caught what he'd said, he meekly replied, "Good as..."

"Oh, My God," she said in utter surprise, "you want to marry her, don't you?"

"I never said that."

"No, not exactly .... but you do want her."

Joseph's words and the proceeding deafening silence sent her over the edge and like a jack-in-the-box she surprised them both by screaming, "And what about me? You can never marry another. You belong to me!" She frantically got off the bed.

Joseph was pushed out of his depth. He'd never expected her to be so clingy and realised that even after all these years he really didn't know this woman. It frightened him to think of what she might be capable of. In his mind, he saw DNA tests, a broken-down Dan and a suicidal Lucinda. The future looked bleak, but anything beyond the present crisis was just too far ahead for him to discern. Right then, he needed to get back some control, and it was essential that he took those steps immediately.

Unsure of how to respond, he decided to take the friendly approach, hoping to bring back some sensibility and re-address the balance of their relationship, which she quite clearly had taken to another level.

"Calm down," he said, "you're acting like a psycho." He got out of the bed and approached her as gently as a tamer would his wild, unpredictable animal. "Why would we get married? Isn't it perfect just the way it is?" he asked, reaching out to tenderly touch her face.

She aggressively pushed his hand away. "What is it, Joseph, am I not the marrying kind? Am I just the murder accomplice kind?" She intensely glared at him, hoping that bringing up the past, the hold that she had on him, would make him remember that he owed her.

"Oh, for fuck's sake. I can't believe you're bringing that up again. You always...."

"Yes! I always. You took me from a pure place into your sordid depth and disease," she said, trying to hold in her tears.

"Ha! Pure? Not likely. You were a murder about to happen." He paused as he remembered back and added. "You egged me on, remember?" Mimicking a girl's voice, he proceeded to imitate her, 'Oh, Bianca The Wanker should get it sometime.'"

"How dare you!" she said slamming her hand down onto the dressing table for extra effect, before pointing her finger at him. "You planned it. You made me do it. From that day on, there was never going to be anything other than an us. You and me. So, fuck Dan! Fuck Lucy Linda!"

"LUCINDA!"

"I know her fucking name," she said scornfully.

Joseph felt things were getting out of control. He had to keep his cool and not defend Lucinda in any way. Somehow, he had to make Magnolia feel as if she was special to him - that he even loved her. "For Christ's sake, what is it with you? I thought you liked this whole secrecy thing. It's our thing, our secret, just like all our other little secrets. We have a world that...."

"Is SHIT!"

"You love Dan. You told me so, remember?" he said, falsely adopting a tone of betrayal.

She was duped, and in a softer tone said, "Not anymore," adding sulkily, "he bores me. The whole doctor status novelty has worn off. Ever since I had our baby, I just want you more and more."

226

The dread that spilled out of those words cascaded towards Joseph like war planes, and he knew he had to put a stop to this battle. At least she had calmed down a little and it gave him the confidence to believe that he still had the power to manipulate her. "Magnolia," he said, "it's never going to happen. You're like my sister."

"I'm nothing like that retard!"

"You can be such a bitch," he said and shook his head in his disgust.

"Oh yeah, really? You're the bitch! Daddy's little bitch that liked to suck on his cock!"

Joseph raised his hand to hit her but stopped himself. "Fuck this," he said and started to dress.

She seductively pulled him towards her and said in a baby voice, "I'm sorry. I hate it when we fight."

He pushed her away. "We don't have those kinds of fights, Magnolia."

She grabbed his hand and placed it onto her breast. He pulled it away.

"What's the matter don't you want to suck on Mama's titties?" she asked, adopting a baby's voice again.

"I don't want to fuck you right now."

"Oh, c'mon grumpy, just a quickie. You used to be able to go all day," she teased, "you getting old?"

"Not likely. I've already banged three whores today and to be honest..."

"What!?"

"Oh, don't get all righteous on me. Join us next time."

"Why would you even want to mix me up with that! Does Lucinda suck whore's pussy? Ha! I doubt it."

"Don't bring her into this!"

"Always her, her." She sat down hopelessly onto the bed.

Most of the time she could ignore Lucinda's presence in the relationship; it had always been her and Joseph.

Lucinda had come much later, and since they had never met, it was easy to pretend that she didn't exist. Until moments like the one she was being faced with, where it became clear that Lucinda was winning his heart and tearing her own in two.

This validation was like a chemical reaction, transforming her love to a hate that spilled from the wound of her broken heart, dripping bad blood into the canyon their relationship had formed over the years. They were on opposite sides now, and she desperately struggled to contain her bloody fury as it rebelliously splashed around like a wrathful wave. She knew once unleashed it would create another ocean between them, where already she was frantically swimming to get closer to him.

Joseph also felt the silent rage eat its way through the dense air and fall like bricks around him. He didn't want to be trapped in the tower with an evil Rapunzel, and quickly tried to bring an end to the conversation.

"Magnolia, it was only a suggestion," he said jovially, trying to laugh away the tension.

Magnolia found nothing about his suggestion humorous. The bed that had previously been soaked in their passion, now felt like a coffin, and she quickly stood up, tripping over articles of clothing that lay scattered about like victims hurled from a car. Delicately picking up each one, she put them on. Somehow, she had to bring them back to life.

Fully dressed, Joseph lit a cigarette and swigged the last of the red wine that had lightly intoxicated them both only a few hours before, when the mood had been as rich and sensually fragrant as the drink.

Even though Magnolia couldn't bear the sight of him, as he stood dressed and ready to leave, she didn't want him to go. Knowing that she should just shut up, she

228

couldn't help spitting out the next words that dropped like cement solidifying the bricks of the wall that Joseph already felt trapped in.

"Am I not special to you?" she asked.

His eyes filled with vengeance, and he said, "You are special. My special friend. My favourite fuck buddy."

His firm words stung like nettles, and the heat of the rash burned her. She was losing him. Destitute, there was nothing she could do. Joseph had never been within her control. With no idea of where this was all leading, she felt herself falling, unable to stave off the rushing ground that rose to meet her. There was no point in struggling. The end was coming, and nothing could save her from the inevitable blackness she was falling into.

Joseph bent down to tie the laces to his shoes and caught a glimpse of her small feet nervously comforting each other. He felt sorry for her and endeavoured to soften the blow a little.

Standing up, he held her by the shoulders and said, "I'm sorry. Listen I don't want to hurt you. Of course, you're special to me. My oldest friend." He smiled lovingly at her. "I just thought an extra person might be fun. You know, something a bit different."

It worked.

Sorrowfully, she asked, "Are you bored or something?"

"Nothing to do with that," he said compassionately, and playfully added, "you know, variety is the spice of life."

In essence, it wasn't the variety that he craved. He had enough of that, what with Lucinda, Magnolia, and the countless number of other one-nighters and prostitutes who fed his narcissistic needs. The truth was, he just didn't want to be alone with her anymore. Over the past few months she'd become increasingly more psychotic, behaving as if she had some kind of right over him. And there was absolutely no way that he wanted to be with, or even near, a woman that wanted to control him. He guessed a third party might be a distraction from the intensity he felt clawing its way through her, to reach him.

He guessed wrong. Her reaction rang large warning bells, and he knew that it had been a big mistake to mention it. She had changed, and though it had been happening for some time, like the gradual aging process of a fruit, Joseph only saw it then - when she had become well and truly rotten.

His Magnolia: the once attractive, fiery beast that he'd adored, sat looking like a broken Lucinda. It didn't become her, he thought, in the same way that it did Lucinda, whose melancholy aroused a deep need in him.

Shaking his head, he thought, this baby has ruined her. He tried to be tolerant of her new post-birth hormonal state and despite this, the desire for her had gone. Once he'd seen a weakness in a person that he admired, it was hard for him have the same respect for them again. He could be very unforgiving in that way, and Magnolia for all her years of friendship had not even been saved from this.

#

Magnolia was well aware that her behaviour was driving Joseph away, in just the same way as her mother had forced her father out. As a then eight-year-old girl, she remembered repeatedly saying to herself, "I won't be like that, I won't be like that..." But it was impossible, nature and nurture worked together to make her an exact replica. She even read from the same script. Now an actor rather than a spectator, she'd lived out the drama a few times in

230

her adulthood before she saw the pattern. Even then it had made no difference - she couldn't stop it. There was a dark pleasure in suffering that she was addicted to.

If she'd read further into the script, she would've seen what it was that Joseph had already detected - that once she'd gotten him, she wouldn't want him anymore.

She wasn't quite there yet. Only halfway through the act, the stage of life was a dance of devastation, where she was unprepared for what followed. As the curtain fell, it exposed her for the whole audience to see, and to her horror, there in the front row, sat her once-biggest-fan-turned-critic: Joseph.

#

Joseph turned away from her and looked out of the window. He wasn't that surprised with the way things had turned out. He'd always seen the mild insanity hidden behind the curtain. At one time, it had been exciting to be the master of this - when it could be mastered. But since the birth, her emotions had risen dangerously, mastering themselves and pushing through the layers of sanity to surface like fungus, until an ugly mutation overwhelmed the delicate balance of attraction and psychosis.

#

Silently, they stood with their backs to each other: Joseph facing the window, where freedom awaited him, and Magnolia the wall, facing a picture of Dan at his graduation ceremony. His happy, proud face glared at her, and she resentfully remembered cringing when he'd hung up the picture, delighted at being the king of his castle. At the time, he'd suggested putting her picture next to his, and she'd almost vomited. It was bad enough that they were living together. She didn't need to live in a museum of their 'love.'

Everything was going wrong; her plan wasn't working. If Dan had suggested inviting a prostitute into their sex to spice things up, she wouldn't have cared.

Even through her angst, the thought of Dan with prostitutes made her smile. She was sure it would be his worst nightmare. He would never see a prostitute due to his moral and ethical high ground. Her smile broadened, and she even chuckled to herself at the comical sight of Dan nervously standing in a whore's room.

This vision magically brought her back to a happy place, where the elation lifted her, and she floated like a witch on a broom towards Joseph. Standing in front of him, she looked up with puppy eyes, and smiled.

He held her shoulders to keep some distance between them and kissed her on the forehead. It was like the kiss of death. The death of bondage. The death of the hold she had on him. Before she had a chance to say or do anything else, he stepped away from her and backed out of the room.

She heard the door slam shut and burst into tears. Her own sobs competed with Ruby's wails, and she said, "I swear this kid's going to fucking kill me.'

Wiping away her tears, she walked over to the drinks cabinet and poured herself a shot of whisky. She downed it and poured another. "Fucking miserable, ungrateful, little bitch," she said and stormed towards Ruby's room. She stood outside for a second shaking with fury, not knowing what to do, and then shut the door.

The wails were drowned out somewhat. Not satisfied, she stumbled over to the music system and switched on the radio.

# Twenty-five

Joseph felt sad. Endings were always so difficult. And although he hadn't cut the cord completely, he knew that it wouldn't be too long before he did. He hadn't planned it like this, or at all in fact. This ending had been evolving for some time now.

Maybe it was just a coincidence that this mood of change should occur on the same day as the anniversary of his mother's death. Either way it was a sad day. Magnolia had been in his life longer than his mother. But with the change in mood, came the tide of change, and he was ready to grow up; ready to lose his childhood love in a way that he'd never been ready to lose his mother.

He dreaded making the yearly pilgrimage to her graveside; predominately because it was a ritual that he did with his father and mentally challenged sister.

It was the only time that he made the effort to be in their company. Somehow, on that day, the force of his mother's spirit held them together for a moment in time.

When he was younger, and had less freedom, he'd reluctantly joined them by her graveside. As he got older and more powerful, he chose to sit in the car amongst the other stranger's graves. He couldn't bear the sight of the two remaining members of his family. They were losers as far as he was concerned and being anywhere near them only exasperated the pain of losing his mother.

His sister, Pamela, had grown uglier and more disgusting in his eyes. Having gotten fatter, she wobbled when she walked, like a pig with Parkinson's disease. His father, beaten down by years of alcohol abuse had lost his power, his soul drowned in intoxicants, so all that remained was the smouldering rage that teased Joseph with the possibility of turning into a fire again.

Even though Joseph was a man now, with one look, his father could strip the layers off his protective shield, and with the same power as a time machine, was able to make Joseph feel as scared as the six-year-old boy he had once been. The fear only lasted for a few seconds in normal time, but the memories were so ingrained, and the trauma so vast that it felt like an eternity.

His father's eyes shone with a light empowered by dark forces. It amazed him how, in all these years, his father's eyes had not changed; age had neither softened him nor made him wiser. Age had however, transformed his body. Even though his father had kept his form for many years beyond his peers, his muscles started to sag when he stopped working as a builder.

Joseph remembered when he was a very young boy how much he had admired his father's branching arms and had fond memories of swinging like a monkey from them. Back then, his father had been as strong as an old oak, rooted in the soil of his wife's fertile, organic love. When she died, the soil dried up, and the roots became unearthed. The old oak began to die. Joseph first saw him die inside. It took many years for his body to break and catch up with the shattered pieces of his heart.

234

Sitting in the car, Joseph remembered those moments tenderly. It was odd how he was graced with them, and he had the sudden notion that his mother had gifted him with these memories. He felt her by his side. Very quickly, he shirked away this thought, and his mother stepped back. His mother was dead, and once a person is dead they are no longer; not in body or spirit, he told himself firmly, trying his hardest to believe something that his heart beat out a different tune to.

He started growing impatient as theories of a possible afterlife infiltrated his mind. Under no circumstance did he want these stupid thoughts invading him and turned his attention back to the graveside.

The visual distraction, though a respite from the theoretical torture, was no better, and he distastefully surveyed his sister, who was oblivious to any pain and smiling; smiling at what, he had no idea? The falling autumn leaves that hit the ground with the same velocity as her drool? The squirrel hopping by their side hoping for a treat? The sun that shone, lighting up her bowl face? Or the emptiness of her thoughts that created the space to be happy?

With no answers to these questions, he shifted his gaze onto his father and saw something different. For the first time, he noticed how weak he looked. He was only nearing sixty, and could potentially live for another twenty years, although he doubted very much that would be the case, for it was clear that his father had lost his will to live. To punish him, he hoped life would demand he stay in it to experience weakness and fragility.

Joseph wondered if he had it in him to care for his father in old age, or if he would choose to abuse him like his father had done to him when he was a fragile and vulnerable child. The vile thoughts of making daily visits to his father's house to repeatedly beat him, lock him in

235

a room, and deprive him of food, excited him as a means to purge his anger. The pleasure from these visions only lasted a few seconds before he thought, I'm as sick as he is, and got out of the car and lit a cigarette.

Leaning against the bonnet, he eyed up a newly erected gravestone and flicked his ash onto the grave: "MICHAEL BROWN - LOVING HUSBAND AND FATHER."

# Twenty-six

The Formless Voice announced, "Mr. Brown, please stand."

Mr. Brown closed the magazine that he'd been reading and stood meekly, sobbing into a handkerchief.

"Enough tears, Mr. Brown," said The Formless Voice severely, "your remorse has been well documented, but upon which basis is yet to be determined. Exactly why are you so sorry? For the deed? For the loss? Or just plain old sorry for yourself?"

"I err, err," and breaking down again into sobs, Mr. Brown shook his head to indicate that he could not go on.

"MR BROWN!" shouted The Formless Voice.

Joseph's thoughts projected onto the large screen, *"What a useless being."*

"Ok, ok I will try, but I never want to return. Never," cried Mr. Brown pathetically.

"So, you never want to love again Mr. Brown? Is that what you are telling us?"

"I never can. Not the person of my dreams. Not the forbidden fruit of my sweet, sweet child..."

Joseph thoughts projected onto the screen: *"Great. Another fucking paedo."*

"The first time I held her tiny body in my arms, I loved her. I loved her like any father loves his newborn child. Her tiny fingers and toes curled with each touch, each kiss. Her soft cheeks pressing against me filled me with a strong desire to love her, to protect her, and to always cherish her. I loved her so deeply, I became soaked by her powerful innocence, and I never wanted to put her down.

"When she screamed in the night, to be fed, to be changed, to be held, I ran to her side like her servant obediently tending to her needs. I kissed her soft palms, and the soles of her feet washed me with the sweet scent of baby skin. Her open mouth, reaching for her mother's teat, found my lips instead, and I couldn't help but slip my tongue in for her to suckle. The sweet juice of her baby mouth aroused me, and though I knew to never let it happen again, I had been touched by the drug of baby juice, and like an addict, was transfixed."

Joseph's angry thoughts flashed onto the screen, *"Fucking wanker! Get addicted to something that will fuck only you up."*

"More and more, I wished my wife would leave us alone. I even resented her for holding my sweet child; she was mine. I wasn't willing to share her. Jealousy rose in me whenever my delicate daughter smiled sweetly at another, and it drove my addiction further; I needed her more."

Mr. Brown sobbed uncontrollably into his handkerchief for a moment, before he composed himself and asserted, "But don't you see, she encouraged that desire with her beauty and devotion."

*"Fucked up loser! Selfish pig! Irresponsible tosser!"* appeared on the screen.

238

"The next time I got to be alone with my sweet child was when my wife became sick. After successfully managing to get paternity leave from work, I served them both: my wife with wet flannels for her soaring temperature, and my sweet child with the wetness of my mouth."

Mr. Brown unconsciously licked his lips, and Joseph shook his head in disgust.

"It was the first time that I would bathe her alone, without my wife's interfering presence hung over my shoulder like the good angel. And though my wife was nervous about my doing this, she was too sick to do the task herself."

*"Manipulative, scheming arsehole. I can't believe the world is full of people like this!"* flew Joseph's angry thoughts onto the screen.

"Like a child excited about their parents leaving them alone for the night, I couldn't contain myself, as I prepared the room for our night together." Mr. Brown paused and looked around before saying a little more quietly, as if he were revealing a secret. "I had to make sure we wouldn't be disturbed, so I gave my wife a little extra medication - a sleeping tablet, which she trustingly took from her faithful husband."

With a little pride, and adjusting his sloppy stature, Mr. Brown delivered the next comment as if he deserved an award for it. "You see, unlike other men, I never had the desire to cheat on my wife. Before our baby had been born, she was my everything."

*"Obviously not Paedo Papa. You were and are your everything,"* shot Joseph's words onto the screen.

"With my wife finally asleep, I took our little bundle of joy to the bathroom, stripped her naked and gently eased her into the baby bath. Supporting her head with one hand, whilst the other was under her bottom, I dipped her in and out. Then, slowly, I washed her soft, meaty skin."

Joseph's thoughts streamed like tears onto the screen, *"It's a baby, you weirdo! A beautiful, innocent being...Fucking perv!"*

Mr. Brown imitated the movements of washing his baby and then continued to act as if his baby were right there in his arms. "Taking her out of the bath, I laid her onto the bed and kissed her. I was filled with such a strong desire to hold her close to me."

Mr. Brown's face contorted with the pain of forbidden love, but lost in the emotion, he shamelessly carried on, "It was a genuine love I felt for her, but somehow it became mixed in with a sexual desire."

*"I think I'm going to fucking puke up,"* spewed Joseph's words like vomit onto the screen.

Mr. Brown paused with a faraway look in his eye; the memory of that time having removed him from his present place.

Joseph's thoughts ran in circles on the screen as he rose to leave the room, *"That's it, I've had enough. I don't know where the fuck I am, but I'm going somewhere else."*

"Sit down Joseph, there is nowhere for you to go," said The Formless Voice tiredly.

Joseph didn't listen as his thoughts carried on scrolling across the screen, *"Nut-cases, psychos'. My worst fucking nightmare.... Shit what did I do that was so bad?"*

"Ah Joseph, Joseph where do I begin?" mocked The Formless Voice.

Joseph ignored this remark and screamed, "Let me the fuck out!"

He ran up to the wall and punched and kicked it. His fists and feet just bounced off as if it were made of rubber.

"Joseph, don't make this harder on yourself. Sit down, and stop wasting everybody's time," said The Formless Voice.

Joseph looked at the screen and saw that for a second he had no thoughts. Reluctantly, he returned to his seat. As soon as he faced Mr. Brown again the word, *"Cunt,"* repeatedly appeared on the screen, and he smirked.

Eager to continue reliving his devilish pleasure Mr. Brown said, "After the explosion of ecstasy, I was consumed with guilt and was barely able to look at her. So, I dressed her quickly in her nappy and baby grow and put her to sleep without holding her to my chest or rocking her. Having sucked from her, her sweet juice and power, I pushed her away. In fact, for the remainder of the night I hated her. Somehow, I managed to blame her for what I had done. Somehow, it had to be her fault."

Joseph's words crawled across the screen like a baby escaping from a lustful embrace, *"When is this going to end? Why the fuck am I here?"*

"After that, I stayed away from our baby," said Mr. Brown, proudly adjusting his stature so that he stood more upright.

*"Thank fuck for that! That's the first decent thing this prick has said,"* danced Joseph's thoughts on the screen.

But then, remembering the weight of his lustful love, Mr. Brown dropped his shoulders and hung his head. "My wife complained that I never helped out and was not being a loving father or husband. You see, after that night I became unable to maintain an erection, and my sex life with my wife became non-existent. Over the years, I threw myself into my work and alcohol, whilst she had numerous affairs."

*"Oh, my God! Can you blame her?"*

"As my sweet child grew, my desire for her did too, and when I felt that she was old enough not to tell, I started to go into her room."

Fire blazed across the screen.

"Drink fuelled my courage, and I became a loving father again for the few minutes of sexual play we shared together."

*"Take her to the park, you sicko!"*

"This time she could receive more from me and take part in the acts...You see she enjoyed it too," asserted Mr. Brown in his defence.

Joseph's thoughts entered the screen in a way that indicated that they were tearing the gentle material, *"If you're going tell me that you raped her, then I just don't know what I'll do."*

"Then I slipped out of her bed."

*"Ah no. Ah noooo,"* fell Joseph's words like a fainting child from the top of the screen to the bottom.

"I never held her, apart from during the act. After the sex, I never took her into my arms or stroked her hair. I only ever pecked her on the cheek on her birthday, and I rarely looked into her eyes. Our secret love affair continued until she got her period, and good to her word, she never told a soul."

*"You wrecked her life, you tosser. Where is she now?"* jumped Joseph's thoughts onto the screen.

"Then she fell in love. My sweet child fell in love with the first boy she slept with, and he broke her heart."

*"Err psycho, I think you did that a long time ago,"* stuttered Joseph's thoughts.

"Although I had used her for years, she never expected anybody else to."

For the first-time Mr. Brown was taken aback by a remorse that felt genuine to Joseph.

"This boy she fell for wanted to have sex with a virgin, and my daughter, who was no virgin, either forgot her past, or believed it didn't count. Either way, she embraced her first night with her boyfriend as her first night of real sex."

Mr. Brown broke down in tears again.

Just as Joseph began to worry that this would never end, an unusual feeling stirred in him and although he could not predict the ending, he nervously sensed that he was a part of it.

"She had worn her favourite jeans that night, and her mother's old, pink, original Woodstock top."

"Oh, My God... it can't be..."

"Her new, red, cowboy boots."

"boots," said Joseph at the same time.

"My Jennie."

"...nnie," uttered Joseph in dismay as a picture of Jennie appeared on the screen.

"I don't know why," continued Mr. Brown sorrowfully, "but after that night she killed herself. In her note to me, a private note to her father, she said, 'I just wanted him to hold me afterwards, but he left me in the bed, wet from his love, and walked away.'"

Joseph's thoughts blew chaotically over the screen like a monsoon, *"Oh Jennie, I was young. I was stupid. I never knew you topped yourself."*

Mr. Brown noticed that Joseph was crying and looked to the screen. After seeing the thoughts, he lunged towards him, screaming, "You bastard! My baby is dead because of you! You fucking bastard!"

"Mr. Brown! Order in the court," shouted The Formless Voice. "Security, restrain him!"

At The Formless Voice's request, Formless Forces' (just like invisible bouncers) pulled him off Joseph, and he slumped to the ground in a flood of tears.

Joseph couldn't contain his words anymore and screamed back, "It was you! Because of you! You started it you fool. You sick evil arsehole! You ruined her!"

"Shut up you piece of shit! You think you're so pure, do you? Have a look at this Mr. Picture Perfect."

Mr. Brown threw down the magazine that he'd been holding earlier. It landed by Joseph's feet.

Joseph turned away to protect his eyes from what he was sure would be some nasty act of child abuse and just caught an image of himself as a small boy, naked, on his knees, looking directly up at him. He stumbled back in shock and said, "What the fuck!"

"How is Daddy these days?" asked Mr. Brown and smirked. "Oh sorry, you wouldn't know because you are dead!"

Joseph's sorrow turned to bitterness, and he spat, "Just like your Jennie."

Instead of feeling better it dawned on him that his own actions might have led to Jennie's death. Was he no better than Mr. Brown or even his own father for that matter? Tearfully, he blurted, "Shit! I wished I'd known. I wished I'd cared. I was seventeen, man, and all I wanted to do was have sex. Poor Jennie....Can you ever forgive me?"

The Formless Voice spoke with a little more compassion than before, "That is not the question you should be asking. Can you, Joseph, forgive yourself?"

Returning as the voice of fearful authority, The Formless Voice addressed Mr. Brown, "Now, Paedo Papa." He paused and looked at Joseph and said, "I like that line of yours. Glad to see that your copywriting skills haven't gone to waste here."

Joseph was pleased at first for the recognition, but then felt sad to remember that he'd had a life before.

"This is supposed to be about me. It's my turn!" said Mr. Brown glaring at Joseph.

"Oh, this is about you," said The Formless Voice, "Don't you worry about that. In fact, you've revealed yourself superbly. Your outburst and attack on our newcomer, shows me that your remorse has nothing to do with the acts that you performed but rather with the loss of your true and only love. Even as you retold the story, you got sexually aroused. Were you aware of this fact? You enjoyed telling the tale.... hmm? The only part of your story when you were not sobbing was during the re-telling of your sexual misadventures with your child. Then, Mr. Brown, you were excited, happy, and full of love."

Joseph's thoughts appeared on the screen as *heart shapes with exclamation marks in the middle of them.*

"Yes, Joseph," said The Formless Voice, "it was love, albeit a twisted, sad, pathetic abuse of love bound to a condition, a pattern, an addiction of some sort. A selfish representation of love. Would it shock you to know that your father loved you? Because in his own way he did."

"Oh, leave it out. The man's an A Class Tosser. Love... it's a fucking joke."

"Conditional love is complicated by the mere fact that it is conditional. One of the Seven Universal Laws, The Universal Law of Polarity tells us that everything is dual and has an opposite, a positive and a negative if you like, which only appears different through one degree of separation. But you see, when positive and negative come together, light is born and light is a metaphor for love."

"That sounds like a load of rubbish to me - hippie commune crap, detached from anything real," said Joseph.

"Real. There's that word real - so questionable as to what is real. But let me break it down to you in real terms that you may understand. Joseph, when a person experiences a negative emotion in their life, let's say sadness, but then opens themselves to acknowledge the equal positive emotion that co-exists with that, since as I explained everything has an opposite, then the negative experience is dissolved and love is born."

Joseph looks none the wiser. "You're losing me here, old man."

"Let's say you get angry or sad because you lose your job. Instead of wallowing in your suffering about it and feeling hurt, angry or betrayed, think of all the positive things about no longer having that job - maybe the job was holding you back from your bigger dreams, maybe the hours weren't great, maybe your boss was, and to use one of your owns words here: a tosser. Think, now that you don't have that job you can go for what you really want, have more time, shift your perspective, change your direction, etcetera etcetera. The key to this Law is that if every experience has an opposite then *you* have the power to turn it around. Bring positivity into negativity and turn it into love. So, you see there is no point or purpose to judgment. And my dear boy, I must add that you are not in a position to question Mr. Brown's love for his child. Nobody here knows love in its True form, otherwise, my dear Joseph, they would simply not be here."

"I've been with enough women to know about love."

"Oh really? What's love when it's about fulfilling your needs only? What's love without sacrifice?" Joseph pondered this. "You simply wouldn't know."

Re-addressing Mr. Brown, The Formless Voice continued, "Your sickness will take many years to cure. You are so in love with yourself, with a possession of yourself, that your own flesh and blood in the form of your daughter became a part of your twisted self-obsession. However, you can redeem yourself, you know."

Mr. Brown's eyes lit up at the possibility of being forgiven by the Almighty he felt both bound by, and identified with.

"And so, I give you a rare option," continued The Formless Voice, "either you can choose to stay here or be reborn. Though I warn you now, the family will be a difficult one and you shall have to endure the pain you have inflicted onto others, unto yourself."

"I want to suffer. Let me suffer," affirmed Mr. Brown pathetically.

"Mr. Brown, you do not remember, but you said that the last time that you were here," scolded The Formless Voice. "You are addicted to this suffering, so you choose it again, but not with the intention of working through it. You have a desire to be absorbed in madness and debauchery, and that is why you make this choice. So, I take your options away. Be grateful that I have decided that in your own best interest, you shall be required to stay."

"No! No!" shrieked Mr. Brown desperately.

"For another hundred human years," continued The Formless Voice, "and three hundred sittings. May you be washed of your sorrow, your lust, and your perverse ways. May you be touched by other's stories in a way which moves your heart to feel deeply beyond your reactions and desires. May you grow to feel universal love."

#

In the Female Courtroom, Lucinda was shocked to see

247

the seat next to her suddenly occupied by a girl wearing a pink, Woodstock top and jeans. She looked curiously at her, and the girl, Jennie, turned to her and said, "I loved him too for a short while."

Lucinda tried work out what she meant. Her thoughts were interrupted by a grunt from the front row.

She and Jennie looked to see who it had come from, and saw Magnolia, flick the long hair off her shoulders and proceed to give them the finger.

# Twenty-seven

Joseph stubbed out his cigarette and noticed a much older gravestone next to Mr. Browns: JENNIE BROWN - GONE TOO SOON - ALWAYS IN OUR HEARTS.

He took a step closer and said, "Nah. Can't be," and took a step back. He heard muffled sobs and looked over to see his father crying by his mother's gravestone. "Dick. No point in crying now," he said and walked back round to the driver's side of the car. Just as he was about to get in he recognised the Homeless Man from before, sitting on a bench with his back to him. "Mr. Sewage Hole," he said quietly to himself and walked towards him.

"Watch you don't step on that shit," said The Homeless Man, still looking straight ahead.

Joseph looked down. His foot was hovering over a clump of dog excrement. He stepped over it and playfully asked, "Metaphor for my life?"

The Homeless Man laughed and replied, "That's up to you."

Joseph sat down next to him and offered him a cigarette. "How did you know that I was about to step on that? Got eyes in the back of your head now have you?"

The Homeless Man smiled and ignored the question and the cigarette, and offered him a spliff.

Joseph took it and looked it over. Impressed, he said, "You're doing alright then, for a homeless bloke I mean."

"Homeless but not soul-less. Wifeless but not loveless. Childless but not with regret. That life's not for everyone."

"So, what have you done with your life?"

"I've been a diving instructor, businessman, Teacher...and a lover, oh so many times. But I like to keep moving. The less attachments I have, the freer I am."

Joseph took another pull and passed the spliff back. "Freedom's an illusion," he said at the same time as letting the smoke evacuate from his mouth.

"No. The cage is. You're stuck in this wall-less, door-less cage. It's up to you to fly away from all this hidden rage."

The loud sound of a car alarm startled them both and Joseph turned to see his car lights flashing. He got up and turned towards The Homeless Man and said, "I be..." He was gone. Joseph did a three-sixty spin and said, "What the...again?"

He dashed towards his car and felt something splatter beneath his foot. "FUCK!" he shouted and stormed off whilst trying to smear the shit off his shoe.

#

Joseph furiously walked into the flat holding his shit encrusted shoe and glared at the scene before him of Lucinda snuggled on the sofa, cradling the baby wrapped in a blanket.

"I've had enough of this shit," he said.

Lucinda looked at the shoe, and stifling her laughter, asked, "Bad day darling?"

"You know what I mean."

"Shhh," she whispered, more seriously, "keep your voice down, or you'll wake Boo Boo." She got up and gently put the baby in the pram and cooed, "It's ok, Mama's going to get your bottle," and walked off towards the kitchen.

Joseph threw his shoe to the ground and stormed over to the pram, shouting, "There is no fucking Boo Boo!"

Lucinda frantically hurtled towards him as he pulled the bundle from the pram and flung it across the room. She screamed when it hit the ground and saw a small hand and leg poke out from it. Quickly sprinting towards it, she threw herself onto the floor and unravelled the blanket - inside was a baby doll.

'He's dead! Dead, Lucinda. This isn't fucking real," screamed Joseph.

Lucinda stroked the baby doll's face and cried, "It's ok. Daddy's just angry now."

Joseph shook his head and stormed out of the flat. He leaned against the door, exasperated and listened to Lucinda wailing inside. The pain in her cries broke him, and he slid down the door until he was slumped on the floor. Tears streamed down his face as he took out his phone and dialed Dan.

After three rings, Dan picked up and Joseph said, "Mate, I can't do this anymore, they're killing me. All of them.... Yeah, send me the info for the nuthouse. This is way out of my league."

#

Inside the flat Lucinda sat on the floor rocking the baby doll to her chest. "Lucas!" she screamed, "Lucas!" In her head, she saw him intermittently transform from a 'real baby' to a baby doll and back again. Her tears dripped over his face, and she despairingly cried, "You are real. You are real. Please don't leave me."

# Twenty-eight

*Six Months Before*

Lucinda, heavily pregnant and beaming with joy waited on the underground platform. A train pulled up and the doors opened. Passengers piled out, and she entered the crowded carriage.

A middle-aged woman immediately got up from her seat and offered it to her. Lucinda gratefully sat down and said, "Thank you."

"Oh honey, you're welcome," replied the middle-aged woman. Looking at her bump, she said, "not long now."

Lucinda stroked her belly and said, "A month, but anytime I guess."

"Do you know the sex yet?"

"I want it to be a surprise."

"Like the good old days."

"I've got names though. Well we haven't settled on a boy's name. But we have a girl's name - Ruby."

"Beautiful name."

"Yes. My favourite stone."

A few feet away, Magnolia was standing with her back to Lucinda, squashed in-between the passengers. She put her hand over her much smaller bump and stroked it.

The train pulled into the next stop. Lucinda got up.

"I wish you the best in your new adventure," said the middle-aged woman.

"Thank you," replied Lucinda heartily and walked out of the carriage with Magnolia just a few paces behind her.

Lucinda got on the escalator unaware that Magnolia was following her. At the top, she walked through the barriers and towards the next set of escalators. She sighed when she got there and saw that they were out of order. Sluggishly, she approached the packed stairs.

Magnolia raced passed her trying her best to keep hidden amongst the crowd and got to the top first.

Lucinda was three quarters of the way up, when Magnolia pretended to stumble and pushed several people, including Lucinda, down the stairs.

Lucinda fell backwards as some other passengers tried in vain to grab her.

In all the mayhem Magnolia slipped away unnoticed.

#

Joseph was standing outside a room in the maternity ward listening to a Doctor who solemnly shook his head and said, "I'm sorry, Joseph. We couldn't save him."

"Oh no," said Joseph and flopped into a chair, burying his face into his hands.

"Lucinda will still need to give birth. She's in labour now. But the baby will be stillborn." He gently placed his hand onto Joseph's shoulder and softly said, "I'm so sorry."

Joseph walked into the labour room and watched as a lifeless baby was handed to Lucinda. She didn't seem in the least bit affected and cradled him. "Hello, my precious Boo Boo," she whispered and then sang, "Mummy loves you."

She noticed Joseph staring at her and said, "Don't just stand there. Come and meet our son. He's beautiful."

Joseph warily walked over.

"He looks like a Lucas. Lets call him Lucas."

Joseph nervously looked around at the medical staff for some support.

"Darling, don't you want to hold him?" she asked and held the baby out to him.

He looked at her in surprise and said, "Lucinda, he's dead."

"How can you say that. Look at him. Look at our gorgeous Boo Boo. What's wrong with you?" She snuggled the dead baby to her chest.

The doctor walked in and motioned for Joseph to follow him out.

Taking him to one side he said, "Joseph, she's in shock. Her hormones are all over the place right now."

"Shock! This is more like psychotic! The thing is dead. How can she think it's alive?"

"She just needs time. I'll get a counsellor to come and speak to you both."

"Both! I accept it's dead!" He held onto the wall for support and said, "This is all too much."

"Be patient. There is a chance that she could develop postpartum depression or even postpartum psychosis. We need to support her and tread very carefully."

Joseph was only half listening and said, more to himself than anyone else, "I've got to get out of here. I can't breathe," and raced out of the ward.

*3 Days Later*

Lucinda was frantically running around the maternity ward, looking in all the baby's cribs and screaming, "Where is he? Where is my baby? What have you done to Lucas?"

Several nurses and doctors tried to calm her down as she fell to the ground in a flood of tears.

#

*1 week Later*

Lucinda shuffled out of the psychiatric ward with a blank expression on her face and wandered around until she found the maternity ward. There, she stood by a large window looking at the cribs of the newborns, and placed her hands onto the window as if she was trying to reach them.

A nurse recognised her and tried to coax her away. Lucinda let herself be pulled away from the window but then stopped outside a room: 'Pregnancy Education.' She shrugged the nurse's hand off her and walked in and over to a 'baby boy doll' laying on the table. She picked him up and cradled him to her heart and whispered into his ear, "There you are. There you are, my love."

#

Lucinda, clasped the baby doll tighter in her arms. Through her muffled cries, she could still hear Joseph's voice on the phone outside. It just saddened her further, and she kissed the baby doll on the forehead and placed

256

his plastic lips to her warm nipple and cried for him to cry back at her. Slowly the realisation set in that he wasn't real, and she screamed, "I wish I were dead..."

# Twenty-nine

"...anywhere but here."

The Chair walked up to Lucinda and said, "Still saying the same thing then? Can you not see that it's the running away that has put you in this place? Can you not see, that as quoted in the works of Persian Sufi Poets that, 'This Too Shall Pass?' The Law of Rhythm tells us that all things rise and fall; the pendulum-swing manifests in everything."

The Old Caww cackled and sung, "What goes up must come down." Her face twisted with sourness, and she resentfully said, "I've been down long enough." She looked at The Chair with eyes that conveyed this injustice and spat, "Pendulum swing my arse. It's stuck in the fucking gutter of hell - blooming Universal Law!"

Lucinda wiped her tears with the cuff of her sleeve and said, "You know what? You're starting to get on my nerves. No wonder you're still stuck here."

"Oh, and what you think you won't be? You won't get far without me, love."

"Ladies! Enough!" shouted The Chair. "All you need to know is that you gave up, Lucinda. At every hurdle, you gave up when you should have kept fighting. For if you stay positive even when things appear to be negative then no matter how far back this transitory law pulls you, you can transcend it.

"If you allow yourself to be dragged into the depths of despair, then you just fall deeper into the wells of hell. And when you do eventually garner the strength to pull yourself out, it just takes longer to recover.

"Life is full of up's and down. If you understand this, then you won't play out the victim - you will surrender instead to the vulnerability and fragility of being truly human. Now that my dears, is an act of maturity; one that evolves into wisdom."

She floated from one end of the room to the other. "It's very boring, you know. If you could see yourselves in all the lives you've led, you would see how none of you have changed. That's why you keep returning. And as is the case this time - often together."

She stopped in front of Lilly. "Next to take the stand is our young Lilly."

Lilly excitedly leapt from her seat, still holding the ball she'd earlier manifested. Eyes beaming with childish joy, she proceeded to speak.

"I had been seven, as I am now, and he only four years old, when I decided that it was time. Having been in this world long enough we didn't need to suffer anymore."

She looked across the crowded room to penetrate each person's gaze with the promise of her own power.

"The bottle was large and bright blue. It had a child safety cap that was easy for me to open as I'd watched my mother like a hawk for days in preparation for this moment.

After deciding that he had to go first, I gave him the bottle, and he put it to his lips. The vile smell singed the delicate hairs of his nostrils, and he squinted his beautiful, angel face in disgust and looked at me. I nodded, urging him to drink. His trust in me was so secure that he pressed the bottle closer to his lips. Tilting his head back, he reluctantly swallowed then immediately gagged. I gently supported the bottle from underneath and raised it to his lips again, which he parted with the gentle softness of a newborn.

"I waited .... nothing happened," said Lilly quietly. "He rubbed his belly and looked a little green." Making circular movements with her hand over her own belly, she swallowed hard as if she was trying to keep down the rising vomit, and continued, "Maybe it would take longer than I thought." She stopped and a solemn pause followed. "I could wait," she went on, "I had to make sure that it would begin to work before I took it too, just in case he needed more. If I had taken enough and he not, then he would be left behind to suffer, and I couldn't be that cruel."

Lilly drooped her lower lip and shook her head. Her large, soft brown eyes watered and tears fell, not from her ducts but from the ceiling, drenching all those in the room.

"After some time, we were called for lunch, and I forgot for a while," she admitted, as she spun on the spot with her hands open wide and her tongue out, catching the drops of her own tears that fell harder and circled her like a tornado.

In a sharp motion, she stopped spinning and scrunched up her face with revulsion. "Ewww," she said, "it was like a river of green bile violently spurting from his mouth and nostrils. He dropped to the floor and started shaking as if an earthquake had erupted inside of him."

Lilly stood, a picture of fear. More quietly, and with remorse, she continued, "My mother couldn't understand what had happened and rushed him to the car. I stayed at the top of the stairs while his eyes searched for mine, pleading with me not to leave him alone. He didn't understand what was happening. I could see the fear wash through him, adding to the scratches already carved in his heart .... scratches that I didn't put there but knew would never disappear."

A graveness came over her, like the dark shadow of death, and the tears falling from the ceiling dried up and streamed down her face. "As they drove off, I reached for the bottle. Instinctively, I knew he wouldn't make it, and put the bottle to my mouth and swallowed. That's how I came to this side. But that's not all I did. You see, even though I loved my brother, I used to hurt him."

Her bright eyes filled with tears again, as she searched around the room for someone to connect with. She found Lucinda. Looking into her eyes, she spoke as if she was trying to convince herself of what she was saying. "I remembered thinking it was normal, otherwise I wouldn't have done it in front of my friends. But you must understand that he had to be disciplined. Not because it was right, but because I loved him. He was taking risks, and there was a chance he could get hurt. I told him time and time again not to climb on the cupboards...but he never listened." Sadly, she confessed, "You see, I was afraid that he would fall, and I would be left all alone."

Lucinda knew why Lilly had looked at her. She, too, couldn't bear being left by the ones she loved. She understood Lilly, and a layer fell from her mask.

"I had to stop him, and the only way I knew how was to beat him," declared Lilly, looking down in shame. Then, as many a child does, she acted out the scene whilst saying, "So I kicked him hard in the stomach." Raising her hands in the air as if to push back the judgment she felt from around the room, she asserted, "But I never touched his face, and she only touched mine once with the buckle of a belt...because she loved me."

Quietly, she stood remembering her mother, whom she'd loved, but in a desperate attempt to get away from had taken her own life. Feeling the room wouldn't understand her actions she tried to explain further. "I learnt to hurt those I loved. I also chose to take two lives: my brother's and my own, to save us. I know now that it was not my choice to make. A misuse of my power and misunderstanding of my right to life."

Lucinda couldn't believe that there before her was a young child with the energy and physical appearance of a seven-year-old. Everything about her spoke of youth - her actions, intonations and pitch - and yet she possessed the ability to articulate such great wisdom.

She wondered if other children on the earthly level also possessed these nuggets of wisdom, but only lacked the words to express them. Then, through time, by living in a world conditioned not to feel, they lost them.

The buried treasure within each human being became something Lucinda started to feel, as her own trunk of treasure slowly crept open.

With no worldly knowledge about the Law of Universal Mind, Lilly's wise words were revealing to Lucinda that all beings, including herself, had access to all knowledge, known and unknown.

After giving a small pause to allow Lucinda's golden thoughts to emerge, Lilly said, "I was very sad when I came here initially because I missed them all, but now I am truly happy to be as I am."

She looked at Lucinda and giggled. "You don't remember me, do you?" she asked. "But I bet you remember this song: 'Oh the trees are wild reaching up to the sky, Lilly and Lucinda, friends till the day we die.' Except, as we now know, there's more to life after death."

Lucinda did remember that song, and in her mind, saw the image of Lilly dancing in her garden. A tear dropped from her eye, and for a second she felt both saddened and comforted by the presence of an old friend.

She walked over and knelt in front of her so that they were the same height and said, "Lilly, you were my friend, weren't you? And that's why I have the doll called Lilly."

"Yes, I gave that to you for your fifth birthday. You insisted on naming it after me."

"Wow. I had no idea."

"And you used to always sing our song to it. I think it was the only time I saw you happy after he died."

"After who died?"

"Why, your brother, silly. Don't you remember? I mean of course maybe you don't. But didn't they tell you?"

Lucinda was shocked. A brother? She'd had a brother? No. It couldn't be possible.

Lilly turned her attention back to the room and carried on speaking with a renewed confidence brought about by her heartfelt confession. "I have learnt here that I create what I want from a desire in my heart to have it, and I am happy."

And with that, little Lilly disappeared, and the manifested ball she'd been holding in her hand fell to the ground.

"Wait," called out Lucinda, "tell me about my brother?"

"Dear Lucinda," said The Chair, "you did have a brother - Lucas. His death was a tragedy they say. One you allowed to happen."

"What?"

"Close your eyes and let me take you back."

Lucinda hesitated then asked, "Is this going to be like Scrooge, Ghost of Christmas Past or something?"

"Something like that," replied The Chair and smiled. Lucinda was eager to understand more and so closed her eyes.

In a flash, she found herself standing in her first family home. The sounds of laughter ran through the corridors, and she followed them to the living room, where she saw her father on the sofa tickling her mother. In front of them were two squealing babies, joyfully catching the splatters of laughter that fell from their parent's mouths.

"Is that baby me?" asked Lucinda pointing to the female infant child.

"Yes, Lucinda, it is indeed you," replied The Chair.

"And I suppose the baby boy next to me is my brother?"

"Yes. That is Lucas."

"My parents look so happy," said Lucinda, both surprised and saddened by the image before her. She never remembered her parents laughing like that when she was growing up.

"How old are we there?"

"Oh, I would think about one. Cute, weren't you?"

"Yes. I was. We were." Lucinda paused. "So, what happened?"

At that moment a tall, robust, overweight woman marched into the room looking perturbed by all the happiness wafting through the air. In a swift, sweep she scooped both children into her arms and said, "Time for their naps now. We need to run a tight ship here."

Lucinda's parents tried to compose themselves, adjusting their positions as if the headmaster had just walked in on them canoodling.

264

"Oh yes, of course," said Lucinda's mother, trying desperately to repress her laughter.

The Nanny briskly left the room, leaving behind a small chill in the air. As soon as she was gone Lucinda's parents burst into laughter.

"Ahoy!" cried Lucinda's mother and fell back onto the sofa.

Lucinda's father held her down, delicately kissed her lips and softly said, "I love you so much. So very much."

Lucinda's mother smiled lovingly at him. "I know, my darling. I love you too." She looked towards the door. "Do you think we can get away with a quickie right now?"

They could both hear Lucinda crying.

"Well, I think Lucinda will keep Nanny busy for a little while longer, so..." said Lucinda's father as he undid the top button of her blouse and buried his face into her chest.

"Erm Chair," said Lucinda "I think we can move on. I don't - "

She stopped talking as the room spun around her, and she found herself in the children's bedroom.

The mood mirrored the grey, wintery day, visible through the gap in the closed curtain, where a malevolent force teetered on the tips of the heavy clouds, filled with sadness and about to erupt like thunder.

Lucinda walked over to the playpen and saw a two-year-old Lucinda curled up in a corner, sitting in her own excrement and crying. Lucas reached into the playpen from the outside to touch her hand. She let it drop down so he could take it.

The dense, tender moment between them was shattered when the Nanny entered the room with the force of an unwelcome hurricane and bellowed, "Get away from her, Lucas. She's a very, very bad girl." The

Nanny pulled Lucas away from the playpen, and he reluctantly let go of Lucinda's hand, his own now covered in her excrement.

Lucinda wailed. Her twins touch had been a small comfort to her and without it she felt void. The Nanny lovingly picked Lucas up and warmly said, "Now, you have always been a good boy. You never cry and you are a happy chappy." The warmness in her voice transformed to hatred, as she looked coldly at Lucinda and said, "Unlike that devil's spawn in there."

Lucas snuggled deeper into the Nanny's arms. The betrayal was too much for Lucinda, and the tenderness she felt for her brother evaporated.

From that day on she despised him. Whenever she could get away with it, she would bite, pinch and kick him. He never told on her. Silently understanding her; he loved her anyway.

By the time Lucinda was four she'd convinced herself that Lucas' favourable treatment was because he was a boy, and so she tried to turn him into a girl. Everything was a game to his light spirit, and he willingly dressed up in dresses, put clips in his hair and did everything that Lucinda asked of him.

Even when the Nanny was sacked by the parents after they cottoned onto the fact that Lucinda was being neglected, Lucinda didn't stop. She'd already been damaged. Nobody knew how much, until it was too late.

Lucas died the week before Christmas. On that day their mother had been on the phone frantically trying to recruit another Nanny, when Lucas and Lucinda had crept into the back garden towards the small pond that their father had made them that summer, and was now covered in ice.

Lucinda grabbed Lucas's Action Man model and threw it onto the frozen pond.

"Aw Lucinda! That's my favourite one." he cried and looked pleadingly at her.

"Go and rescue him then," she said.

He sighed heavily. Shoulders drooped, he trudged through the snow towards the pond. Lucinda followed. She had no idea of what would happen next. No conscious idea that is, and yet each one of her steps carried the imprint of the Grim Reaper's. Inside of her was an evil force – it was only a matter of time before something bad would happen.

Lucas stepped onto the frozen pond and turned back and smiled. She smiled and nodded back, urging him on. He took another step and slipped. They both laughed as he tried to get up. Once on his feet again, he took another step and another. Then the ice cracked, and he fell through the middle of the pond.

Lucinda gasped and quickly turned around to see if their mother had seen. Lucas's hands grasped the edges of the ice, as he frantically tried to pull himself up, steam pouring off the top of his head. For a second their eyes locked, mirroring each other's fear, and a second later he slipped further down, and the fear in his eyes slipped into her heart.

She stood as frozen as the ice on the pond with a gaping hole in her heart like the one he had fallen through. She knew she should get help. But maybe, just maybe with Lucas gone, they would love her more.

Seconds passed to minutes, and still she stood there, a part of her hoping he would re-emerge and another part feeling freer with each moment that he was gone.

Lucinda's mother charged into the garden and scolded, "What are you doing out here without a coat on?" She saw the hole in the ice and Lucas's Action Man near the side of it and screamed, "Lucas! Lucas!" and ran towards it.

The room spun around again and Lucinda found herself downstairs in their living room; the same room that she'd first entered when her father had been playfully tickling her mother. In the place of the sofa, was Lucas' tiny, open coffin. There were lots of people standing around morosely and talking quietly.

Infant Lucinda was sat on her new Nanny's lap trying to avert her eyes from the pitiful gaze of the mourners. Her father didn't look at her once. Her mother tried. At least she tried.

The whole house started to rapidly spin. When it slowed to a halt, Lucinda found herself in a large, stoic, cold house, that was as comforting as Lucas's coffin.

Pain, bitterness and sadness emanated from the walls as her parents walked around like empty shells. The house lacked the warmth of the previous home. There weren't even any photos. Not even one of Lucinda or Lucas. It was as if they were starting their lives again. This time as death warmed up.

It was enough for her parents to barely exist. They couldn't really live again without their son, and they couldn't really love their daughter – the one who'd watched him drown and done nothing to help.

# Thirty

Lucinda ruffled through the drawers of the baby wardrobe, and pulled out the old raggedy doll with 'Lilly' embroidered on the front of the dress. She threw it to the ground and continued to search through the baby clothes until she found the one she was looking for - a baby grow with, 'Mummy's Little Bunny' printed on the front.

She crouched onto the floor next to *her* baby doll and gently took off its clothes. Staring at its body, she cried, "What's the use? It's my fault you're dead." She blamed herself. Joseph had never wanted the baby.

#

*15 months earlier*

Lucinda had been so afraid, that during the eerie silence, whilst she'd waited in a state of delusion hoping that Joseph would surprise her by saying, "Darling, how wonderful!" she'd done a quick rerun in her head of what she was going to say. To her dismay, when she tried to regurgitate her rehearsed lines, she found that the words evaded her like a group of children afraid to face the punishment they were about to receive.

Timidly, she attempted to walk closer to him, hoping that a tender touch might soften the blow, but the heat of his fiery disposition, circling him like body guards, kept her at bay, and she silently, took a few steps back and cautiously sat down a few feet away from him.

After finding her voice which had hidden like a ghost from the seer, she urged it to step forward and pitch the options. With a stutter she said, "Well... a woman in such a situation has two options."

Upon hearing the word 'options,' Joseph slowly, and in disbelief, turned his head to face her. She didn't have the balls to look at him directly and before she was gagged by fear, carried on, "She can either have the baby, or she can have an abortion."

No sooner had the words left her mouth, they were violently shot down with daggers of hatred that flew from Joseph's penetrating glare. Like a knife throwing event gone terribly wrong, she was pinned to the spot. Hostility blazed from every cell in his body, and he coldly said, "The first one is not an option." His words lingered like a slow death, as he continued to glare at her with a conviction conveying the hatred of a thousand Nazi's towards one Jew.

And she cracked.

Her strength was pulled from under her, and the tree top that the unborn baby was precariously balanced on, broke. And just like in the nursery rhyme, "Rock-a-bye-baby," down came the baby, cradle and all. Lucinda, heartbroken, wanted to fall with it.

With that one look and sentence, she knew it was over. There was no further discussion about it.

Joseph rose like the almighty himself and left the room filled with the weight of a death summons.

She made the appointment for the abortion, and even went on the day but just couldn't go through with it. She managed to keep it a secret for another two months before her bump started to show.

In those two months, her relationship had grown stronger and when Joseph finally found out, he surprised her by not reacting in the same way as he'd done before. The baby's spirit, she believed had softened him.

#

Now she blamed herself. The lie she'd told was her karma. If only she'd told Joseph from the start, been strong enough from the start, then maybe her baby would never have died.

She looked at the baby doll's face and saw his lips move. In her head she heard him say, "Mummy," and she broke out in tears of joy. She reached out to him, and her happiness evaporated when she felt his cold plastic arm.

The ache in her body to hold her baby absorbed her with the pain of a thousand mothers mourning their dead children. The throb of their cries stampeded through her body like a harem of horses separated from their young, and the madness that accompanied the loss, strangled her from within, urging the hooves to press deeper into her throat. In her desire to die from the pain of her loss, she welcomed the lack of air. Death wouldn't come so easily, and her absorption in her own sadness empowered it to draw her to the window, where she gasped, sucking in the oxygen to further feed the mourning mothers screaming inside of her.

# Thirty-one

Magnolia hunted through the drinks cabinet for more alcohol and found a bottle of sherry. She quickly unscrewed the top and took a large swig and gagged. "Tastes like shit," she said and screwed the top back on and reached into the cabinet again and pulled out another bottle – dessert wine. It'll have to do, she thought and walked into the kitchen to get a bottle opener.

At that moment, she heard a car park up, and her heart leapt for joy, thinking that it might be Joseph coming back. She ran to the living room window and peered outside. When she saw a happy couple exit their car, her heart sank into her gut – so much so that she wanted to shit it out.

She was even more depressed now, and as the day's emotions piled on top of her, she wearily dropped onto the sofa and fell asleep.

#

She was woken by Ruby's screams and looked around

disorientated. She checked her watch: one-thirty am. At least the little shit had slept for more than five hours. She was probably hungry, thought Magnolia, but had neither the energy nor love to feed her child.

She looked over at the unopened dessert wine, and shook her head. No amount of alcohol was going to suppress her emotions. What she needed was a spliff. She was sure that Dan would have some weed stashed somewhere. Ever since the pregnancy he'd kept it hidden from her. Joseph often left her some but his infrequent visits meant that of late she'd hardly had a toke.

With the hope that she might find a few crumbs in her weed box, she first went to the bedroom to have a look. It was empty, not even a few specks of weed dust, just a couple of rizlas. Fuck. Where would Dan hide his supply?

The other night she was sure that he'd been mildly stoned. He claimed to have been at work and was tired. Could that have been a lie?

She walked into the bathroom and rummaged through the overflowing laundry basket and found the jeans he'd worn the night before. Searching through the pockets, she felt a tiny lump of something and pulled it out and screamed, "Yes!" She examined the small piece of hash as if it was a priceless diamond.

Always wanting more, she continued to search like a scavenger and pulled out another pair of jeans. Foraging in the pocket like a child searching for their last sweet, she felt a square plastic shape that before she'd even pulled out, knew was a condom.

She cautiously removed it from the pocket and furiously screamed, "The shit!" She stared at it as if it might transform into a gauze instead. Shocked to the core she couldn't believe that trustworthy, beaten down, honest Dan was fucking around.

This find sobered her up in an instant, and she walked determinedly into the living room and grabbed the bottle of dessert wine and furiously tried to open it. It finally popped, and she took a large swig, then another.

She stormed up to the table and took a rizla from the weed box, then dumped herself onto the sofa to roll a spliff. Her hands were shaking so much that the simple task became an enormous feat, and her normally perfect spliff looked like a giant, deformed penis instead. So long as it got her high. She lit it and took a big pull into her lungs. It calmed her down - enough to be able to think straight.

She racked her brains trying to think of possible times where she'd missed the signs. They must have been there; she was normally so astute. Dan claimed to work a lot, and to be honest she was grateful to have him out of the house as much as possible; no matter how lonely she was his presence only made her feel lonelier.

She hated him, and now more than ever. She took another drag, this time it hit her harder, and she sighed with relief. Maybe this was her way to get out of the relationship. She could get rid of him once and for all. After another long drag, she picked up her phone and called him.

Dan was walking through the hospital corridors when his phone rang and was surprised to see that it was Magnolia calling. She never called, and he thought that either something was terribly wrong, or in his deluded mind, that she missed him.

He immediately answered. "Hello darling," he said

"Get the fuck home," she screamed.

"What's happened? Are you ok. Is Ruby..."

She screamed louder into the phone, "I said get the fuck home!"

"Are you drunk?"

"Are you fucking deaf?"

"Ok darling, calm down, calm down. I'm only halfway through my shift."

"Now, you cunt. Now!" She ended the call.

Dan's hand was shaking as he put his phone back into his pocket. He was filled with dread, and knew that somehow, she'd found out. The anger in her voice had the same effect as food poisoning, and his stomach churned. He felt as if he was going to pass out or shit himself, or possibly even both.

His phone rang again. Magnolia was calling him. Tears filled his eyes, and though he couldn't bear another lashing, he answered it anyway.

"You cheating cunt!" she shrieked.

"What are you talking about?" he said with a squeaky voice that screamed - guilt.

"Oh, you know what I'm talking about. How long have you been fucking her?"

"I… I haven't?" He quickly slipped into the toilets for privacy, and also, in the event that he couldn't hold himself any longer.

"I found the condoms. We don't use condoms. In fact, we don't even have sex! Who is she? And you'd better tell me the truth?"

Dan was silent. Should he tell her?

"I know already that you're a lying cunt so -"

"Prostitute," he blurted, "I never made love to anyone. It was just a prostitute, just once. It meant nothing, Magnolia, nothing. You are my everything. You and Ru..."

"You'll never see us again!" She couldn't bear to hear his voice; his honest, disgusting voice. He'd actually admitted it. Silver tongue Joseph would have found a way out of this. "You disgust me," she said. "Where did you even get the idea?" Then she remembered her conversation with Joseph. Did he have something to do with this?

"You went with Joseph, didn't you?" she asked. The silence on the other end of the line was the only answer that she needed, but she wanted to hear him say it. "Didn't you?" she yelled.

"He took me. It was just once, we were drunk and a bit stoned and -"

And there was the confirmation - Joseph and Dan best friends. She really was in another league now; a league all on her own.

# Thirty-two

Joseph walked into the flat to find Lucinda curled up on the floor next to two dolls. He delicately picked her up and carried her limp body to the bed and slipped in next to her. She snuggled into his arms, and he dozed off feeling her warm breath gently stroking his chest.

In the sweet moment just before deep sleep, his heart thumped inside of him. Enlivened by an unusual force, his unconscious leapt like a man jumping from the blaze of the rising sun, as it dawned on him that he felt ready to love her. She needed help, but if she did recover, then he would at least try to be faithful and for that Magnolia had to go – to get completely out of his life.

He leant over and opened the drawer to his bedside table. Reaching in, he pulled out a small, red ribbon and stared at it, then got out of the bed and threw it into the bin.

A weight lifted from around his heart, and he walked back and climbed into bed.

With the decision made, and the cord partly severed, he peacefully fell asleep.

The loud ring of the phone startled them both. Joseph quickly answered it and checked the time. Only Magnolia would be crazy enough to call at two in the morning. He put the phone to his ear and was surprised to hear not Magnolia's, but Dan's frantic voice on the other end of the line.

"Shit, Joseph! She's gone nuts after finding condoms in my jacket pocket."

Joseph was relieved but still felt some apprehension, feeling certain that considering the content of this call that the next one would be from her. He shimmied to the edge of the bed and whispered, "Ok, but why are you calling to tell me this shit at two in the morning, man?"

Dan cringed with shame and hesitated before blurting out, "I told her it was all your idea."

"Ah Dan, you fucking pussy," said Joseph.

"I know, I'm an idiot, but she scared me. She started to say she would run off with Ruby and..."

"She's going to do no such thing, mate. She's bluffing. She's just vexed. Trust me, Dan, calm down - she won't do a thing."

Joseph knew Magnolia would never leave, and felt the cloak thrown over the dead, fall around him like a cascading avalanche, as he was taken by the ice-cold realisation that Magnolia would never leave *him*. And if he stayed in her manipulative clasp, then he would stay trapped under the heavy weight of her daily, decomposing love. It wasn't enough that he wanted to leave her, he had to move away, somewhere far and take Lucinda with him.

Although he felt for Dan and what he was going through, having made his decision he wanted out of the Magnolia drama once for all. "Mate, I'll talk to you again

278

when I wake up in a few hours. Trust me," he said, "she's not going anywhere."

He turned off his mobile. There was no way that he wanted to hear from Magnolia that night. He just wanted to hide under the snow, in the dark, until he found a way to shovel himself out.

# Thirty-three

Magnolia slammed the phone down in anger, muttering, "How can it be engaged at this hour?" She poured herself another glass of dessert wine and lit a cigarette. Like Sherlock Holmes, she tried to solve the mystery.

Joseph never switched off his phone. Ever since the baby, she'd insisted that he kept it on in case something should happen to her. She'd always used fear to control him. Why wasn't it working now?

After an agonising hour, the phone rang. It had to be Joseph, she thought, calling her back after switching on his mobile and seeing one of the many texts messages she'd sent him. Quickly answering the call, she said, "Hello."

"Magnolia, listen -" It was Dan.

She screamed as if stabbed in the heart and threw the phone down, furiously shouting into the empty room, "Fuck you, Dan!" repeatedly, before collapsing onto the floor and crying for Joseph.

Drunk and desperate, it took everything she had to stop herself from racing over to his house and breaking down his door. Even in her crazed state, she knew that if she did that then she may as well sign off her relationship with him forever. There was no other choice but to wait for him to come to her. The same old story; she was always waiting for him.

To preoccupy her mind and give herself hope, she sat trying to think of ways to get rid of Lucinda. Murder even came to mind, though unlike before, this time she would have to do it alone. As the fantasy of the dead Lucinda grew, she imagined being the person that Joseph turned to in his time of grief. The one who was there to save him.

Magnolia took comfort in this reverie. But nothing could shut out the incessant torture of Ruby's screams that ripped through the walls and tore at her nerves.

Unable to take the noise any longer, she rose from her secure spot on the floor and reluctantly fell out of her fantasy. Stumbling a little from the intoxication, she embarked on the pilgrimage towards Ruby's room.

Just before entering, she paused and braced herself as if she were about to walk into a frightening place. Sighing deeply, she swung the door open and fell back as she was hit with a torrent of screams. Reluctantly, she forced herself to wearily walk through them.

When she arrived at Ruby's crib, she saw that her face was red and her head covered in sweat. Her nappy had expanded from not being changed in over five hours and looked as if it was about to explode. Magnolia had not picked her up or fed her since she'd heard that Joseph had taken Dan to prostitutes. She couldn't bear to look at their creation and even had an urge to destroy it.

Ruby's dummy was by the side of her head next to a ruby stone Dan had given her. She thought about shoving the stone into Ruby's throat but knew her baby didn't know how to grasp yet. She'd have to wait a few more months before accidents like that could happen.

Not because she cared for her baby, but because she wanted quiet, she shoved the dummy into Ruby's mouth. The force of her cry spat it out again. Insistent on some silence, she took the dummy and stuck its teat into her dessert wine before placing it into Ruby's mouth again. Ruby scrunched up her face and tried to resist. After the seventh wine dipping, she eventually calmed down and with her eyes rolling back and lips painted red, she fell asleep.

Magnolia watched Ruby's small body peacefully rise and fall, hoping to see it suddenly stop. Cot death only happened to people who wanted to keep their babies, she bitterly thought, and even resented Ruby for sleeping since she could do no such thing.

Instead, she felt compelled to sit up all night calling Joseph, every hour, on the hour. To her dismay, each time the response was the same. She knew something was terribly wrong for both the home line to be engaged and his phone switched off.

After what seemed like an eternity the night gave way to day but didn't take with it the demons she'd been facing for the duration of the darkness.

#

In the early hours of the morning, a petrified Dan returned home from work looking meek and weary. The mere sight of him made her stomach turn, and she looked at him with hatred. Dan assumed this loathing glare was because of his infidelity with prostitutes, and felt terrible for betraying her trust and hurting her so much.

"Pack your things and go!" she screamed at him, stumbling over one of the empty bottles that lay strewn on the floor next to a torn picture of Joseph.

She couldn't bear to see Dan's face anymore. Finally, he had done one good thing in their relationship by succeeding in giving her a reason to get him out of her life.

Dan looked at the floor, and after seeing Joseph's picture in tatters, assumed the picture of him had already been chewed, spat out, or burnt in some hellish fury.

He was afraid of the sight before him. Magnolia looked like one of the crazy women he'd tended to on the psychiatric wards. Her hair was running in all directions trying to get away from her head; her clothes hung off her as if they were trying to escape from the mad fumes her body was exuding; and her make-up ran down her face, fleeing from the war that raged within.

He had no idea what she was capable of, but was too weak to make a real stand against her. Instead, he guardedly edged past where she was standing, and with his hands held up in surrender, tried to placate her by following her requests. "Ok, calm down", he said, "just let me pack a few things." He backed away. Not once daring to take his eyes off her.

Thankfully his clothes were in the wardrobe on the far end of the room, so as he packed, he could still face the door; the door that he could feel Magnolia hovering by, hopefully without a weapon.

He had to say something though. To at least try and reason with her a little, but he was too afraid to speak; whatever he said was sure to aggravate her further. He wanted to ask about Ruby, but that was another sore subject, and he daren't even go into the room to check on her. In truth, he was afraid of what he might find. The silence in the baby's room could be the silence that either heralded or followed death. The lack of action on his part just confirmed to him that he was a pathetic partner and a poor father. At a complete loss, he just chose to pack his things in silence.

Magnolia watched him through the crack in the door and scoffed in revulsion. She wasn't disgusted with what he'd done. No, she was just disgusted with him. With his fear of her and with the ease with which he let her dominate him.

Once Dan had a small holder (of exactly what, he didn't even know) he edged back out of the room and towards the front door. Comforted by the fact that he was near the exit, he mustered up the courage to speak. "Let's see a marriage counsellor," he said, the shake in his body reaching his voice.

Magnolia laughed at this hilarious suggestion, and Dan, who thought that he could fall no more, dropped further into humiliation. Breaking down into tears, he pleaded with her, "Magnolia don't give up on me. Please give me a second chance."

She shook her head and walked over to the music system. In just the same way as she drowned out Ruby's wails, she turned on the radio to full blast and faced Dan. She found an immense pleasure in watching him grow paler, as he desperately mouthed some words that became lost in the bass of one of favourite rave tunes.

Outwardly, and with no reason to hide her true emotion, she laughed as he stood crying in the doorway. Neither of them showed any embarrassment for the way they felt: Dan, a sorry mess of tears, and Magnolia, a malicious bitch, pleased with the destruction that she was instrumental in causing. She genuinely enjoyed the fact that Dan held himself responsible for everything. It was even more of a victory that he had no idea about her sordid affair with his close friend. It took a great effort on her part to stop herself from telling him there and then. But she knew that if it all came out, her chance of

284

having Joseph would be gone, and she couldn't take that risk - not even to hurt Dan.

The pleasure from this dark secret soothed her own angst from the past five hours of not being able to contact Joseph. Truly, he was the one she was livid with. How could he keep a secret from her? And to make matters worse, a secret with Dan. That betrayal was worse than anything. It showed her that Joseph was not containable or trustable, and she wasn't (as she had once thought) ever special to him.

#

Dan watched as Magnolia changed again, her smile fading as she stood looking through him. There was no fire in her, no emotion at all, and in that instant, he missed even her abuse; it was better than nothing. Defeated, and with his head bent low, he shuffled like a prisoner going to his cell, out of their door.

#

Magnolia was pleased with the outcome. Taking another cigarette from the box, she lit it and blew the smoke in Dan's direction, which followed him like a ghost out of their home.

# Thirty-four

*Joseph and Lucinda's last day alive - 10 am*

"Fucking hell, Ruby, SHUT UP!" screamed Magnolia and stormed into Ruby's room and over to the crib. Ruby's baby-blue eyes widened in terror at the sight of her fierce mother. For a second the sound of silence hit the air like a stink bomb, but Ruby, hungry, wet, thirsty, and most probably hung over - screamed even more loudly than before.

"Shut Up! Shut Up! Shut Up!" spat Magnolia, her venomous words spurting all over her.

It was pointless. Ruby was relentless. Desperate for some peace, Magnolia reluctantly pulled off her soggy t-shirt, soaked by the ripples of milk that streamed out of her nipples and down her belly. The bizarre twist of nature that her crying baby could rouse her breasts to drip milk, never ceased to revolt and infuriate her.

She begrudgingly picked Ruby up, and her drenched nappy fell off. In no mood to hunt for another one in the cesspit of a room, she wrapped a cloth around Ruby's lower half and stuck her nipple into her small mouth.

Ruby's red, wine-encrusted lips clasped onto the nipple with a fierce devotion to live. She had been saved by her father - her real father - Joseph, whose phone call had brought some humanity back into Magnolia's cold frame.

After waiting eight hours for her call to be returned, he'd finally called back at ten am. She thought he'd sounded a little weird on the phone; a thought that transformed into a feeling of doom that lingered after the call. Disturbed by this unwanted sensation, she sought to find somebody else to punish for her pain. Ruby was that outlet.

She was the big mistake. She was supposed to bring them closer together, and with that purpose unfulfilled, Magnolia had no need or fondness for her. She even hated the child's name, chosen in malice to hurt Lucinda, it now only reminded Magnolia of her.

More than a year had passed since Joseph and Lucinda had met. Nothing compared to the fifteen years she'd shared with him. But somehow Lucinda was winning. Despite all her scheming, Lucinda was his priority, and as the days went by, she felt him swimming further away from her, like the shark in his oceanic blue eyes.

Magnolia's panicked thoughts chaotically splashed through her. She needed more alcohol to drown them and pulled Ruby of her teat.

Ruby screamed.

"Fuck off," screamed Magnolia back at her and walked off into the living room. She grabbed the bottle of wine from the table and took the last swig. The numbing effect of the alcohol eased her pain a little, but not enough. She lit a cigarette and walked over to the faded vision board and kicked it. The board fell forward to reveal a camera. Lights went on in Magnolia's head.

Blackmail. She'd blackmail him into staying with her. For the first time in hours she smiled.

She picked up the camera and stood the vision board back up. Pausing for a moment, she bitterly stared at the board, at her lost dream - and stubbed out her cigarette onto one of the babies faces.

.

# Thirty-five

*Joseph and Lucinda's last day alive - 12 noon*

Joseph pulled up outside Magnolia's house and turned off the ignition. Not one part of him wanted to go in: into the realms of her madness. He had no idea how she would react to what he was about to tell her, or whether she would even believe him.

Placing his head onto the steering wheel, he racked his brains trying to work out what to say. He thought about saying something short and sharp like, Magnolia, it's over, but he choked on his own words. She would ask why, and he didn't want a big discussion. He didn't want her words in his head, crowding in on him like an army of angry bitches.

He thought about just telling her straight out, in one sentence, Magnolia, I love Lucinda. This also carried its risks. In his head, he saw Magnolia's face twist and realised that he was afraid of her. She wasn't as docile as Lucinda, and he didn't put it past her to grab a knife and stab him in a wild frenzy. No, there was no way that he could mention Lucinda's name, or that he loved her. It would kill Magnolia, and there was no telling how she might take her revenge.

If she were sane, he might be able to say, Magnolia, let's just be friends. But in his head, he heard her sarcastic laugh at the ludicrousness of that clichéd line; they'd never been just friends.

He thought about softening her first by making love to her, and then telling her with whatever words came out of his mouth. Shaking his head, he decided that wouldn't do either. They shouldn't make love. It might intensify the emotions. Hers, of course, not his.

In the end, and after much deliberation he knew that he couldn't pre-empt what he would say as he had no idea what kind of Magnolia was going to greet him. This notion took away the responsibility, and he relaxed and just prepared himself for whatever was thrown at him. Knowing he could handle it, whatever it was.

Ready for battle, he lifted his head up from the steering wheel and told himself, "It's over. It's over. It's over," then got out of the car.

Someone was singing Kumbaya My Lord, and he looked around for the culprit. There, sitting in the park opposite, was The Homeless Man, eyes closed and singing his heart out. The sight of him distracted Joseph from his own turmoil for a second, and he smiled to himself and said, "Jesus, who the fuck does he think he is?" He chuckled and thought that he did look a bit like Jesus.

Without opening his eyes, The Homeless man stopped singing and called out, "He who commits adultery lacks sense; he who does it destroys himself. Proverb 6:32."

"What the fuck." Joseph couldn't believe what he was hearing.

The Homeless Man smiled and said knowingly, "If a man is found lying with the wife of another man, both shall die, the man who lay with the woman, and the woman. Deuteronomy 22:22." Then he went back to singing with even more vigour than before.

He's completely lost it, thought Joseph and turned and walked towards Magnolia's house.

Each step he took sent waves of nausea to his stomach as the truth in The Homeless Man's words fell like bricks in his gut.

He approached the front door, his heart, thumping with the beat of a thousand warriors urging him on. Ready for war, he rang the bell and waited.

Excited by the shrill ring of the bell, Magnolia salivated like Pavlov's dogs in anticipation of the meal. Having showered, and even applied a little make-up she was ready for her seduction, and opened the door, oozing with a confidence that was bursting with desire.

Joseph walked in and looked her dead in the eyes. To not see the truth, she covered them with her hand, pulled back his head, and devoured his neck with the ferocity of a hungry vixen.

He hadn't anticipated this, and he surrendered; he would let her have him one more time. And so one last time, he kissed her back and grabbed her round buttocks, slipping his fingers into her already wet hole. He loved her. He hated her, and he was ready to let her go.

His cock grew harder, and he picked her up. She clasped her legs around his waist with such desperate force that he felt trapped. Today would be the last time that he'd be her prisoner, he told himself.

His fingers still inside of her, he walked them both to the bedroom and threw her onto the bed.

Under the watchful eye of the secret camera, he gave her one last meal, which she ate up with the passion of an impending finality.

#

Lying in his arms, she was not ready to hear the next few words that Joseph found slip from his mouth with the same ease as her pussy had done moments earlier. "Magnolia, I'm very fond you," he said.

"Fond?" she whispered quietly, and thought, Nothing like the word, love. "Fond?" she said again, letting each letter of the word seep in like a knife slowly puncturing her heart.

"But, don't you see, Magnolia, this has to end. I can't live a double life anymore. It's tiring me, and it's time for us both to grow up and out of this." He paused, expecting her to fill the silence - nothing - unable to bear it himself, he continued, "you will always be in my heart, but focus on Dan - on your family."

Magnolia jolted up as the previous night's pain came speeding at her like an unstoppable train. "My family? she shrieked like a wild street cat. "This," and pointing to the space between them, she screeched, "this is our family!"

Joseph knew that this would never end; knew that he would never able to reason with her and quickly started to dress. Pulling on his jeans, he said, "There's nothing more to say, Magnolia."

She felt tears well up in her eyes like an accelerated cancer, and started to cry. "You can't leave me. I don't love Dan. You are my life."

Joseph looked at her sitting like a small child on the bed, peering up at him in desperation. Unexpectedly, a rare phenomenon occurred, and he felt all her pain.

The warriors beat in his heart, giving him the strength to end it, once and for all, and taking a deep breath, he said, "I love Lucinda. She is my life. She's the one who's going to be my wife."

The release of those words were like explosives from a bomb, and the whole room shuddered in shock. Magnolia was stunned from the blast. Her face turned an ashen grey, as death crept up before his very eyes.

He waited for her to say, I'll tell Dan, I'll tell Lucinda, I'll ruin your life, but she surprised him by saying nothing at all. Her silence, though a welcome relief, was out of character. A part of him saw this as his opportunity to leave, another part wanted to understand what her next move would be.

He sat down next to her and held her soft, clammy hand. She turned her head towards him, and her eyes, heavy with the weight of darkness, called out to the spirits to take her. Still burdened with the vision of him, she told him, "Just go! Go now and never come back."

Her words slid like shards of glass from her mouth, slicing the cord attaching them. The shrapnel from her blasted heart blew into the space between them, and the ashes of fifteen years dispersed into the air.

Finally separated, Joseph, one half of a Siamese twin, walked out of the room. Moving freely away, he glided like a dove towards the door.

And then there was one.

#

Seconds turned to minutes before Magnolia moved from her spot in front of the drying cum stain on the bed. In that time, her life flashed before her, and she laid it to rest. Her future was a blank space that she didn't know how to, or want to fill. No matter what she did, it was over. Joseph was not the type of man to verse finality if it were not really the case.

Whatever revenge she decided to take was futile. Joseph had had enough. He was finally ready to be free of her and accept the consequences, whatever they were.

Detached, Magnolia rose, the second half of the severed Siamese twin and took the camera from its spot. She attached it to the computer and with nothing to lose, burned their sex onto a CD.

Joseph was gone and with him her desire for life. He'd ignited her flame, and he'd put it out. The control had always lain with him, and despite all her manipulative attempts to control him, he had the final say.

She didn't care for Dan or her baby. Whatever became of them was of no interest to her. Surprisingly, Lucinda was the only one she had an ounce of emotion for, and she wanted her to know the truth. She wanted her to suffer. Would Lucinda leave him if she knew? She doubted that very much but didn't have the energy to care.

With her other missions failed, she resorted to putting her life energy into this last one, and used all her reserves to parcel up the CD. After addressing it to Lucinda, she called DHL and with nothing else to do, stripped the bed.

# Thirty-six

*Joseph and Lucinda's last day alive - 2 pm*

Lucinda stripped off and stood naked in front of the mirror to examine her frail, bony body.

At the same time, seven miles across the city, Magnolia stood naked in front of the mirror and looked at herself one last time.

#

Lucinda's ET-like fingers moved like stick insects following the contours of her bones. Her ribs, obviously visible, brought a smile to her thin lips, as did her concave belly, dipped like a ditch to reveal two hip bones jutting out like mountains and standing proudly by the valleys of death leading to her crotch.

#

Magnolia's shorter, softer hands, slid gently over the smooth, meaty skin of her body, caressing her large bosoms, which hung like full moons. Her hands, slightly quivering from the effect of the alcohol and the shock of unrequited love, moved down to her waist that curved in to form a crescent on either side of her body.

#

Lucinda slipped her hand down one of the valleys of death and walked her fingers along the plank of her pubic bone, before dipping them into the folds of her pink, soft lips.

#

Magnolia's hand slipped over the meat of her hips and the other reached behind to grasp her large, firm buttocks. Their roundness reminded her that she'd never felt whole, and the emptiness pressed all around her. Quickly, and to move away from the impending suffocation, she slid her hand to the front of her body and glided it over her bald, neat pussy. But she dared not go inside; she still felt Joseph and wanted to keep that sensation for as long as she lived.

#

Lucinda let one of her hands fall behind to take her small round cheek and squeeze it, like a mother might on her beautiful cherub's face. Reaching down to her thighs, as fragile as branches sprouting from her hips, she admired their stick-like forms.

#

Magnolia squeezed her hands around the tops of her

thighs, which stood strong like tree trunks. She felt the muscular power of the force that lay within. Her body responded to her touch, and just as she started to feel, she stopped.

#

Lucinda, satisfied with her tiny form, threw on her dressing gown. Ignoring the groan in her belly, she walked away from the mirror.

#

Magnolia slipped on her silk negligee and ignoring the cry from her baby, picked up the parcel and waited by the door.

# Thirty-seven

*Joseph and Lucinda's last day alive - 2 pm*

With Magnolia finished with, it was time for Joseph to face Dan.

He'd called him earlier, but the laborious sex session with Magnolia had lasted much longer than he would have liked, and he was late for their lunch appointment. It was at their regular spot: a cheesy, cheap cafe they'd often frequented for their hangover, recovery breakfasts.

Joseph walked in, and was surprised by Dan's bedraggled appearance. He'd never seen him look so rugged before. His hair, normally gelled to the right side, was sprouting in all directions; his smooth skin was covered in facial stubble; his clothes were creased, sitting awkwardly on his body in shame; and his normal erect posture was slumped towards the ground, as if he were carrying a dead weight.

Again, like earlier, Joseph tried to prepare for this meeting but there was no easy way to tell Dan, and it couldn't have come at a worse time.

He approached the table where Dan was sitting and took a deep breath before cautiously sitting down opposite him. Smoke blew in his direction, and he was startled to see Dan with a cigarette in his hand. The righteous non-smoker (spliffs didn't count in Dan's book) was obviously in dire straits.

"Thank God I have you. Magnolia's kicked me out. I'm so fucking...." he broke down into quiet sobs.

"Mate, it's going be ok. Magnolia, she -"

"She fucking hates me, that's what," wept Dan, as he wiped his tears with the quivering cuff of his shirt. His phone rang. "Maybe it's her," he said, frantically pulling it out of his pocket. His face dropped when he saw that it wasn't. "Someone calling from the hospital," he said disappointed and silenced the call.

"Mate, don't lose it."

"I'm going to call her," he said, still desperately clutching his phone.

"No, leave it. Good to keep her on her toes. Like I told you before, you shouldn't be too available. Treat 'em mean, keep 'em keen."

Dan knew that he was right and put his phone onto the table. "How do you do it Joseph? You always come up tops. You can treat them anyway and they still want you"

"Not always. Just seems that way."

"When have you ever lost a woman? Never, right?"

"I lost my mother. Nothing hurt more." A soft silence permeated the air. It was the first time that he'd ever talked about his mother and Dan felt even closer to him. "Sometimes I see her in Lucinda," said Joseph, more to himself, "maybe it's what's keeps us together. There's something different about her. It's almost like she borders between life and death. It's as if she touches both worlds." Dan's quiet sobs brought him back into the moment. "Sorry mate, going on like that."

"You see, your life is on track, man. I'm a fucking failure."

"My life's on track? Are you fucking serious? I'm living with nutter, and I can't even leave her, cause I, well I think I love her."

Dan couldn't believe what he was hearing and for a second, stopped sobbing.

"I called that place you told me about," continued Joseph, "think I should go with her. You know support her and shit for a few days at least." He sat back in his chair and lit a cigarette. "Then I need to get away for a while."

Someone else leaving him, thought Dan and sobbed louder. Joseph edged closer to him, aware that people were looking at them and put his hand over his, hoping to comfort and quieten him. It had the adverse effect and Dan only cried harder. "Why did I do it? I had a good woman." He looked pleadingly into Joseph's eyes hoping for some clemency. He just wanted his friend to tell him that it was all going to be ok.

"She wasn't an angel," was all Joseph could bring himself to say. It was also a way he thought might lead into the dreaded truth that he had come to reveal.

"Yeah, all right, I know she was a handful. I mean, everyone has their difficulties, right? But at least she never cheated on me," said Dan, his large, brown eyes full of regret and sorrow.

Now was Joseph's chance. He had the opening he needed. It couldn't have come more easily. The pause that followed precipitated the perfect path that was abruptly diverted when Dan's pager bleeped, startling them both.

Dan hurriedly grabbed his pager, praying that it was Magnolia. In this case, Joseph was the one given the reprieve. "The day couldn't get worse," he said, getting up from the table after reading the message, "I've got to go to the hospital. Fucking disaster. Some nutcase has thrown herself off the bridge into oncoming traffic, causing a pile up. Ah, shit man, I haven't slept a wink, I need some coke or something." His voice oozed with desperation, as he viciously rubbed his tired eyes.

"Don't be a fucking idiot, just have a red bull," said Joseph, half pleased, and half pissed that he didn't have to go through with telling Dan... yet. Perhaps, he conjectured that he was destined to talk to Lucinda first. Lucinda, who he knew – no matter what – couldn't live without him.

# Thirty-eight

*Joseph and Lucinda's last day alive - 2.30 pm*

A knock at the door interrupted Lucinda's scouring of the five newspapers that had been delivered that day. Rising from her comfortable position, she was pleasantly surprised when she opened the door to find a man wearing a DHL uniform and holding a parcel addressed to her.

Quickly signing the form, she excitedly tipped the courier, unaware that this wasn't part of the custom. Nevertheless, he received the gift with pleasant surprise whilst she opened hers with images of a sexy negligee, a necklace or diamond ring crossing her mind. The fantasy came to sudden halt when instead she found a CD with the words, "U HAVE BEEN DECEIVED," written in black marker across it. Her stomach sank. Already, without playing it, she imagined what she would see.

The courier shared the same vision and said, "Sorry, love." She looked vehemently at him as if he were somehow responsible. "Don't shoot the messenger," he said and scarpered off.

Lucinda stepped back into the house and over to the computer. She took a deep breath and put the CD in. Sitting apprehensively on the edge of the chair, she squeezed her eyes shut, praying to see a wedding proposal from Joseph instead of what her intuition warned her was about to be revealed.

Opening her eyes, she pressed play and saw her worst fear jump from the screen. She only watched for a few minutes, but it was enough to see Joseph in doggy position, passionately bent over and kissing the neck of a girl with large breasts and long, dark hair.

Before she saw who it was, she retched and ran into the bathroom, holding her hand over her mouth to catch the spurts of vomit that shot like sewage from a burst pipe. Covered in her undigested lunch, she stumbled into the bath, crying and scrubbed her body raw like a rape victim - the rape of her heart and her soul. Despairingly, she screamed, "I can't live like this; I can't live like this!" and slumped down into the bath as water from the shower rained down on her.

After an hour in this position, she eased herself out and grabbed Joseph's towel hanging from behind the door. Wrapping it around her body, she buried her face into the soft folds of the material. Joseph's smell seeped into her, and she let the towel drop to the floor by her water infused feet that had wrinkled like an old lady's. Out of nowhere she heard the same voice from the reincarnation book in the library say, "Oh, thank fuck for that. Finally, you're on your way."

Lucinda didn't understand where the voice had come from or what she meant. One thing she did understand was that not even with the evidence in her face could she stop loving him.

There was no point in confronting him. He would talk her round, and she would still not leave. With no self-respect left, she had nothing. Her reservoir of pain spilled over, and the fallout paving a slippery, bloody path that once stepped upon, took her like a conveyor belt towards death.

She stepped out of the bathroom and into the hallway where she saw the baby doll appear as a real baby again, standing near the cupboard in the hallway, smiling and nodding its head. Lucinda remembered what was inside: Joseph's prize possession – a hunting rifle. Peace filled her as she imagined the sound of the gunshots - BANG, BANG, BANG.

Her ears became deafened by the imaginary blast, and her eyes, already burnt by the truth on the tape, closed, as the smell of gunfire filled the air, and she tasted death.

She took the gun from the cupboard and walked into the bedroom and sat on the bed. Still perceiving the baby doll as a real baby, she saw it run to her side and say, "Come to me, Mama."

She reached down to touch him, and he disappeared. "I'm coming baby, I'm coming," she said as she undid the safety cap on the rifle and looked inside to see if it was loaded. It was. She flicked the rifle back into place and put it to under her chin. Eyes squeezed shut, her finger on the trigger, her whole body was shaking. She was so close, and then in her head she saw an image of Joseph and took her finger off the trigger.

Breaking down into sobs, she let the hunting rifle drop to the ground and looked at the empty space where the baby doll had just been. "I'm coming my love, I'm coming," she said, "but I'm not coming alone. We'll be a family again."

She got off the bed and slipped the hunting rifle under it.

# Thirty-nine

*Joseph and Lucinda's last day alive - 3.30 pm*

An hour later, Joseph returned home to find Lucinda sitting at the table, cutting out articles from a newspaper. He touched her gently on the back of her neck and leaned over her shoulder to read the headline. *The Bobbitt Effect – Mrs. Prim Loses her Rag and Kills her Cheating Husband.*

Lucinda claimed her hobby of collecting newspaper articles moved her in some way. It moved Joseph in some way too: moved him closer towards her. He liked her idiosyncrasies, and this one in particular. Although he knew she cut things out, he'd never actually bothered to see what the articles were about. Seeing the violent nature of the one in her hand aroused his curiosity to see what the others were. He wanted to know what else it was that moved her in some way.

After sticking the cut article into her scrapbook, Lucinda left it on the table to take another shower. She needed time alone. The mere sight of Joseph plunged her heart into a shredder.

Silently, she entered the bathroom which still carried the faint, pungent smell of her vomit, and stepped into the bath. She turned on the tap and let the water fall onto her, soothing her like the tears that she was no longer able to cry.

#

After watching her tiny frame exit the room, Joseph picked up the scrapbook and flicked through. It surprised him to see that all the articles were about death, and all but one had occurred from murder: *The Tragic Poisoning of Infants Lilly and Kyle.*

He continued to skim through the articles until he got to the very first cutting, and the blood drained from his face when he saw the article that he hadn't seen for more than fifteen years. He read the headline out loud in amazement, "Year Head Found Torched and Murdered in Home."

Shaking in disbelief, he scanned the article: *Mr. Bianca, a well-respected member of the community, was found dead in his burning home yesterday evening ....Police are asking any witnesses to come forward... There are no suspects... Police were shocked to find child pornography at the teacher's home, and a thorough investigation is being carried out....*

Joseph put the scrapbook down and poured himself a large glass of wine to absorb the shock. He downed it like a shot and picked the scrapbook up again.

Lucinda quietly crept up behind him, scaring him a little. His rock-solid nerves had already been bulldozed by the day's events and seeing that article was like a punch in the gut that left him winded.

"That guy Mr. Bianca was a neighbour," she said, pointing to the article.

"Really?" he questioned, unsure about whether to believe her or not.

"Yeah. I hardly remember him though. But I do remember that he was a bit weird. I didn't like him at all. Then when I was about eight-years-old I found that article about his death in my mother's cupboard. It was the first one I ever collected."

That bastard probably molested her too, thought Joseph, feeling even more justified for murdering him now.

"They never caught the guys that did it you know," she said with a twist in her voice, which led Joseph to question if she knew that he was the culprit. He immediately dismissed this thought and cursed himself for being so paranoid. Everybody around him was acting crazy. He was determined not to go down with them.

"By the sounds of things, he deserved it. Who cares?"

"So, you think it's ok to take the law into your own hands?"

"Sometimes it's the only way," he said with no idea that he was giving her permission to kill him.

Closing the scrapbook, he noticed that there was one blank page left. He placed it onto the table and pushed it away like a lover he no longer wanted the company of, and quietly wondered what murder might fill that final blank space.

"It's nearly finished," she said, smiling coyly and walked a few steps away from him, stopping in the doorway of the bedroom to gaze at a bird perched on the window ledge.

He didn't take his eyes off her and watched as her towel fell slightly, revealing the delicate frame of her shoulder. He wanted to go over and kiss it, but stood still, feeling the love moving in the space between them.

Everything about that moment confirmed to him that he wanted her, perhaps forever - she was his partner in life.

As if she'd just heard his thoughts out loud, she turned round and smiled at him. He smiled back and walked towards her, took her hand and led her to the bedroom - just as the bird flew off the ledge.

#

For a second, Lucinda thought she felt it too: his genuine love. Then the image of him on the computer shot out at her like a ghost, and she recoiled.

#

At the foot of the bed, Joseph lifted her onto the mattress and kissed her, unaware that the smell of another woman on him was murdering her heart.

Lucinda, The Martyr let the pain absorb her while Joseph took her into his arms, for what he had no idea would be the last time and began to stroke her beauty spot.

# Forty

In just the same way as she'd seen her life in film format when she'd first died, Lucinda saw it again, but this time in the form of a written script. Like a savant genius, she read it in a flash, but with a new perspective of the events that had occurred.

Her experiences in the Female Divine Courtroom had opened her to some truths about herself, enabling her to feel (albeit temporarily) beyond her reactions and delve into the core spirit of who she was.

The position of power she found herself in enabled her to see that she hadn't always identified with the victim. At one time, she had been a fighter and a warrior, with the same spirit as the suicide bomber, and the same delusion that came out of a need to be loved.

It was in fact when intimate love (within the realms of a relationship) entered the arena of her life that her foundation instantly weakened, and she crumbled.

One of her major limitations was that she never owned herself in that destruction, instead seeing it as something happening to her, rather than as something she was instrumental in causing. Thus, Lucinda became a victim of her resignation. A victim to the sorrow that had absorbed her time and time again in her relationships with men, and in her relationship with life itself.

She wasn't so unlike Joseph in that respect. However, in his case, his limitations were born from anger, and an adolescent need to break free from all ties. He didn't want to be held down by the illusionary trap that he saw in everything, especially in his relationships with women. Never wanting to be owned by them, he didn't own himself in the process and the very real truth that his connection to life was what bound him to people, and the relationships that he felt trapped by.

Joseph and Lucinda's dramas played out separately, attracting one to the other, and they found comfort in this mix. It was in this way that their egotistic addictions seeped out like glue to bind them together.

But not once on earth did they make use of their wisdom or heart intelligence. So, instead of growing beyond, they grew deeper into those patterns, where neither was able, nor willing, to break free.

That was until they entered the Divine Courtrooms and were given another chance.

# Forty-one

"We have a guest speaker," said The Chair, "who will reveal to us the last of the Universal Laws. You won't see him, but you'll hear him."

"Bloody typical! said the Old Caww, "after years of being in ere, you wanna torture me with the sound of a man, but not the sight, or smell or feel.. "

"Shut it Granny!" shouted Magnolia.

"Oh, well let's see *you* in a few hundred years when you're gagging for it," said the Old Caww, knowingly.

Magnolia went a shade paler; it was after all quite possible.

A loud cough resonated throughout the room, refocusing the attention, and The Formless Voice started to speak. "The Universal Law of Gender states that everything is male and female - and what I mean by that is that everything has masculine and feminine elements from humans to plants. There are no exceptions. The elements must work together. In just the same way as you need two hands to clap, you need both masculine and feminine elements in the world. There needs to be a union of the two, a cooperation, collaboration and a dance. Sadly, men and women in today's world have forgotten how to dance, preferring to battle in a fight that can never be won, instead of dancing together in the music of life.

"The Law of Gender has another interpretation for it is not just about this union but also about patience. You see the Law of Gender is also the Law of Creation and everything that is created needs a gestation period to come to fruition. It is the same with our goals. When the time is right they will happen."

#

The lights went out in both the Male and Female Divine Courtrooms, as if it were the end of a stage performance, and then came on again. Joseph stood baffled as he watched the men change the order of the room.

He had no idea what would follow and didn't like the not knowing. The familiarity of the Courtroom had started to feel like a safe place and now with that gone, he was afraid that he might go down a level, rather than up.

Lucinda, too, was confused. Where was she supposed to go now? Everybody else seemed to know what to do.

With both Lucinda and Joseph looking lost and bewildered, The Courtrooms merged. The invisible ethers shifted onto the same dimension, and Joseph saw the females wandering out through the males, and the males through the females, totally unaware of each other.

Lucinda saw the same scene, as she watched the Old Caww move through a man with a huge cock tied to a chain around his neck. The circus she witnessed stapled her further to the ground, and she looked down at her feet, urging them to move.

They didn't.

But she did see another pair of feet in front of hers. Cautiously, she looked up and saw Joseph.

"Joseph! I, I'm sorry," she said, a multitude of emotions washing through her.

Joseph lovingly stroked her face and passionately drew her into his arms and said, "Why did you do it? I was going to marry you. You were the one for me."

She sobbed uncontrollably and buried her face in the crease of his neck. Gently peeling her face away from the bedding of his skin, she stayed locked in his arms and said, "I love you so much. Please forgive me."

Joseph squeezed her tightly and said, "I played my part. Maybe it was always going to be this way. Maybe not"

"If only you hadn't cheated so much," she said in a baby voice.

He pulled back from her in utter disbelief. It was clear that she was sorry but it seemed not sorry enough. Releasing her from his grasp he said, "This has nothing to do with me Lucinda. You chose to kill us in the end. I didn't put the fucking gun to my own head and blow up my face, did I? You did!"

"Calm down Joseph," she said and started to cry again. "I said I was sorry, and I truly am."

"What's the point of being sorry if you're going come out with crap like that?" Lucinda looked baffled, and he shook his head and said, "Jesus Christ, didn't you learn anything?"

"Well, yes. Stuff. So much stuff. So many stories. I just haven't been able to digest it all."

"Well maybe if you stopped crying you'd be able to."

"Please don't be mad at me. I love you."

"You love me? We're dead, Lucinda! Dead!"

"But at least we're together," she said, meekly tilting her head to the side and looking up at him with doey eyes, "forever."

"Together forever in hell! What does it matter now anyway? I've accepted what I've done. Have you?"

Lucinda was quiet. Her time in the Courtroom had been intense, and she felt as if she had grown. But was it enough? Perhaps not, thought Joseph, and he let go of her body, he let go of her heart, he let go of the responsibility and took a step back.

Together they floated above the Courtroom, as the people below them started to exit, moving through each other like ghosts. The more sensitive souls sensed a disturbance when another energy moved through them. But in the same way on earth when humans feel a sudden shiver down their spines, the dead too shirked it off, and carried on their way.

New people arrived into the Courtroom, no longer Joseph and Lucinda's living room but Magnolia and Dan's.

Lucinda and Joseph stood staring at each other. After some time, they were drawn to look below.

The ethers separated again, and, as before, they saw what appeared to be the same space, each only seeing one dimension of it: Joseph saw the males gathering in one ether and Lucinda, looking in the same direction, saw the females gathering in another. She noticed that although the room was different, some of the same characters were still there. The Old Caww, for one, was still bitching as it was announced that a young woman would be the first to take the stand.

#

Magnolia sat and waited in what looked exactly like her

old living room and watched new people arrive. They were mainly strangers to her, except for the Old Caww, who was there again.

"Fucking just wanna punish me, don't they? How long am I gonna have to wait for her to get her arse back 'ere? Oh, oh, I killed my lover. Get over it! What's it been ten years in earthly time since the last time I was 'ere?"

"Ten years," murmured Magnolia quietly to herself.

"Welcome again everybody," said The Chair. "We're just waiting for our new participant. Let's see where she is now."

#

Ruby, ten-years-old, and wearing the heart shaped ruby stone as a necklace around her neck was sitting with an Indian Yogi on a beach in Southern India and diligently listening to him talk.

"You become what you mediate on, ya," said the Indian Yogi. "One of the great Esoteric rules, a little like the Universal Law of Vibration we talked about yesterday."

"What about the patterns? What about the monkey mind?" she asked.

"Ah, ya… the monkey mind." The Yogi laughed and said, "It takes years to calm him down. Just stop feeding him the bananas." He smiled at her, and she smiled back. "Another Esoteric rule, ya, is what you don't use becomes obsolete. Just don't do and the mind will follow."

"I thought that you said that the thought comes first."

"Ya, ya, but the action solidifies the thought. You can't always stop the thought, but by being aware of it you can bring your attention back to the breath, and the thought slips away - and even if not, you can choose not to do the action. Practice Ruby, practice."

Ruby sighed. He made it sound so easy.

"Anything and everything is possible," said the Yogi, as he collected the books off the sand. "Be happy anyway. Go play." He put his hands into a prayer position and said, "Namaste."

Ruby smiled and put her hands into prayer position and repeated, "Namaste."

"We carry on later."

She nodded and skipped into the sea.

Small waves crashed around her, inviting her to ride them. She did and body surfed like a pro.

Nearby was a Young Woman standing in the water and crying. Ruby stood still and looked over at her and asked, "Heartbroken?"

The Young Woman wiped her tears and asked, "Are you a mind reader or something?"

"No. Not really when you believe that there is only one mind - one consciousness."

"Cor dear, that's a bit deep for a kid," she said, a smile creeping up onto her face.

"It's the Law of Mentalism. But don't worry. Today you love him. Tomorrow, you'll hate him."

"Is that so."

"Yes, the Law of Polarity."

The Young Woman looked puzzled.

Ruby swam over to her and grabbed her hand, "Be happy. Let's have some fun. Come. I'll teach you to catch waves."

The Young Woman shrugged and together they started to catch the waves.

After a while the sea became calm, and The Young Woman chaotically carried on trying to catch the small waves.

316

Ruby was standing still and watching her, "If you keep going for all the small waves," she said, "you're going to miss the big one."

The Young Woman stood still. Something about what Ruby said hit her.

"Let me teach you how to catch waves properly," said Ruby. "Just copy me."

She stood with her legs and arms apart in the Yoga Warrior position, her face turned towards the horizon. "Stand still and imagine the waves moving towards you; focus on one wave - your wave. Become that frequency to attract that wave. It's there, you can call it to you. The Universal Law of Vibration."

The Young Woman looked at the bumps of waves heading their way and said, "They all look the same to me."

"That's because they are. So are we. There is no separation in anything. The Universal Law of Correspondence."

"But then how will I know that it's my wave?"

Ruby shook her head from side to side, like an old Indian yogi and put her hand over her heart and said, "Because you will feel it."

The Young Woman instinctively put her hand over her own heart.

"But then, even when you feel it, whatever it is, remember that it won't last. Everything comes to an end and begins again. The Universal Law of Rhythm."

"So, if he stops loving me and I still love him, will he love me back?"

"Maybe he won't. But you'll be loved back. What goes around, comes around. The Universal Law of Cause and Effect."

"Ah Karma! I know about that."

"Knowing is one thing. Believing is another, and patience is key. You must be patient and trust that what's for you won't pass you. The Universal Law of Gender."

The young woman laughed and asked, "Are you some kind of yogi prodigy?"

"No. But I spend a lot of time with the yogis here in India."

"Lucky that you learn these things now."

"One day I'll forget them."

"What makes you say that?"

"That's what happens when you grow up. You lose the magic and then spend your whole life looking for it in another person or thing, when it's already inside of you, is you. Except most people don't believe that because they are afraid."

"Afraid of what?"

"Dying. It's crazy really. From the time we are born there is only one thing that is guaranteed and that is that we will die."

"Are you not afraid of dying?"

"I don't know. I guess so. But I'm learning that love is the magic and love and loss are connected. So, everybody is afraid to love because no matter what, they'll one day lose what they love. So that's why we don't truly love and that's why we lose the magic."

"You won't," said The Young Woman assuredly.

"There's a long road yet," said Ruby and winked. A large wave came towards them, and she raised her eyebrows as if this was the one, then waited for the right moment - and caught it.

The Young Woman watched as it carried her to the shore. "Weird and wonderful kid," she said to herself. Then a large wave came towards her and just as Ruby had done, she waited for the right moment - and caught it.

"That's just a glimpse," said The Chair. "Silly girl, she could have avoided coming here. Her script could have been so different. She had many crossroads. Many opportunities to take another path, for she was shown."

Levitating a foot off the floor, The Chair floated like a light paper plane past those nearest to her and ran her soft hand over their faces. "To be born," she said in a measured voice, "is like winning the lottery." She paused in front of a girl and firmly took her face into her hand. Looking deeply into her eyes she said, "It gives you many opportunities, and though there is an element of destiny, it's not restricted by limitless possibility."

Letting go of the girl's face, she hovered over to the next one and said, "You, like Lucinda, had many choices in your life, but failed to see them as such, choosing to celebrate your failures instead of meditating on the good things. In this way, you neglected your inherent ability to actualize the vision in your mind created by your heart's intelligence." The Chair floated towards another lady. "Feeling the truth in your heart and believing..." she said and paused in front of her, "you never truly believed, and so you became the negative things you meditated on. You created your destiny and yes, you were given a hard life, but you chose it. Just like you will choose the next one. Your soul is your guide. Nevertheless, if you wrap it in cling film, you cannot feel its breath; you become distant from it, and closer to the conditional limitations that cause you so much angst.

"You've all suffered but you chose this life to grow from it. You know this place is not the end. And so, within all your lifetimes, you had the same choices to make: to either take advantage of the opportunity to grow out of your limitations, reactions and reluctance - to truly love, by countering your patterned response; or to do as you all did, which is what you have done for many lifetimes, and that is to be absorbed in the drama and repetition of your suffering. Same old story, just a different stage and actors."

The Old Caww let out a guffaw, as if she were spitting out an unsavoury meal and said, "Not me! I haven't even had the fucking chance to live that many times. I been stuck in this God forsaken place for blooming years!"

The Chair ignored her, but noted her disruption, which unbeknownst to the Old Caww had cost her another three Courtroom sittings, without the privilege of talking about herself and perhaps moving on. The Chair would deal with the Old Caww much later, but for now addressed them all and said, "You know what your choices were. You remember them, don't you?"

#

Lucinda listened from above the Courtroom and thought that she did indeed remember the times when she'd had choices to make. Times when her desires overrode her reason; or her reason killed her passion; or her passion became warped by jealousy; or her jealousy ruled her heart; or when she just didn't listen to her heart. Those were the times when she re-did what it was that she'd done for many lifetimes, by ignoring the pulsing, intelligent heart-conscience that was the source, and which urged her to move on. It was a blessing to feel it and a criminal act to ignore it. Thus, she imprisoned herself with a belief that she was in fact separate from it.

One such crossroad was when she'd first met Joseph. Warning bells had rung out, and she knew that she'd been with this soul before. Their chemistries were so intertwined that she couldn't escape being with him. It was karmic. But she did have a choice, because she'd been given the sign.

Later, when being with him started to break her heart, she'd had another choice: to change her behaviour and perhaps change him in the process, or to leave. She had chosen the easiest, most painful and familiar choice, which was to stay in the same pattern and be ruined.

Somehow in that Courtroom she understood. She was familiar with the concept and the feeling of the crossroads. She knew exactly what The Chair meant.

#

"Now back to the present," continued The Chair, "Ruby chose her path and ten years on in earthly time, she is here."

Ruby, now twenty-years-old, appeared in the front of the room with her back to everybody, holding an empty bottle of whisky and swaying from intoxication.

Magnolia stared intensely at her. Ruby, felt it and turned round - completely off her face and sauntered towards her. Nodding her head in an Indian fashion she said, "So here we are."

"Get her away from me," screamed Magnolia, "it's because of her that I don't have him. Her and that skinny little bitch, Lucinda."

Lucinda was flabbergasted and tried to push herself down from where she was floating so that she could face Magnolia. "You fucking whore," she screamed down, to no avail. Somberly she asked, "How could I have not remembered her name?" Turning to Joseph, who was still by her side, she said, "I get now why I never met Magnolia. Joseph, you're unbelievable. I loved you so much!

"What's love without sacrifice?" he said.

"I sacrificed everything for you!"

"And that's the problem. Everything - everything YOU wanted for yourself. You didn't really love ME!"

"Yes, I did!"

"You didn't love me enough the way I was and you didn't love me enough to let me go. You loved me because you were too afraid to be alone. You couldn't even let go of our dead son."

He moved back further from her and looked down into the Male Divine Courtroom where an older Dan stood bewildered, looking as messed up as he'd been when Joseph had last seen him.

A familiar male voice resonated around the room, and The Formless Voice said, "Dan, please take your seat." Dan looked frantically around the room to see where the voice had come from.

Joseph was saddened to see his friend with the same panic stricken expression on his face as when he'd left him. He didn't know Dan had died, and he thought that he must have done something terrible to be there.

Dan screamed, "That recording! That fucking recording! He was supposed to be my best friend, loyal to me and not fucking my girlfriend." He put his head into his hands and pulled his partially grey, thinning hair. "It drove me insane. I lost her. That fucking bitch I loved so much. It was me that had to look at her broken body in the emergency room after she threw herself off the bridge. And then my best friend, Joseph. That fucking bastard, Joseph!"

Dan looked across the room at the crowd of men. He enjoyed having an audience that would listen and wanted to convince them that he'd had no choice. Deep down, he also wanted to be forgiven. "They left me with their child.... THEIR child, I say, and I raised her as my own. But as she grew, she grew into him. When I looked into

322

her eyes, I saw Joseph. When I looked at her hair, I saw Magnolia. She even had a beauty spot in the same place as her mother. Her temperament was of them both. She had nothing of me in her whatsoever," he said regretfully. "I tried to love her, but she was different, aloof. In the end, they took her away from me and all I had were my whores." He paused and spat out in shame, "Yes! WHORES, is that so bad?" Sneering, he went on, "Joseph, my friend, introduced me to that life, and I became addicted to it. It was my only comfort. After a time, it ceased to be. Once I'd fucked them I could only think of my Magnolia and that wretched Joseph. So, you see those whores got all my fury, and in return I took their lives." Falling to the ground, he cried out, "Please God, forgive me...."

"Oh shit, Dan, what have you done?" said Joseph, shocked beyond belief. He never thought Dan had it in him to kill a fly, let alone a person. He'd had the perfect life. How could it all go so wrong? He felt sad for him and looked down at the wreck of a man, destitute and broken. It was clear that Dan hated him, blamed him even. Joseph knew that wasn't the answer and that it wouldn't help him in the place that he was in now - a place where lessons not learnt in life were dealt with in death.

He wanted to help Dan, and this sentiment resulted in his thoughts being broadcast as The Formless Voice, "Dan, by accepting responsibility, transcending guilt, growing beyond the notion of good and bad, learning love is a wound that must be gracefully endured, that God is not a separate entity, and forgiveness must begin within - are lessons you will receive in this Courtroom."

Dan's eyes almost bulged out of his head in shock. "Joseph, you cunt!" he shouted, "Is that you?" He looked wildly around the room. "Where are you, you son of bitch? Where the fuck are you?"

Joseph watched from above. He knew that he needed to give Dan some more time to adjust. After all those years of shirking responsibility and vehemently fearing control, he now felt the weight and responsibility of so many lives upon him. The consequences of his misdemeanors sat heavily on his heart, and he felt anxious about all that had happened. For once, he didn't blame anybody else, not even himself. Responsibility was a purposeful feeling, but blame - a waste of time. Instead of seeking to dramatize or gratify his feelings in some distracting manner, he sat with them and let them burn.

The fire dissolved into light, and a vast openness spread before him. Nothing mattered to him anymore, and once the wave of regret had passed him by, he floated higher up into the room.

It was no longer necessary for him to be in his body, and as The Formless Voice, he said, "Mate, here in the Narcissistic Afterlife, you..."

Lucinda heard Joseph's voice trail off and was unaware at first that he was not by her side, as she was too preoccupied with the goings-on in the Female Courtroom. It infuriated her to know that Magnolia had been right next to her the whole time, and that she'd had no idea about the sordid affair between her and Joseph.

Anger was a rare emotion for her to acknowledge and something shifted. Acceptance flooded her with warm waters soaked in the essence of magnolias, and she sat with the feeling, waiting for it to burn her.

With no need to question Joseph anymore and no desire to hear the truth (which for a long time she'd felt in her heart) she turned towards where he'd last been floating.

324

No longer there, she looked up and watched him disappear through the ceiling, leaving her behind. To her amazement, she felt no sorrow, anger, or sadness about his departure. Unlike in her life, in her death, she was finally able to let him go...

## Acknowledgements

Thank you to all the people who were a great support to me throughout the writing of Beauty Stone. There are so many of you - you know who you are.

A special thanks to my mum for always believing in me.

Heartfelt gratitude to my spiritual teacher Bhagavan Adi Da Samraj, whose Teachings and Wisdom have made this all possible.

The quote on the back cover: "Before death you make mind; after death mind makes you." was quoted by Adi Da Samraj, during a talk on December 12th, 1988.

## Author Bio

Demet Dayanch is Londoner with a Turkish/Cypriot heritage and currently lives in London (UK).

She has been writing poems, stories and plays ever since she could hold a pencil.

As much as writing, she loves to travel and lived in Istanbul (TURKEY) for nine years, where she wrote BEAUTY STONE.

Her background in psychology greatly influences her style, and her love for drama creates the stage in her mind to bring to life every character she writes about.

She is currently in the process of writing the sequel to BEAUTY STONE.